Jenisjoplin

Basque Literature Series No. 14

Jenisjoplin

by

Uxue Alberdi

2017 Winner of the Academia Saria 111 award

Translated by

Nere Lete

Center for Basque Studies
University of Nevada, Reno
2021

This book was published with the generous financial assistance of the Basque Government.

Basque Literature Series No. 14
Series editor: Mari Jose Olaziregi

Library of Congress Cataloging-in-Publication Data

Names: Alberdi, Uxue, 1984- author. | Lete, Nere, translator.
Title: Jenisjoplin / Uxue Alberdi ; [translated by Nere Lete].
Other titles: Jenisjoplin. English
Description: Reno, Nevada : Center for Basque Studies Press, [2020] | Series: Basque literature series; no. 14 | Summary: "The novel Jenisjoplin tells the story of Nagore Vargas, a rebel on a journey to find her identity and avenge her ancestors"-- Provided by publisher.
Identifiers: LCCN 2020046760 | ISBN 9781949805321 (paperback)
Subjects: GSAFD: Bildungsromans.
Classification: LCC PH5339.A39 J4613 2020 | DDC 899/.92--dc23
LC record available at https://lccn.loc.gov/2020046760

Contributors

Author

Uxue Alberdi Estibaritz (Elgoibar, 1984) is a writer and a bertsolari (improvisational poet.) She is the author of 2 collections of short stories; Aulki bat elurretan (A chair on the Snow) Elkar, 2007; Euli-giro (Sense of Chagrin) Susa, 2013, three novels Aulki Jokoa (Musical Chairs) Elkar, 2009; Jenisjoplin, Susa 2017 which was selected as the winner of the Academia Saria 111 award (Readers' Choice) and Dendaostekoak (Backroom Stories) Susa, 2020. Her essay Kontrako eztarritik (Through the Wrong Pipe) Susa, 2019, received the 2020 Essay Euskadi Award. Among many published works for children, her story Besarkada (The Embrace) received the 2016 Children and Young Adult Euskadi Award Literature.

Translator

Nere Lete is a professor of Basque and the director of the Basque Studies Minor at Boise State University in Boise, Idaho. She holds a bachelor's degree in Basque Philology from the University of Deusto and a Master of Fine Arts in Literary Translation from the University of Iowa. She has published her translations in various American literary venues. Nere Lete's grassroots work was instrumental in the creation of a Basque language preschool in Boise, Idaho where she loves to perform puppet shows in Basque.

INTRODUCTION

by Uxue Alberdi

The novel *Jenisjoplin* tells the story of Nagore Vargas.

I created a character, a rebel who, as the result of the adverse conditions of her childhood, was forced to build a strong identity: Nagore Vargas is the child of Spanish left-wing immigrants, the daughter of bar owners, someone who, from childhood, adopts a sense of class-consciousness and the identity of the oppressed. She comes of age on the streets of a working-class neighborhood and in her parents' eighties bar, as she assumes, at a very young age, the responsibilities and decision-making of an adult.

She experiences the eighties and nineties with no filter, in their full beauty and rawness. The tension of those times mirrors Nagore's emotional state, she even acknowledges that hers is an eighties soul: she has a passion for justice, an inherent tendency for defiance, a predisposition for violence, a posture against authority, an overflowing rage, a need to avenge her ancestors…

The distance, the distortion that fiction establishes provided me with the opportunity to develop a series of ideas that I have shared with only a few people. Before developing these ideas, I built a platform for them, and from that platform only, have I been able to speak comfortably. Together with the political struggle of the Basque Country, I have examined my own experiences, emotions and personal contradictions along with those of my contemporaries. The themes and thoughts correspond to the particular situation of each character, but they create a wider echo: the characters must think of dissidence, violence, struggle, peace, pleasure, surrender, guilt…

At the end of the novel there is a description of a lobster shedding its shell: the old shell is gone, but the new one is not yet formed, it is soft and prone to injury. That is Nagore Vargas's situation, and I believe that that is how we find ourselves as a country too. This is a necessary transition to go through, it provokes fear and lack of confidence but this shedding is fundamental to go on living.

"The story your novel tells is DEEP," my editor told me during our first meeting. "So, I think that the narrative style should be 'LIGHT': fluid, simple, quick, with few explanations, as fresh as water in a flowing current."

I believe I achieved that result: *Jenisjoplin* is a fast-paced novel, full of action and dialogue. Pain is one thing and drama something else. There is pain in *Jenisjoplin*, very palpable; the wound is plain to see. But there is no melodrama; the protagonists are looking at life.

Perhaps one of the main messages of the novel might be found toward the end, in a conversation between Luka and Nagore.

"What does 'living well' mean to you, Nagore?"

"Mostly, it's not feeling guilty."

Jenisjoplin

It was Monday morning and we were headed to Artxanda by car in the last days of the summer of 2010.

"Like Mayor Azkuna, let's go see how Bilbao is doing without us!"

In serious situations, Irantzu resorted to humor as an escape. We two women in the backseat, the men in front: Karra at the wheel and Luka next to him. We looked like four young people on our way to the hills; the smell of the potato omelet that Luka made reinforced that feeling.

"You can't be arrested holding a potato omelet in a Tupperware container between your ankles, it's bad form." Irantzu held the cargo between her hiking boots.

"Try to use Tupperware and arrest in the same sentence. Try it, try it! Did you make it with onion?"

"A little bit."

"Then we're safe."

Karra turned up the music.

"*No pasarán! Los venceremos, amor, no pasarán*!" We all joined Carlos Mejía Godoy in song. "*Aunque no estemos juntos, te lo juro: no pasarán*!"

That day, the theme song of Luka's show was stirring a deeper echo than usual within us. We arrived in Artxanda singing away. There we were, the *Radio Libre* team, while the sun warmed the city. The leaves, in September, wait for their destiny trembling on their branches.

We had discussed everything that had to be discussed. When I got arrested, Karra would take charge of my show and running the station, and Irantzu's replacement was also lined up to moderate the political talk show when the time came. We had decided in our last meeting not to go into hiding but to continue working on our respective journalistic assignments.

If anyone, Luka might be the fortunate one; maybe they didn't have a file on him yet. He had only been working with us for the last four or five months. He was developing our international television website devoted to the Basque youth protest movement. We called him *Transatlantic*; he was a shy, hybrid polyglot. He didn't have a place to stay in the city and I invited him to be my roommate in exchange for collaborating at the radio station. I offered him the pull-out bed because I was using the guest room since Mother, after her last relationship shipwreck, came to stay with me "for a while."

In a short period of time we went from being a marginal, minority media outlet that no one cared about, to appearing in all of the Spanish newspapers as the Basque leftist pro-independence youth organization's "Segi Radio." Just like that, we became the voice of ETA. Our listeners grew as did our critics. A charisma-lacking columnist accused us of glorifying terrorism. We sensed that they were spying on us. Irantzu and I had police in plain clothes following us. Lights and shadows at night.

"I bought my bus ticket for tomorrow," Luka announced.

He was planning to visit a cousin in Madrid and then return to Havana, to a waiting girlfriend and his mother.

"The pigs might deport you for free!" Karra smacked Luka's leg.

We placed the beers and potato omelet on a picnic table.

I looked at my friends. Was it my imagination or did they look better as the arrest got closer? Though really, I always thought they looked pretty good.

Karra and Irantzu had been my lovers, one off-and-on for many years, one for a short and intense period. I believed that having shared such an experience gave us a kind of kinship. I wasn't looking for children in exchange for sex. I looked for brothers and sisters, the more the better. For me sex was truly a type of pact, one that had to be cherished outside of the bedroom too. I believed that the nights that we shared exclusively, the two of us, built bridges that only we could walk on, from me toward each lover and vice versa. The bridges of La Salve, La Merced, La Ribera. Complicit bridges. Bridges for two. Ours was quite an in-bred office, to tell the truth.

"It's your fault, obviously," Karra used to point out.

He was the elder brother, the radio station's first paid employee, the senior member, the one who, a year earlier, when he became a father, left even paid jobs aside. He hardly showed up at the studio anymore. I knew him from my first days in Bilbao.

Luka grabbed the camera and walked toward the overlook. Soon, that photograph would become a distant memory in a hot Havana bedroom.

Irantzu and Karra began running, like nervous dogs that scatter in all directions when the car door opens. I lit a cigarette as I watched them. I saw Irantzu standing on Karra's shoulders, trying to climb an old oak tree. She held on to a branch with both hands and climbed it with the sheer strength of her upper body. Karra embraced the trunk of the tree and made a little jump, placing the soles of his feet barely above the ground on each side of the trunk and, with another quick movement, he hugged the tree a little higher. He jumped again and with his feet placed like a big frog, went up another eight inches.

"Arrivederci!" yelled Irantzu from atop the branch. "We'll just live up here!"

Bringing us back to reality, Karra fell flat on his face on the grass.

"Are you OK?" he turned and asked me.

"Calmer than you two monkeys," I teased him.

"They won't be violent arrests, Nagore," he reassured me.

"Is there such a thing?"

There were no objective reasons to be calm. A high percentage of those who had been arrested lately had reported being tortured. We had received direct testimony at the radio station of young people who had been badly beaten. Beatings. Rape. Humiliation. Strangely, I wasn't afraid. I felt safe among my friends, as irrationally as a child holding her father's hand, I thought that as long as I was with them, nothing bad could happen to me.

Irantzu opened a beer and cut the omelet.

"Eat some," she ordered me, "you look as if a gust of wind could sweep you away!"

I had just spent a month and a half hardly eating anything due to a fever induced by an esophageal infection that the doctors took forever to diagnose. If I was slim before, after this illness, two of us could fit in my pants. The fact that as soon as I began feeling better I started working at the perfumery during the day and the city festival pop-up txosna street-bars at night, didn't help me gain much weight. Neither did the menacing shadow of the raid and the infiltrations.

"Let's have them come tonight!" I exclaimed, completely convinced. "Let's be done with this and get back to normal."

I took a puff of my cigarette. After some silence, the others burst into laughter.

Luka suggested we take a group photo at the lookout, with the tripod. The sun illuminated the dust motes dancing in the air. They brought me memories of my childhood, of how I tried to catch those sparkles on the desolate street by the railroad tracks and how they would escape as soon as I closed my hand.

—

When I arrived at the perfumery, I found Mother packing anti-wrinkle cream jars. She looked like a converted bartender who had just begun the transition from booze to cosmetics. She moved behind the store counter with the reflexes of a server; too fast, too abruptly, without sophistication. She played the music too loud. She dressed up in an esthetician's lab coat, in an effort to hide the stench of manure but in essence, deep inside, she was a farmer full of complexes, clumsy.

"We're returning them."

The sales weren't bad, but not enough to pay off our debts. I blamed it on Mother's pessimism but I didn't mention it to her. I was used to living with my nose barely above water: we were the kind of people who pretended to have full pockets but had overdrawn checking accounts, we were people programed to be rich day to day and spend the year poor. A mess of a family, but trustworthy.

I asked Mother to take a break. A client was coming at five for an exfoliation treatment and I would close the store at seven. Mother lit a cigarette before she left the store. I scolded her.

"By the way, the hospital called," she said while pushing the smoke out of the store with her hand. "You have an appointment for your tests at eleven."

"Tomorrow?"

"You can't make it?"

"No, sure, great." As great as it was for Luka to take that bus trip to Madrid.

The lady that came for the treatment had a very porous face. She was a new client. I had her lay down on the massage table and I prepared a green mud, aloe-vera and argan-oil mask. "The weather?" I sent Karra a text while the mud dried on the woman's orange-peel-skin face. "The sea is calm," he replied.

After twenty minutes, I removed the mask, and sold her two jars of the anti-wrinkle cream Mother had packaged to return to the distributor.

I received a text message from a number I didn't recognize: "The pigs are squealing."

"You should come back next week for another session," I suggested, "after that you'll be able to continue the treatment at home."

I wrote down her next appointment in the book. The fuller the upcoming days looked, the more unreal the arrests seemed. If they took me away, it would be good for Mother to keep busy until I returned. I phoned her to ask if she could spend the night somewhere else.

"I have plans," I told her.

I didn't want Mother to be home if the police knocked the door down.

"I have to hang up, I have customers."

It was seven thirty by the time I closed the store. Just in case, I wanted to leave the bookkeeping updated. I would do some shopping for dinner and go home.

The supermarket was packed with last minute shoppers. Eggs, ham, bread, two bottles of wine, and after hesitating for a while due to its price, I bought some Irati sheep's milk cheese too. While I was waiting in line to check out, I thought I saw someone spying on me from the other side of the store's automatic doors. I saw two men watching me. I returned the shopping cart and returned the gaze. "What do you want?" I mimed back at them, raising my head and eyebrows. By the time I paid for my groceries and left the supermarket, they were gone. The games, certainly, had begun. I hardly had to walk two hundred yards uphill to get home but had to rest my grocery bag on the ground three times. I hadn't completely healed yet, I got tired quickly. During one of the stops, I spotted a man on the other side of the street: a pig, a six-foot-two young man, a member of the secret police, standing next to the entrance of another apartment building. I thought he was going to offer to help me carry my grocery bag. Having him notice my feebleness infuriated me. I grabbed my bag and stood in front of him. Aware of the domestic ridiculousness that the grocery bag brought into the scene, I looked him in the eye. He did not blink. I held on to that rude, mocking gaze, and left.

I found Luka standing in the hallway.

"They're onto us."

"I know. "

He followed me to the kitchen. I uncorked the bottle of wine and poured it in two glasses. I asked him to cut the cheese, I held out my glass for a toast.

"Let's make a deal."

"OK."

"Let's turn off our phones and enjoy these two bottles of wine in peace."

"One will do. You might want to keep the other one for another special occasion."

I pulled out my cigarettes. I asked him about his Cuban girlfriend.

"Her name is Lilian. Lili."

"You'll be in Havana soon."

"I'll miss our TV nights."

During the four months he stayed at my house, we binge watched *Mad Men*, *Breaking Bad* and *Carnivale,* one right after another. In the evenings, along with Mother, we enjoyed ourselves sitting on the sofa, though a socialist, he sure passed his love for American TV shows on to us. He would soon need to make do with Cuban soap operas.

"After being used to this life, you'll get bored in Cuba."

"Don't be so sure, I like the slow pace."

We filled our glasses again.

"And you? How is it going with Igor?"

I had to pound my chest with my fist not to choke on a piece of bread.

"With Igor?"

He was a collaborator that lived in Donostia, a political analyst. My interest in him apparently was more obvious than I cared to admit.

"Unfortunately, he is a rigorous monogamist," I took a sip of wine, "for now, anyway."

I knew it was a matter of time, but I was getting impatient. For weeks, we had been making senseless appointments to meet in bars in Bilbao or Donostia as an excuse to consult on different topics or compare political perspectives. But since he was the one with a partner, I believed that it was up to him to make the first move. I wasn't used to waiting. If sexual tension and similar wars were not resolved quickly, I slowly began to lose self-respect. I was better at surviving in the battlefield and accepting any collateral damage than managing the uncertainty of a truce. Igor, on the contrary, handled the wait stoically.

"Waiting is an art," Luka lifted his glass, "another type of pleasure."

"Let the chips fall where they may, the sooner the better," I told him, leaving him unsure if I was talking about the arrests or Igor.

Both issues provoked the same physical reaction in me.

At the beginning of summer, after the lunch we had for all collaborators, and after everyone else had gone home, I ended up swimming half-naked in the ocean with Igor. Since we didn't have towels, we lay down in the warm night to dry. We didn't touch or speak to each other. Our lips and fingertips held on to our desire, we spent two hours looking at each other, smoking, testing how tightly the rope could be stretched.

After dinner I made some coffee, since we were half dozing off by then.

"I need to take a shower," I told Luka.

I washed my hair and put on street clothes. I spent some time choosing my outfit. It was midnight by then. I saw Luka lie down on the pull-out bed, his jeans and sweatshirt on. He didn't realize I was looking at him. His knees trembled.

"Would you like to sleep with me?"

I held his hand and took him to Mother's bed. We left our shoes by the door. It wasn't comfortable to sleep in street clothes, it was a nuisance to feel the rubbing of the sheets against my jeans, but we got into bed and pulled up the sheets. He held my hand.

"Nothing will happen."

He was talking to himself. I hugged him and stroked his back on top of his sweater. Men's fear aroused me.

We undressed slowly; we ended up naked under the sheets; the pants, t-shirt, socks and panties I selected for the moment of the arrest now thrown on the floor. I'm not sure when I fell asleep, but by the time we woke up it was daylight.

I woke him up.

"They didn't come!"

I felt like complaining to someone. They made fun of us. I picked up the clothes from the floor and got dressed quickly. Luka followed me.

"Should I make some coffee?"

I didn't answer, I was getting a bunch of text messages.

"They arrested Karra."

I opened the window. No pigs under the apartment building. It had happened four hours earlier, while Luka and I were asleep.

The streets looked normal. An old lady entered the building across the street holding the newspaper and a loaf of bread under her arm.

—

It was a strange morning, like the day after a death or falling in love. You, feeling so moved, yet heaven and earth looking as usual, numb to trembling, in absolute conflict with your reality, clashing cruelly, as if one deed would cancel out the other, sunrise against death, death against sunrise.

"They came close," said Luka.

We were free and I felt my muscles tense with rage. I prepared myself to be arrested, to measure my resolve. The wasted adrenaline felt like an insult. I felt like someone who received a break she didn't deserve. Once again, the burden of impunity that I felt when I was a child kept haunting me: while those around me were punished, I was left to manage the privilege of going unpunished.

"Should we go window shopping?" I texted Irantzu.

We met at ten outside of Zara. I kissed her and we went in. We stopped at some flowery blouses.

"They just took Karra," she held up a hanger, "it was an uncontested arrest."

"And the radio station?"

"They searched it. Turned it upside down."

We walked to the jacket section.

"Have you been there yet?"

"I spoke to the neighbors."

"The computers?"

"They took them."

"All of them?"

"I think so."

We walked to the shoe department.

"We'll need to hold a press conference," I said.

"Will you take care of the statement?"

"O.K."

It was ten thirty.

"I need to go," I said.

"Where?"

"To see the doctor."

Irantzu went up the escalator. I walked by the theft detector without attracting anyone's attention; the security guard didn't even look at me. I felt guilty taking the bus to go to the hospital, in debt to the healthcare system because it gave me an excuse to keep the morning occupied. I wasn't sure what type of testing I was going to have done; I didn't care either, as long as it kept my mind busy for a few hours. I was convinced that if I slowed down, the recent events would take care of themselves. At that moment, I wasn't concerned about my health, I had more important worries.

I received a text from Luka: "On my way to Madrid." I imagined him wearing the clothes I had taken off of him the previous night. I replied: "At the doctor's, killing time."

The bus was a mass of hoarseness, coughing and weariness. The crowd reeked of sweat. I felt so separate from them: young, clean, healthy.

The just-passed summer seemed far away. I remembered those feverish twenty days as one very long day. I stayed with Mother in the city with all those who couldn't afford a vacation. She was having health issues too, a broken collarbone, the result of a fall. We were doing our best, trying, without success, to take care of each other.

Gradually, day-by-day, the achy feeling and sore throat turned into delirious fever. When I began complaining about painful breathing, Mother decided we had to go to the doctor. I didn't have the strength to argue with her. She, with no driver's license, I, not able to get out of bed; she finally called an ambulance. "Who is the patient?" the EMT asked while Mother, using her good hand the best she could, helped me put my street clothes on over my pajamas.

Mother and I visited the clinic three times and each time, after running a few tests, they sent us back home. The crippled Mother and her wasted daughter, the *Odd Couple*. Father ended up having to come, hurrying but still late, to take me to the main hospital in Bilbao. He threatened a doctor who, in the name of peace, agreed to see me without an appointment. All that for him to have me open my mouth and inform me abruptly that I had a yeast infection; that in two weeks the infection had spread from my mouth all the way to my esophagus and that the infection was the source of the ache I felt in my lungs. He wanted to run other tests to find out how I had developed an infection of such magnitude.

The bus was filling up.

We had to prepare the statement denouncing the arrest and the temporary shut-down of "*Radio Libre*." I would write the first draft of the statement once I was done at the doctor's office.

I turned in my paperwork at the counter and was sent to the infectious disease unit. A nurse told me she had to do a blood test.

"Do you get dizzy?"

"Only in the car."

"You have good veins. You need to come back in two hours to get your results."

Once outside the hospital, I tried to find a bar that didn't smell like sick people. I found an Irish place nearby. I was used to writing, words flowed easily, automatically, faster out of my hand than my head. I lit a cigarette. The last rays of the summer sun warmed my back through my leather jacket. I was overtaken by an expansive sensation of well-being, the feeling you get when the wind blows at your back. I tried to ward off the guilty feeling spurred by that pleasurable moment and took a deep breath. The wait to be arrested was over, so was the hidden anxiety. Things seem to indicate that Karra would be released soon. They did not have any evidence against him. Everything would be over in two or three days. "I'm working on the statement," I let Irantzu know.

A guy walking down the street smiled at me shyly; probably charmed by the image of a young woman writing in her notebook. A romantic, I thought and returned the smile. I was happy. After all it was a Tuesday morning after having had sex.

I returned to the hospital at the appointed time. There was no one in the waiting room. The bearded man that must've been the doctor, signaled me to enter his office. He began shuffling and reading documents, his back turned. He pulled the results of the tests and placed them on the desk.

"Nagore Vargas."

"Yes."

"Age?"

"28."

He looked at me as if he were searching for something.

"You tested positive."

I waited for him to continue.

"Haven't they told you?"

I didn't know what he was referring to.

"We tested you for HIV."

"What?"

"We tested you for HIV and the results are positive."

"You're joking."

"I do not joke with this type of information."

That is the last sentence I remember in any ordered way. Instead of feeling devastated, I became focused, I gathered around a point inside of me and a mind-set transformation took over me. I began carefully registering all kinds of details. His beard had begun to turn gray on the sides, by his jaw, and some reddish hair peeked out among the gray. He wore small, gold-rimmed glasses on his aquiline nose. Deer eyes, seagull eyebrows. A few discreet wrinkles in the corners of his eyes. In contrast to his chiseled face, a double chin. His breathing slowly pumped up his starched white lab coat. That detail brought me back to reality, that I was in front of a doctor and not a judge. I recognized the smell of his cologne: *Blue*, Chanel.

"Nowadays, things have changed a lot; don't worry, you'll be fine."

I lost my concentration. I lost the doctor's face and his smell. The colors and shapes around me no longer formed reality. I heard AIDS. My aunt. *Adiós lucerito mío* (Farewell my little bright star). Walls covered in wallpaper, ochre color flowers, vinyl. The smell of soup. Grandma Rosa. Childhood rain crashing on asphalt. Big, fat, dirty river. The train passing close by. Father. Mother. Angel. The lost colors and lines returned to form the doctor's profile once again.

"Am I HIV-positive or I have contracted AIDS?"

"You were already sick when you came in."

"I feel fine."

"You have AIDS. That is how you got the yeast infection."

The walls in the office were decorated with children's drawings.

"It's impossible!"

He waited until I calmed down a little. I buried myself in the chair.

"You won't die."

"We all will die."

"We have succeeded in making AIDS a chronic disease, however, with all the complications that a contagious chronic disease implies. People have a hard time accepting that they are contagious."

I grabbed my purse and stood up, ready to leave.

"A piece of advice: be discreet about it."

He stretched his hand.

"I will see you tomorrow at eleven, to run some more tests."

—

My aunt, Karmen Vargas, died of AIDS in May of 1987. She was twenty years old. Seven years earlier, one morning in 1980, Rosa Moreno, my grandma, found a syringe inside the umbrella stand at home. She was cleaning when she saw it stuck among the checkered umbrella rods. She held it in her hands and looked at it, unable to understand how a syringe made it inside the umbrella stand. She put it on the kitchen table, next to the fruit basket, until my father, Rafa Vargas, returned from work. She heard the word for the very first time from her son: heroin.

Karmen began sticking her veins at school recess, behind the red and white gate of the cement soccer field, when she was eleven and while her mother still sewed cloth dolls for her.

The child that played with dolls began communicating by screaming and slamming doors. She drooled while speaking to her parents. Grandma was afraid one day her own daughter might bite her.

Grandpa and Grandma didn't have the slightest idea about what was headed their way. They didn't know what an addict was. When my father explained what the syringe was for, "I will get her on the right track," my grandma said. But by then, Karmen was lying in some dark street, her shoulder against a friend's, in a faraway, lost land.

It was 1980, by then Karmen had been hooked on drugs for two years. My father was the first one to suspect. He saw his sister hanging out with older people, people with whom she hardly had anything in common, except where to get the next fix. But he didn't say anything to his parents. At that time, heroin didn't have a fatal reputation. It was only later that it became connected to the down-and-out, marginal people and death. In those days, they called it *the White Lady* and it had the voice of Lou Reed, Janis Joplin and Jimmy Hendrix. It brought new ways of loving and sex, peace marches, anti-establishment and anti-bourgeoisie positions. Images of US parks, long hair, flowers, music; London's anti-cultural movement.

Apparently, Grandma felt that for a while she had forgotten to look at Karmen and by the time she realized it, Karmen had turned into someone else, an untamable beast with a sad, unfocused stare.

She first started stealing at home: a watch, a pair of earrings, a vase… They didn't own much of value. If anything, theirs was a home lacking material goods. Karmen sold the items to get money to buy heroin. She easily fooled her mother, would promise her she wouldn't do it again, would get on her knees. She asked for forgiveness, until the next time. As time went on, she stopped lying and resorted to raw confessions. For Grandma, the lies were easier to deal with.

Awakening to the world of heroin was a cruel blow for Grandma. Her daughter explained to her that as a motor requires gas to function so she needed heroin. That she could not get out of bed unless she had a fix. She ended up with a needle at breakfast, lunch, dinner and bedtime.

When she ran out of punishments, confinement, threats, love-declarations and pleas, Grandma began giving my aunt money to buy dope. Grandma knew that if she didn't give her money, she would steal it from somewhere else, Maritxu's pharmacy, Jose's tobacco stand, in any purse that was at hand. She would run into trouble with police and her suppliers would beat her up for not paying them on time. She gave up, above all, because she could not stand Karmen's pain, that painful void, that only heroin could satisfy.

Grandma's efforts were in vain. More than once the police came looking for Karmen while she lay in bed screaming from withdrawal. They accused her of robberies and vandalism. At merely fifteen, all Grandma saw was a child in pain; the police saw an unruly junkie. She promised them that she would take her daughter to the police station, that she would have her there by nine in the morning, begged them not to take her like that.

For three months, they confined her to a Madrid juvenile detention center and, when she became of age, they locked her up twice. Even her energy to steal waned. She was hardly able to get on her feet to go get her fix. She gradually spent more time at home, in bed, under the covers. She would plead with her mother to hold her in her lap. And so she did, she sang to her, caressed her feet.

"She was so young when she got hooked on heroin that she grew more than four inches during that time," Grandma would say.

Grandma Rosa even ended up helping give Aunt Karmen heroin injections. As consequence of having to shoot up her arms every day, it made it increasingly harder to find a vein. All the body parts she used to stick herself were blocked, her hands shivered. Aunt Karmen taught her mother how to melt the drug, how to take it in with the syringe without air, how to clean the needle, how to stick it in the vein. She took care of her daughter like a nurse would.

At home, they hit rock bottom. Grandpa asked Grandma to kick Karmen out of the house and Grandma would respond by threatening to leave with their daughter.

Grandma pulled down the window blinds and didn't open the door to anyone nor did she answer the phone for three months. The only thought that would calm her down was the hope of ending that hell alongside her daughter. If more than twelve hours passed since her last dose, Aunt Karmen would start to sweat and throw up. The irises of her eyes would expand, she would shiver violently, have convulsions, cramps in her arms and legs, tachycardia. A few times while everyone was asleep at night, Grandma turned on the gas and got into bed next to her daughter who felt cold, shivered and moaned. She hugged Aunt Karmen with all her might, but her body was no longer enough to calm her daughter. The daughter's flesh hurt her mother's flesh. It was too late. Karmen's body longed for heroin; it was too late for tenderness to penetrate that child's skin. After a few minutes passed, feeling regret, Grandma would get up from bed, walk to the kitchen, inhale the last poison breath, shut off the gas, shut her eyes and push open the balcony door.

—

My mother, Arantzazu Alkorta, came to town in 1979. Originally, she is from a lost corner of Goierri. Born by chance in a farmhouse known as Bernarats into a poor family. The youngest of eleven siblings, germinated too late inside her mother. By the time she was born, her parents were elderly. Her father didn't get up from bed since the day he said "no more" and her mother had enough on her plate running the farmhouse. Her older brothers and sisters took care of her. They made her do all the difficult chores. The caresses of the hazel tree branch are still visible on her legs. She learned to be subdued and obedient and not to show her feelings.

When she read in the newspaper that Zirimiri Bar in town was looking to hire someone, she left the farmhouse on the first bus out, never to return. The rust of the industrial town, its grey color, the stench of oil and stuffy hidden corners, the rumbling of factories, sirens, the rattling of Spanish-speaking tongues, the smothering urban landscape crammed with row after row of community housing… became a fresh breath of air for the young runaway farm girl.

She met Father at Zirimiri Bar. He was known as the "Syndicalist." He was a foreman in the largest workshop in the area, and a member of the workers' committee. He must've spoken passionately about general strikes, closures, about meetings and assemblies while drinking wine and smoking cigarettes. That tanned, long-haired young man must've charmed Mother with all that talk about the proletariat and the working class while looking at her with the idealization of the subjugated as he spoke in plural with his revolutionary hammering cadence.

They made a nice couple: both tall and brown haired, ridiculously young, with no apparent flaws, beautiful. Mother serious and slim, Father quick to smile and carefree. When they married in 1980, they were penniless. A month before the ceremony, Aunt Karmen had stolen the 50,000 pesetas they had saved for the wedding and Father had been fired for been involved in some protests. All of them are nothing but smiles in their wedding pictures: Mother and Father in the middle; Grandma Rosa and Grandpa Manuel next to Mother; Karmen linked arms with her brother. Without a penny to their name, they went to live with Grandma and Grandpa, at 21 Lasalde.

Soon after Mother got pregnant, Karmen began her detox process. They had arrested her for theft and sentenced her to three months in prison for stealing from a jewelry store in the neighboring town. The police arrested her at the store when she returned to get her leather jacket that she had left behind. They took her to Martutene. When Grandma went to visit, her daughter acted as if she were out of her mind, as skinny as a street dog, trembling and frightened. Karmen had taken more heroin while inside, worse quality but more expensive.

"I'm very tired," she told Grandma.

She implored Grandma to get her out of there. But Grandma and Grandpa did not have the money to pay for a detox center which cost eighty thousand pesetas a month, and they already lived in debt. They resorted to selling arid land that Grandma and her siblings owned in Granada to pay for treatment at the Patriarca Center. They took her to the Cortijo de Santa Elena in Valencia. That is where she began writing her first letters to Grandma. She told her that her whole body hurt, that she vomited often.

"*There are 86 of us. We don't do anything but eat and work. They make us get up at six in the morning and put us straight to work: tilling the garden, pushing dollies and unloading bricks for a shower room that we are building. The house is quite unkempt and needs lots of repairs. Those who cannot work because of the terrible consequences of heroin withdrawal are taken to complete a "marathon:" They make them put on a backpack full of bricks and make them walk, until they fall from exhaustion. The ones in charge are people like us, junkies, who are clean now. They manage the money, take our tobacco away and give us only five cigarettes a day. I do not like it here.*"

I was born on March 15, 1982, while Aunt Karmen was at the Cortijo de Santa Elena. She asked about me in her letters. She asked Grandma to send her pictures of me. She worried about my weight and wanted to know if I had caught a cold, if I had a good appetite, if I had any teeth yet.

She spent a year and a half in the community at the Cortijo de Santa Elena and she not only improved her health but successfully kicked her heroin habit.

She returned in 1984, healed, apparently. She looked beautiful, radiant, pretty and smiling. I was two years old.

As soon as she came into the house, she held me in her arms. She felt a special attachment toward me from the beginning and since my parents were working at the bar, Karmen offered to take care of me. She fed me, rocked me to sleep and took me for strolls. People she knew stopped her on the street to welcome her back and share pleasantries about me. They told her I resembled her.

Grandma says that Karmen followed an ordinary routine, a calm one, with only one goal, to live. She didn't want to go far, didn't want to do anything special. She just wanted to live. Eat, go for walks, sleep… She felt a renewed love for people and nature, free of demands and contempt: she tried to be conscious of the moment summer turned into fall, to let the rain soak her skin, to feel the warmth of other bodies, to hear her parent's footsteps close by, to press her face against a child's cheek, to breathe… She did not ask anything special of life.

The photos of the two of us together during those days became immortalized in Grandma's house. There was one taken in the neighborhood of the 1985 snowfall: Aunt Karmen making a snow angel; in a summertime photo of both of us, by the train tracks, sticking our tongues out at the camera, I must've been about three and my aunt nineteen.

Not long after those photos were taken, she began to lose weight. Her cheeks turned pale and deflated. The dark circles under her eyes deepened. The following winter her legs gave out. Suddenly, she vomited the first bite of lunch… same thing happened at dinner.

"I can't swallow anything," she told Grandma.

They went to see their family doctor and got a prescription for vitamins. As they noticed that she began doing worse, they took her to the hospital in Donostia. The doctors there did not hesitate in their diagnosis: AIDS.

They informed her that she was going to die and apparently, she did not cry. An eighteen-year-old girl had recently died of

AIDS in the area. The *Bug* had taken already three boys in town. She asked for Grandma's forgiveness.

During her illness, she continued to take care of me as best she could. The antiretroviral treatment left her shattered, to the point that at home they wondered if it would be the AIDS or the medication which would take her first. She could hardly walk after she took her medication. They had to carry her to the bathroom. Mother became annoyed because I spent so much time with her. She was afraid of how deeply I was attached to my aunt. There was a major confusion in the town about how AIDS was transmitted, rumors ran wild: that it was dangerous to be in the swimming pool with a sick person, to drink out of the same glass, to wear the same slippers… Mother harshly criticized all the whispering; she said that people spoke carelessly, but she did not know, in her daughter's case, what the appropriate distance was. For Karmen to caress me, kiss me, breathe the same air in that closed bedroom day after day… was too much for Mother. She often argued with Father about it. She had some disagreements with Grandma too. Grandma knew that other mothers in the same situation took harsher preventive measures, like setting aside the patient's silverware and dishes or washing their clothes separately with bleach. She knew that those mothers avoided being close to their sick children, but she refused to treat her daughter as if she had the plague.

Grandpa Manuel moved to Aunt Karmen's twin bed so my aunt could sleep with Grandma. At the beginning of 1987, Mother and daughter slept in the same bed for four months. Aunt Karmen felt terribly cold no matter how many blankets and electric heaters Grandma used. She almost always preferred Grandma's company and mine. Grandpa's presence at home reassured her but she did not dare to call for him. Manuel did not dare to go to her either. She pleaded with Grandma and me to climb into bed with her, she needed us to touch her constantly. I remember that she used to ask me to hold her in my arms.

I spent many hours with Aunt Karmen during the final months. I would play music and pretend I danced flamenco which made her laugh. Grandma says that I helped Aunt Karmen and Grandpa to reconcile. She explained that, one evening, I called Grandpa from Aunt Karmen's bed. I asked him to sing one of his songs so I could dance to it. Apparently, I brought him into the bedroom by pulling him by his shirt. I dragged a chair from the kitchen and improvised a flamenco stage by the bed. Grandpa Manuel, after a moment of hesitation, began clapping, cleared his throat, and began singing. By then Karmen was damaged. He sang *Adiós lucerito mío* (Farewell my bright star), I twirled incessantly, holding up my arms and stomping my shoes against the floor.

Grandma and Aunt Karmen never spoke about death. When she was close to dying, they took her to Arantzazu Hospital. The nursing assistants organized a party to celebrate her birthday: It was May 5th, 1987, she turned twenty. We brought her presents and a cake, she smiled. By then, though, she did not have enough strength to blow out the candles. I felt scared. I saw her for the last time at that birthday party. Apparently, I kept my distance from Aunt Karmen that day though she did her best to bring me close to her.

"Let's leave," I asked Mother.

Karmen died four days later, on a Monday afternoon, while holding Grandma and Grandpa's hands.

—

"Wake up, Jenisjoplin!"

I had been in bed for hours, perhaps days. Father pulled up the blinds and opened the window. The room was stuffy. Outside, it was dark.

"It'll be light soon. Get up."

"But…how did you get here?"

"We made it in five hours from Coruña to Bilbao. I was caught speeding by at least three traffic radars."

"Did you bring Josune with you?"

"She is asleep in the car; long trips kill her."

"What did you tell her?"

"What was I going to tell her? It was our first time staying at an all-inclusive hotel. We had to grab our suitcases just as we were about to get in line for the free buffet, and we left."

"Shit, dad."

"She's my girlfriend."

"We hardly have a relationship. She doesn't know me."

"I have always been truthful."

"Yes, a sincere-icide."

"Whatever you say. Go take a shower."

It was the first time since I had been diagnosed that I saw my body naked. *She who has a beauty mark, will always have a certain spark.* Grandma used to tell me when I was a child.

I came out to the living room with my hair wet and wearing my bathrobe. Father was sitting in an armchair, smoking a cigarette. He made a movement with his hand so I would push my hair back.

"You have the *Bug*."

"That's what they say."

"So, that son of a bitch is still alive."

"Where is Mother?" I wondered.

"In the kitchen."

"How is she?"

"She's overwhelmed, we are going to kill her with so many disappointments. Yesterday when you came into the store, the world came tumbling down on her. She knew it before you told her. I would bet my life she suspected something."

He blew a smoke image in the air that resembled nothing so much as absence.

"Do you remember Aunt Karmen's First Communion photo?"

I did, it was hung in Grandma's hallway. "That nun's habit suits you really well," my friends told me when they came to visit, though surely, they knew that I didn't make my First Communion.

"It's the way you look at the camera."

"What?"

"It is how you two look at the camera that make you so alike. A half shy smile, half daring, and that split gaze: as if you held questions in one eye and answers in the other. Janis Joplin and Amy Winehouse."

He blew two smoke rings, one smaller than the other, which disappeared with the third puff.

"You will not die. You can't."

"No."

"Treatments have evolved."

"It's the same shit. Your friends who are taking antiretroviral medication, how are they doing?"

"Better than the ones who didn't have a chance to take them."

He looked me in the eye, harshly.

"You were the apple of your aunt's eye."

"I'll make some coffee."

I walked into the kitchen and put the Italian coffee maker on. Gardening advice on the radio, I turned it off.

"Do you know what she used to say? 'This child and I have the same stream running through us.'"

I leaned my back against the kitchen door. Father was lying on the couch, I was only able to see his boots and his cigarette smoke.

"The Earthworm," I said; that is how we referred to the brown colored river we saw from Grandma's window.

"Always about to overflow. Always about to be clean, yet always dirty."

"Father…"

"It's true."

"Father."

"We're the Basque lumpen."

"Don't exaggerate."

I thought he seemed happy, or perhaps there was a small sense of inner enjoyment in the pain. I could tell by his way of smoking.

"Sometimes things make sense, what do you want me to tell you; better difficult to understand and yet making sense than easy to understand and senseless. You have always been rational."

"Are you telling me that it's rational for me to have AIDS?"

"Don't twist my words."

"Me? Dammit, Father, do you hear yourself?"

"I didn't expect this. You don't deserve this…"

"So?"

"You must've suspected. You don't even weight a hundred and ten pounds."

The Italian coffee maker was gurgling. I couldn't see Father's face, but I could picture it: he was smoking while observing his hand, as if looking in a mirror.

"You have always wanted to fight against it. Now you can avenge your aunt by your own flesh. Perhaps it's an opportunity for you. And for the two of us. We had started to become middle-class, you know? Vacations, mortgage, the perfumery. This will put us back where we belong. We'll fight from the mud. And we will win," Father assured me.

"It sounds like you are going to thank me for getting sick."

A smoke cloud raised from the back side of the gray sofa: an old whale.

"If it didn't sound so cruel, I would say you sound as if you were proud of me."

He sat down, his back to me. He lit another cigarette.

"What's the plan for today?" he asked me.

I walked to the kitchen. I answered him raising my voice.

"I need to give a press conference. What do you say?"

"It sounds great."

"Ah, and then I have an appointment with Doctor Puertas. Nothing important. A formality: he will measure my defenses and viral load."

"Sarcasm is bad."

"You're a fine one to say that."

He stood up from the sofa and walked to me, finally.

"You haven't offered me any coffee. It smells good."

"Would you like some coffee?" I asked him.

"No, thank you."

"Then with no sugar."

"I'm leaving. I'll be around. Call me if you need anything."

"OK."

"Will you call me?" He asked me.

"Maybe."

"And promise me that you will keep your chin up."

"Yes, of course."

“Promise me, Jenisjoplin.”

“I promise.”

—

I went out for the first time in my diagnosed body, as if I were carrying a bomb inside my pocket. The street, the people, the day’s light had a new hue. It reminded me of the day I aborted: how I walked the streets carrying a spark of life inside me, hidden from the world and knowing that it would soon disappear. Now I carried a spark of death, in a body part that could not be identified.

It was early and I took the bus to the hospital. I felt closer than the day before to the general ugliness that filled the bus. On the other side of the window healthy people were on their way to work. I felt an urge to talk to Luka.

“Nagore!”

“Luka”

It felt good to pronounce his name.

“I’m waiting for the attorney at the bar across the street from the courthouse.”

“Has he seen him?”

“Not yet. But they assured him that he’ll be with Karra when he enters his plea.”

“Today?”

“Hard to know. He’s pacing the hallways in the meantime: that’s where cases get decided.”

“Karra’s photo is in the paper.”

“I’m looking at it as we speak. How are you?” he asked me.

“Fine. I’m doing fine.”

I thought the call got cut off.

"Luka?"

All of a sudden, his voice came back on.

"We had a nice night."

"What?"

"That we had a nice night."

"Suspenseful."

"Tender."

The old man next to me was trying to clear his throat. He kept coughing. It kept me from hearing what Luka was saying.

"Irantzu called me. She said that since yesterday you are nowhere to be found."

"I'll call her," I said.

The old man with the cold motioned to me with his hand to get away from him, his eyes bulging. A loud sneeze propelled his body forward.

"I don't want to give you my cold, child!" he said, bringing his handkerchief to his mouth.

I stood up.

"Where are you?"

"On my way to the doctor's."

"Again?"

The bus stopped and I got off. The bus-shelter was deserted. It resembled a scene from a movie, waiting for the main character to speak. I lit a cigarette and released my words together with a trail of smoke:

"I have the *Bug*, Luka."

Silence.

"AIDS."

He didn't say anything, or perhaps the bus's roar covered it.

"I didn't know, I swear. You'll need to get tested, Luka."

It felt like I was interpreting lines that someone else had written for me. It wasn't enough to tell the truth, I wanted to sound believable.

A woman approached me, in a hurry.

"The bus?" She asked.

I signaled that it had already left. She sat at the bus shelter grumbling.

"I can't talk now, Luka. I'll call you later."

"I'll come back to Bilbao."

"No."

"I'm serious."

I tried to sound believable, once again:

"You must stay there with Karra."

"So then, you come here."

"I can't," I said.

"I'll wait."

He hung up on me.

—

In neon lettering: Ataka. It was the third bar my parents were running; after Zazpi and Media Luna. Four years earlier, the summer after my aunt died, in '87, they took a bar located in the filthy heart of town, on a corner of its small cement plaza.

They hired two young friends like themselves, skinny and leftist, and opened a two-story bar that they kept open day and night in that dead-end neighborhood. The bar on the ground level, a sound booth together with a dance floor; and a pool table, pinball machine and a small bar in the basement. At first, Angel and Father ran the main bar. People called them *Zipi* and *Zape*, like the cartoon characters. Angel was Father's best friend. He was a musician from Madrid. He had enviable straight, blonde hair, and the looks of a nice boy, in contrast with the *enfant terrible* looks of his friend. He was a substitute bass player in a few *movida* bands, though his dream was to be able to become a member of a Basque rock band.

"The Madrid vibe is nothing but smoke and mirrors!" he used to complain.

Father acted as his manager and they went down to Madrid together every time Angel had a gig. They always returned grinning with big, dark circles under their eyes. Angel would summarize their trips as "well played," since, besides having concerts in the capital, he had lovers too. The fourth friend ran the "catacombs," but as soon as they realized he was spending the bar profits on speed and trafficking drugs under the stairway, they decided to kick him out and run the business among the three of them.

"Sweetheart!" Mother greeted me.

She was wearing a ripped Hertzainak band t-shirt.

"Have you had lunch?"

"It's six in the evening," I pointed out.

"I already gave her an afternoon snack," Grandma replied.

Angel served me a lemon soda.

"What is that?" I asked looking at the walls.

They hosted monthly photo exhibits, the current one covered the wall behind the bar with snapshots of body parts: breasts, penises, backs, mouths, navels, tongues, fingers, thighs, vaginas and butts. Flesh and hair.

"Your father's idea!" Angel laughed. "I dare you to guess who is who!"

I tried to disguise my embarrassment. There were about seven or eight penises.

"Are they yours?"

"Bar workers and our buddies. We look good enough to eat, don't we?"

"You, lazy and crazy," Grandma scolded him.

"What do you think, should we go downstairs and shoot pool?" Angel asked me.

He was my private pool teacher.

Mother lit a cigarette.

"Homework?"

"She'll do it later!" Angel interrupted. "Let's go!"

We went down to the catacombs and placed our beer and lemon soda on the pool table. Angel put three balls in the pocket with one shot. He was quite an artist. I was trying to decide how to hit the striped 13 ball.

"You have to imagine an invisible ball next to the one you want to hit, lined up right with the pocket, and you aim the white ball toward the imaginary one."

He walked to the other side of the table and drew an imaginary ball with his finger. I aimed there.

"Right on!"

I decided to try with the yellow 9 ball.

"They organized a karaoke session for kids at the culture center."

I had heard something about it. They put up some posters in school, and the teacher told us about the event organized by the Basque language association in town.

"Ugh!" I said, unconcerned. "Those are events for students attending Basque schools."

"Don't you want to participate?"

He left the cue sideways on the table. I shrugged my shoulders.

"There are three songs to choose from: *Lau teilatu* by Itoitz, *Aitormena* by Hertzainak and *Iñaki, ze urrun dagoen Kamerun* by Zarama.

I didn't know a single one.

"Which one is the best one?"

"*Aitormena.*"

On our way up, he took me straight to the sound booth. They had more than 2,000 records, organized by genre. It was the only bar in town that had its own music booth. They kept Basque music on the bottom shelf; Angel pulled out a record from there.

"Learn it," he told me. "And while you're at it, tell me what it says."

I pulled out my handwriting homework and placed it on the bar counter. I began working on my cursive worksheets. The door opened and day light came in. It was later in the afternoon and though the light had begun to dim, it contrasted with the darkness inside the bar. It was Father, bed sheet marks on his face. He held me by the waist from behind the bar stool.

"What are you up to?"

I raised my hands, pointing at the evidence.

"Only priests, nuns and children write like that," he said, infuriated.

He explained that I had to write each letter individually, while he lifted the pencil off the paper each time he wrote a letter. He guided my hand, I felt his warm chest against my back, while we wrote *karramarroa* one letter at a time.

"You're no longer a child."

Truth be told, the word looked elegant. It was an adult's way of writing 'crawfish', no doubt. Next day I would be scolded in school but it wouldn't bother me a bit. I saw Mother put on her leather jacket.

"I'm done, dear. Let's go home."

I put my worksheets inside my backpack and jumped off the stool toward Mother.

"See you tomorrow" I told Father.

"Bye, beautiful!" Angel said from the warehouse and covered his ears with his palms to remind me to listen to the song.

Grandma grabbed the bag full of dirty towels and bar cloths, to wash at home. She beckoned me to come to her.

"Your father's is that ugly one there," pointing at one of the snapshots.

—

I stood in front of the hospital's automatic door, searching my purse for the document the doctor had given me the day before. I found it among my notes for the press conference and some delivery receipts from the perfumery. "Diagnosis: HIV." An autumn breeze almost blew it from my hands. The mere image of me chasing down my own diagnosis exhausted me.

I saw a young man walking towards me. I straightened myself and sharpened my glare, instinctively. I folded the document and put it away.

"Do you have a light?"

I lit the cigarette he held in his lips.

"Visiting someone?"

That second: the one in which you decide you would sleep with the person in front of you.

"Yes."

That instant: when you know he would say yes. I tried to extend that moment.

"What's your name?" he asked.

"Nagore."

I smoked a cigarette as I stood next to that stranger, until I saw that the reception area was empty. I stubbed out the cigarette and nodded goodbye to the man. The automatic door shut behind me: hardly a whisper. I approached the counter and showed my document to the receptionist.

"The infirmary. Lower level. Section C."

The waiting room was packed. I sat on the only unoccupied seat. Next to me, I noticed a heavily made-up woman with a urine sample cup visible in the half-opened purse on her lap.

"Waiting for blood work?"

About five or six of us raised our hands. The nurse assistant asked us for our documents. She put mine aside.

"Good morning," the nurse greeted me.

I read "virus-load," on the blood collection tubes placed on the table. She left the tubes in front of me, stickers faced up.

"Roll up your sleeve, please."

I stretched out my arm. The fat man next to me also undid the wrist buttons of his plaid shirt and stretched his thigh-sized arm to another nurse.

"I kept a strict diet to lower my cholesterol, you'll see."

The whole infirmary burst into laughter. We were all looking at the short man's red face and his body stuffed into his tight shirt, he looked soft and innocent, as blameless as a lover of blood- sausage.

They tightened the rubber bands around our upper arms.

"You have good veins."

She called a young nurse.

"Will you take care of her?"

A nurse about my age sat in front of me.

"Watch out, don't prick yourself!" a more veteran colleague warned her, discreetly pointing out my diagnosis. The blood-sausage fan looked at me. He displayed broken capillaries on his nose and cheeks.

"The doctor will call you in an hour."

I didn't feel the sting. I saw the tubes full of blood.

I rolled down my sleeve and got ready to leave. The short man was blocking my way; he shoved his chair backwards, and strenuously pushing with his arms, noisily and laboriously stood up in front of me. He put his beret on.

"Take care," the nurse told him.

"Go, Athletic, go!" the man answered, cheering for his favorite soccer team.

—

I rode the elevator to the eleventh floor. It made me feel uneasy catching sight of myself in the mirror, an old acquaintance who observed me from afar. The elevator stopped at almost every floor; people came in and out. I was the only one who got off on the eleventh floor.

A room full of junkies, down-trodden people, a pregnant gypsy… I expected a sample of Bilbao marginality. I found an empty hallway. I realized that, unlike other sections of the hospital, the waiting room for the infectious diseases' unit was hidden; not even chairs in the hallway. I opened the door slowly, afraid of who I would see and who could see me. There was only a thirty-something guy sitting in the small bright room. He was wearing a sports coat and working diligently on his tablet. He entered the doctor's office before me. After about ten minutes, he came out with Dr. Puertas, smiling. They acted as if they were old friends.

"See you next time. Take care," the doctor told him. "Nagore," he called my name, so I would follow him.

Dr. Puertas's deer-eyes observed me from the other side of the desk.

"How are you doing?"

I brushed aside all the possible answers I could give him. He wasn't wearing the same cologne he was wearing the day before.

Jean Paul Gaultier. I was familiar with scents that did not belong to my social class.

"Your results are not good."

Outside, it was raining.

"Yesterday your cd4 lymphocytes were almost at 700, and today they hardly reach 500."

He kept sliding his finger on the paper and reciting numbers.

"All immune-system markers came down."

I looked away from the raindrops that played tag with each other in the window.

"In a single day?"

"It happens after the diagnosis."

He circled a number with his pen, and turned the report around to show it to me.

"The viral load is high. Right now, the infection probability level is very high."

He took off his glasses.

"Have you engaged in any risky behavior?"

I thought of the moment when I slipped my hand under Luka's sweatshirt. His exact body temperature. The initiative had been mine.

"I don't know."

I felt my stomach aching.

"It's important."

I was infected. I was contagious.

"You just turned white."

I brought my hands to my stomach and crouched.

"Are you OK.?"

I whisked away a thought: a smell.

"Why is the waiting room hidden?"

He looked at me from above his glasses.

"To protect your privacy."

The architecture itself showed we had something to hide.

"Ninety percent of the patients who come here come for the same reason."

I thought of the guy wearing the sports coat.

"I can't believe it."

I didn't tell him the exact idea that crossed my mind: I can't believe that sex is over for me. It was a jab, a thought and its physical reflex, in my vagina, pain, concentrated in my genitals. I looked at the doctor as if he were a policeman, a judge, a civil servant. I felt like saying, "If you only knew!" The impulse to say: "I've had such good times." Wanting him to understand: "I have loved so well." I gave myself permission to cry.

"We have to talk about the medication you need to take."

He pulled out a few booklets from the desk drawer. A series of colorful pamphlets showing what looked like smiling young athletes. I read, "Tracking-card," "Antiretroviral treatment control," "Symptom control," "medication A," "medication B," "medication C," "medication D," …

"I would like to postpone taking medication as long as possible."

I knew that they didn't have reliable information about the long-term effects of antiretroviral medication. He looked at me astonished.

"I recommend you start as soon as possible."

"I don't want to."

"We don't want the infection to spread."

I tried to erase the memory of the stench.

"You must do it for yourself and others."

"I feel like throwing up."

He handed me a bag. When I began vomiting, he handed me a few paper towels. He took care of disposing of the bag and left the office.

I stood up and waited for him to return.

"Where are you going?"

"I have things to do. I'll come back some other time."

He sat down.

"Pride won't help you."

"Neither will submission."

"You're wrong."

"That's my problem."

"It's obvious: you are the one in trouble."

I grabbed my jacket and my purse. I looked at the doctor as I was about to leave.

"Could I ask you something?"

"That's why I'm here."

"Is there a way to know when I got infected?"

"In your case, yes. It's recent."

I pictured the car, the bed, the guy. That soft penis. The smell.

"How do you know?"

"I would say that you have shown a 'weak positive;' you are turning into seropositive.

I murmured as if confessing.

"It was two months ago."

"Yes, it could be."

"It's my fault."

When the elevator left me in the main entrance of the hospital, the ghost of death walked along with me, but the automatic doors threw me out, back to life. The man that had approached me to ask me for a light was gone. Cigarette butts on the wet pavement by the hospital entrance. I smoked alone. I let the butt fall, opened my umbrella and started walking.

—

Once in a while, Father would take Tuesday afternoons off. He gave me a call while I was having lunch at Grandma's and asked me if I felt like going to the port in Mutriku to enjoy the nice weather. I left the table without finishing dessert.

There was the black Ford Escort, with the top down.

"Hello, Jenisjoplin!" He greeted me.

As soon as we lost sight of Lasalde, I stood on the back seat and made the rest of the trip with my head in the open air, my hair blowing in the wind, all the way to Mutriku. When stopped at traffic lights, I liked to get on my knees and play the staring contest with the driver behind us. I would always win.

Father stopped the car at a bar at the entrance to town and asked me to wait. I was in a hurry to get in the ocean. Though we lived close to the shore, they rarely took me to the beach. Mother loved the shade and to stay at home while Father preferred to go to the festivals of neighboring towns. He wouldn't rest until he got me the biggest doll at shooting games at the carnival. When I was about five or six, we went to town festivals, to the carnival stands, and Father took me on the highest rides, the ones for adults, like the Roller Coaster, the Viking-Ship ride and the Eagle. He always clashed with the people in charge of the rides, wanting to bring a young child along, but he would tell them firmly that he was the father and to leave him alone. I always felt safe as long as Father held me from my waist, even when the ground was above and the sky under us. Mother would wait for us on the ground, terrified. The few times we visited the beach, depending on the color of the warning flags, Father would take me into the deep waters always holding my hand, we both advanced against the waves, breathing precariously, until a wave would catch us from below and return us tumbling to the shore, our swimsuits, hair and mouths full of sand.

Father returned quickly. We walked down to the port and observed the children who were undressing at the edge of the tidal pool. I took off behind them but Father whistled at me.

"Follow the other group!"

He was referring to the kids who had left the pool behind and were headed to the edge of the dock. I had heard about it before but had never been to what was known as the "drum." The tide was low, I walked carefully to the edge of the pier, afraid to fall into the water that seemed so far below. We climbed the last few steps to get to the "drum." Father sat down on the ground, he spoke to me while holding a cigarette in his mouth.

"Jump!"

I looked at him in panic.

"Nagore, jump!" he repeated, sternly.

I began slowly undressing. I took two steps toward the edge and, began feeling dizzy as soon as I looked down. My vision blurred; the two sides of the dock seemed to come together, and then pull apart. I took a step back. When I was about to turn around and tell Father that I wasn't going to jump, I sensed a big hand pushing me and felt my body falling. I fell, wind- milling my arms and legs. The time it took to fall into the water and emerge seemed eternal. I surfaced with my eyes wide-open, in a panic, but after a few seconds, my urge to burst into tears, turned into a giddy happiness. I began laughing loudly, while thrashing my hands and legs to keep from sinking. I looked up and saw Father's head looking at me. He was applauding.

I proudly retraced my steps to the "drum:" I felt I could smell the admiration of the kids smoking and sitting on the steps and against the wall. I climbed the steps to the dock breathless and with anticipation to see Father. I pictured him waiting for me, holding the towel wide, ready to tightly embrace me.

"C'mon, one more time!" he urged as soon as I walked to him.

The second time I jumped with no push. This time the height of the dock as well as the time between the drop and Father's accompanying round of applause seemed shorter. The kids on the steps did not even bother to look at me. Farther away, in the tidal pool, the children kept playing with a ball. I told Father I wanted to go back home.

"You bet," he said, after making me jump five or six more times.

—

The Lasalde neighborhood had been built, in a hurry, in the northern section of town, between the stream known as the Earthworm and the railroad, to house the wave of workers that arrived in the valley from southern Spain. It was close to town, yet separate. It was located across the tracks, close to the hills, fields of rough grass, burrows, rocks and trees, each area with its own name: *Zaldikoa*, *Sorgin*, *Urpekontzia*. At the beginning of the schoolyear, the bushes next to the banks of the stream were chock-full of blackberries and, at the end of the school year, ducklings hatched.

Grandma and Grandpa's second floor apartment had a balcony that faced the street. That is where everyone lived before I was born. My parents earned a living working at a bar they leased called Zazpi that was located in the biggest town in the area. Mother worked there during her entire pregnancy. They lived for a few months in some friends' house as boarders. Zazpi was a typical dive-bar of those days, mildew stench, a perpetual all-nighter, with no windows or ventilation, with long sofas against the wall. It must've been a dim hole, a take-off and landing strip for the heroin addicts' pleasure trips. Mother went to work under the protection of a mastiff. Her customers were usually polite to her, but calming down the kids in withdrawal, having to oversee the cash register, cleaning the vomit, reviving those who had passed out in the restroom…were all part of her job. On one occasion, when she went to replace a wobbly tile on the restroom floor, she realized that that was where the neighborhood addicts hid their lone, shared syringe. She did not dare remove it.

When I was born, my parents decided to leave Zazpi and lease another bar in our neighborhood. The premises had an apartment and we moved in. It was a humble neighborhood bar, Media Luna: a bar counter, kitchen, appetizers, paper-napkins and olive pits covering the dirty floor. Noise, clanging plates and the on and off faucet. Boisterous men, smoke, TV. The bar was an extension of our home or, more precisely, the other way around: our home was an extension of the bar. While my parents were at work, they kept me in a small crib by the door between the bar counter and the hallway. Apparently, I didn't complain much and the buzzing of the bar helped me fall asleep and take long naps. My parents took turns working: Father worked nights and slept during the day, while Mother opened the Media Luna, cleaned the place and fixed the appetizers. If by chance I cried, she would ask a customer to take care of the bar while she nursed me by the door.

"The youngest bartender in history, right here!" people teased her.

A few months after Karmen's death, at the beginning of June, Grandma took me to her hometown, La Esperanza. My parents thought that getting away and taking care of her granddaughter would help her with her mourning. They took advantage of that time to take over the Ataka and change bars and homes for the third time.

In La Esperanza, we stayed with Grandma's youngest brother. Uncle Paco was a councilman in a town of about one hundred people. He was a member of the Spanish Communist Party. Atop a small hill, the town consisted of a small group of houses lining both sides of the dirt road, squeezed against hilly and washed-out terrain; dusty floors, cracked walls, surrounded by pines and olive trees. We stayed in that small town, without much entertainment, from June to September. Grandma made me a few new dresses, since the clothing that Mother packed for me was too hot for Andalusia summers. I don't know what we did during the day. I must've spent time next to Grandma, drawing on the floor with chalk, or playing with small rocks. In most of the pictures taken during those months I'm usually outside, by the doorway, inside a bucket full of water, eating watermelon or sitting on a small stone fence, dressed up as a flamenco dancer. The pictures are overexposed, taken from a distance. No close-ups, and I'm always alone.

My parents' life, on the contrary, advanced rapidly. Soon after my aunt died, Father began working determinedly. If anyone asked him about his sister, he replied with a quiet smile. He bought the bar, rented an apartment, and filled the fridge in one and the bedrooms in the other.

Grandma and I returned from Andalusia in mid-September, right after the town's festivities were over. Father welcomed me at Ataka's door, crouching down, with his arms open. I didn't let Grandma's hand go. We had lunch, they closed the bar, and I took off toward Lasalde.

"We don't live there anymore."

He took me in his arms and took me to Altzadi, the neighborhood across the stream.

"This is our new house!"

What I remember about that house is that it was located in a neighborhood that I didn't know; that it didn't have a living room or a dining room; that the kitchen had a marble counter with three stools that were too tall for me to reach and that marked where the kitchen ended.

—

In the outskirts of the city, a web of roads of different heights, carrying scrap-metal blood pumped by the rusty heart of Bilbao. I couldn't confirm if the news about the arrest had been covered by peeking at the newspaper of the traveler sitting next to me since he had it open to the sports section. I placed my head against the window and for the first time in many hours, I fell asleep.

The world, sitting in the back of the black Ford Escort, was small and warm. I was lying down, sleeping lightly. I felt something on my arm and sensed Mother's smell on the coat she just carefully placed over me. Billie Holiday's *Strange Fruit* on the car's cassette player. Raindrops against the windows. Father's voice, and a little softer, Mother's. Laughing.

Someone was shaking me as if I were an old rag.

"You're bleeding."

The woman sitting next to me handed me a handkerchief she had pulled out from her coat pocket.

"Here."

I began bleeding while asleep. I looked out of the window, confused. Pancorbo. Spain. It took me a few seconds to stitch together the recent events. When I sat up straight, two big blood drops fell down to my chest. I searched for some tissues in my backpack, while I tried to stop the bleeding with my left hand.

"Wait, let me help you."

She began cleaning the stain on my sweater with a wet towel.

"If it dries out, you won't be able to wash it off."

I felt scared.

"Please stop."

I realized that her hand was stained with my blood.

"Wash it, right now."

"Don't worry, honey."

She used the same wet paper towel to lightly clean her hand and placed it inside the ashtray in her front seat.

“The days when we were allowed to smoke in buses are sure long gone,” she exclaimed.

I formed a little ball with tissue, put it inside my nose and I pulled back my head.

“It’s not good to plug your nose when it’s bleeding.”

I turned my back on her. I felt the phone vibrating in the pocket of my jacket. It was Irantzu calling.

It was cold in the bus. My legs had felt trapped since the passenger in from of me reclined her seat. The discomfort made me want to cry. With my eyes closed, I tried to return to the backseat of my parent’s car, to no avail. Shakira’s *Waka-Waka* playing on the radio. It was long past the eighties! “I’m on my way to Madrid. Sorry. I’ll tell you all about it another time,” I texted her. I turned off my phone.

—

By the time we arrived in Madrid it was dark. The feeling of being in a strange place shook me. I looked around. I didn’t see Luka. Perhaps, his invitation had been nothing but sweet talk, perhaps a few nice words said under duress. After all, we hardly knew each other.

“Your face looks familiar.”

He was wearing the same clothes as when we were together, a sweatshirt with the hood on, under it, his messy hair. I didn’t see him approach me.

He took a step back and narrowed his eyes.

“Do I know you?”

His tennis-shoes were soaking wet.

“Nagore Vargas.” I told him.

"Luka Moretti," he pretended to take off his hat. "Nice to meet you."

He wasn't as Italian as his last name. His mother was from Venice but destiny led him to be born in the isolated Irish county of Donegal; he wandered here and there, going to wherever his mother's journalistic specialty of revealing the insides of freedom fighting movements took her.

"Hats are no longer fashionable."

"Neither are revolutionaries. Are you coming?"

He offered me his arm. I held on to it. The mouth of the metro swallowed us.

"I never would have thought of finding refuge in Madrid."

"If I owned both hell and Madrid, I would live in hell and put Madrid up for rent."

The subway train arrived in no time. People pushed us inside. The movement took me away from sadness, yet guilt frightened me from deep inside. We were under ground. Alive. I stared at Luka: a slim, small young guy, with an ordinary look to him. More than attractive, the *Transatlantic* was welcoming. A lifeboat.

"When is your flight to Havana?"

"I'm afraid of planes."

"The game is over, Luka."

The subway was now packed. We stood surrounded by bodies, pressed against them. Human heat. He grabbed me by the hand.

"Quickly, we have to switch lines."

We came out with a group of passengers. He hugged me.

"I'm sorry, truly."

The ground shook under our feet. He took me down the stairs. We climbed into another subway car, this one a little less crowded.

"Do you like cannelloni?"

"Very much."

When we walked outside, the cold struck me. People walked too fast. I felt dizzy.

"I don't know why I came."

Luka kept walking.

"*Calle del desengaño*" (Disillusionment Street) he read on the street sign. "Fortunately, it's just a little further."

It was the second floor of an old building. I climbed the stairs with difficulty.

"I'm sick Luka," I unzipped my jacket. "I shouldn't have come."

"Well, I think you did the right thing."

"You might be infected because of me."

He opened the door and turned the light on. It was a small apartment, simple but neat.

"Whose place is this?"

"My friends'; they let Mother and me use it when we come to Madrid."

"Are we alone?"

He ushered me to the bedroom. With a determination that was unknown to me, he took off my jacket and after he kissed me on the nape of the neck, he removed my t-shirt.

"I thought you were shy."

"Lie down."

I lay down on the bed and he touched my moles with his fingertips.

"Cassiopeia."

He messed up my hair with his fingers.

"I'm very skinny."

"You are beautiful."

He stood and stared at me.

"It's cold."

He pulled the sheets all the way to my chin.

"Sleep."

"I can't."

"Try."

"It always feels worse when I wake up."

"Nagore, I'm not leaving."

The street light came in through the window. The sound of rain.

"Touch me, Luka."

He lay down on the covers, next to me, both of us looking up.

"Don't be in a hurry for anything."

I only heard fear.

"This didn't begin yesterday, and will not end tomorrow," he placed a hand under my back.

"Let's do things slowly."

He caressed my side. I shriveled.

"Careful."

Once again, he covered me with the sheet.

"Please, on top the sheets," I said.

I felt Luka's nervous nakedness on the other side of the sheet. We made love without touching each other's skin.

—

I heard Luka in the kitchen. I got dressed and joined him. He was cleaning the lens of the video-camera.

"We need to talk," I said.

"Here you are!"

He carefully put the camera away.

"Good morning."

"It won't work," I explained.

He split an orange.

"You got up feeling fatalistic, didn't you?"

"I don't believe in couple relationships."

"A cup of coffee?"

I sat down.

"Luka, you can't act as if nothing happened."

"I agree."

"You're acting out of pity."

He brought two glasses of juice to the table.

"It's not my style."

"If not pity, what other reason could you have to stay with me?"

"Apparently, you can't think of any."

He coiled the camera's microphone cord. He had studied cinematography in Cuba and returned to the Basque Country with a grant to complete a documentary about youth movements. He was going to edit the recorded material in Havana.

"It's not a practical choice, Luka."

He burst into laughter.

"You should've used the first person: *I'm not a practical choice.*"

"Love is not a mysterious, rationally uncontrollable thing."

"You said love?" he asked.

I felt embarrassed.

"It's something measurable and negotiable," I explained.

"Aha!"

"That's how it works," I assured him.

"And you are accusing me of acting irrationally, right?

"Yes."

"Swept away by incomprehensible passion…"

He glared out the window for a minute. Then, he turned around and told me:

"If you were dumber, you would live more calmly."

"If you were smarter, you would shut up," I replied.

He sat down in front of me.

"Listen: All my life I followed one woman. I lived where Mother's assignment took us: In Ireland, Bogota, Barcelona, Bilbao, Havana. I haven't slept in the same bed for longer than three months. I want to pause, to get a replacement woman in my life."

"A replacement woman."

"Exactly."

"That's very practical, certainly."

"Completely. You won't go far now. You have a place in Bilbao and I don't have any money to pay rent."

"So romantic."

"I've always lived in tumultuous lands; you are the right kind of territory for me."

I turned my chair and sat crossing my legs around his back.

"Let's talk about you now."

"About me?"

"Why did you come?"

"I don't know."

"Do you want me to say it?" he asked me.

I lit a cigarette.

"Looking for a fool who won't abandon you."

"Please!" I said, outraged.

He dunked a slice of bread in tomato sauce and brought it to the table for me.

"It sure seems like it."

"Are you accusing me of wanting to take advantage of you?"

"I'm doing the same thing to you. You like theories about love, right?"

"Very much."

"So, here's one: love is never *why* but *what for*."

He stood and put the camera bag on his back.

"I'm off."

"Where to?"

"The attorney called me to let me know that Karra is about to testify."

—

As a child, I found it fun to think about misfortune and play with pain. I would dig my fingernails into my thighs or my forearms, as deep as I could. I wanted to know how much pain I could intentionally inflict on myself. Then, I would release the fingernails and stare in amazement at the dent they left in my flesh while I waited for the pain to subside. Sometimes I bit myself, my arm or the back of my hand. Once, in school, I stuck my pinky finger in the pencil sharpener and, while the teacher was explaining the lesson, I turned my finger. I screamed, not sure from the pain or the shock.

"Why did you do that?" the teacher ran to me, alarmed.

I didn't know what to say.

I loved sharing these experiences with Father. I had the impression that when I told him these kinds of things, I had his complete attention. From the vantage point of the bar stool, I reflected on false happiness with Father; I used to rehearse his sentences when I was alone, and then I'd repeat them in front of my friends, proudly:

"Misfortune can be much more interesting than happiness."

But when I shared the story of the pencil sharpener, what he told me left me completely confused.

"You know that I can't feel your pain, right?"

He taught me to fight false hopes.

"If the soup is cold, you'll waste your time pretending it's hot."

When I was five years old, Father told me that Olentzero and the Three Wise Men didn't exist, and proceeded to explain to me, with all kinds of details, why I should be against those holidays. Due to ideological and practical reasons, we didn't celebrate Christmas. Year after year, I embarked on an intimate crusade against Christmas lights, caroling, presents and happy families. Nevertheless, when Christmas came around, though embarrassed, I would end up writing a letter to Olentzero, cautiously, so Father wouldn't catch me, and I only asked for one thing, nothing very big.

On Christmas Eve, Father and Mother worked late: and it goes without saying, on New Year's Eve too, when they could hardly squeeze in a couple hours for dinner and go back down to work at Ataka. On Christmas and New Year's Day, they slept in and would go down later to clean the bar.

On December 24, they kept the bar open until the evening rounds were over; they used to need five or six servers to handle the waves of people. The bar would be packed, to such an extent that the kitchen workers couldn't even get out to use the restroom and had to urinate directly into the sink and Mother into a bucket. Me too. Instead of going to the march supporting political prisoners, I would stay to help at Ataka: bringing glasses to the bar and getting rid of the empty bottles.

On that day, at the bar, they took the annual employee photo. There's a picture, from when I was about seven or eight years old, where I'm standing on a case of beer and holding an unlit cigarette in my hand next to my parents and their co-workers. Mother has half her face covered by her black hair, looking serious, sad and beautiful, like always.

We used to go home to Altzadi from the bar at about eleven. Angel used to come with us and would hang out with my parents around the kitchen table drinking beer, chatting and smoking cigarettes. They would roll a joint and pass it around. Once in a while, they opened the balcony door to air out the kitchen. I used to sit with them and stayed there until exhaustion and that sweet smoke enveloped me and I surrendered, falling asleep against the table. Father would take me to bed, limp body, arms hanging. That was the only way I fell asleep easily, involuntarily knocked out by fatigue, confident that Father would take care of the rest.

After what seemed a short while, in the middle of my sleep, a hand would shake my shoulder and wake me up gently.

"Olentzero came," Angel would murmur into my ear.

Then, I would open my eyes and find a present in a corner of the bedroom. I would get up quietly, still wearing my street clothes.

"Don't worry, I will keep an eye out."

I would unwrap the gift carefully.

"Did Olentzero do well?" he would ask me.

I would embrace my Guardian Angel as tightly as I could.

—

When I was eight years old, Father enrolled me in the music school, against my wishes. None of my classmates registered and I didn't want to go by myself. I told Father about my fear and he laughed at me for being a chicken. Even though we had moved to Altzadi, they registered me in the Lasalde school, in Urruzuno.

Together with the only Basque-speaking family we knew in the neighborhood, Father fought so we would be taught in Basque. I was the only one among all the students in class who had at least one parent who spoke Basque. I was wary that that fact would not free me from the trap the students sitting in straight rows had set for me. Father accompanied me to the entrance.

"There, in you go!"

I had to climb a bunch of stairs: the music school was on the top floor of an old building. I was terrified. My fear took form between the second and third floor: the *Ikastola*, Basque school students were sitting in the stairway in two lines forming a corridor and I had to pass through it to get to my classroom. I walked slowly through the corridor, my eyes cast down.

I heard someone giggling behind me. I tried to pick up my pace but they stretched their Adidas tracksuit-clad legs to make me stumble. One of the boys began making farting noises. Another one cupped his hands around his mouth imitating a loud speaker and chanted:

"*Urruzuno, no one's really saved, no, no…*" and the rest repeated the chant:

"*Urruzuno, I smoked eight joints and then some mo'*"

"*Urruzuno, Spaniards out of here must go*"

"*Urruzuno there's an AIDS vaccine you know!*"

I walked through the chants, feeling their sing-song against my skin.

"I'm not ready to lose this class struggle, Jenisjoplin."

Father, for many years, wanted to learn how to play the guitar. Every time he had a get- together with his friends, he would take it out of the case though he could never complete a song. He was convinced that his clumsy relationship with his guitar was directly related to class differences.

"The distance between intelligent people and intellectuals," he told me, "is a single step: money."

And obviously, we were the intelligent, the very intelligent. The same thing happened when he would start writing poems or get lost in deep reflection: at first, he easily came up with words, but, suddenly, he would confuse the meaning of *digression* and *regression*, or he would say *diabetis* instead of *diabetes,* and the speech he had built up to that moment would come crashing down, along with its credibility, poetics and allure. His shoes were not fashioned for such a purpose. He could fool his neighbors perhaps, pretending intellectual ways but beyond that, he was exposed.

He signed me up for all the different classes the music school offered. Music theory, guitar, choir… I found my classroom and sat at a desk in the last row, next to a window.

When the teacher called the roll, I lifted my eyes from the desk just enough to show I was in attendance. My pride in the surname Vargas, the gypsy pride that Father always promoted, deserted me. Had the teacher read both of my last names, my embarrassment would have been reduced by half, but no one knew that after Vargas came my mother's name, Alkorta, and they would not find out, from me at least.

The teacher played a pompous melody on the tape recorder and asked us to clap out the rhythm.

"What is it, Mozart or Vivaldi?" I heard a fancy looking girl asking another.

I could distinguish between Camarón and Manzanita, two notes would have been enough. I felt completely ridiculous clapping along in that classroom, among children wearing brand-name clothing. Fortunately, he didn't call on me to walk to the board and draw a sixteenth note, and thus, I was able to survive my first day at the conservatory reasonably calmly.

As soon as class was dismissed, I ran out: at least that first day I avoided the mocking and pushing and shoving of the Basque school kids.

Father was waiting for me at the bottom of the main stairway.

"How was it?" He asked me over enthusiastically.

"OK."

"I told you so."

"Father, are we immigrants?"

He tightened his jaw.

"You are as Basque as those kids, you hear me?" He told me, pointing at the ones coming down the stairway.

I didn't dare contradict him. I nodded, though it was clear to me who the true Basques were: the Basque school students, those who attended after school music lessons, Basque dance classes, and had private English lessons, the ones who didn't wear discount store clothing, the ones who played school league sports wearing uniforms with neat, professionally printed numbers, unlike us, who wore our t-shirts donated by a bank with numbers drawn with markers. Everyone but Father thought those were the real Basques, the ones who did not live in Lasalde, the others.

"Jenisjoplin, I will get you an electric guitar for your next birthday, a shiny red one."

—

An old feeling of guilt runs through my veins, a yearning to be punished, an intimate dialectic with my executioner. It's the same game I play with life: punish me, I tell Life, but we will measure each other. Let's wager flesh, sweat and blood. In the struggle, I feel alive; in peace, I feel dead and that's why I seek violence: because it liberates me from settling down, from stopping, from silence. Because it reminds me that I have a body and that it belongs to me.

Most people try to stay away from violent situations because they think violence is ugly. It has taken me a long time to see that. I think the opposite: violence attracts me. I feel challenged by it; it calls me by my name. Often, it has been me who has provoked the confrontation: with my teachers, bar customers, police, doctors and myself. Defying authority is my basic self. When I'm headed to demonstrations, I look for police road blocks, for them to order me to step out of the car. But I'm never stopped. I want to show those for whom I'm invisible that I'm not afraid of them. I've fantasized about my own arrest, to the point even of wishing for that moment to happen. I pictured them battering the door down, while I stood in my room. Waiting. My body next to a policeman, facing a judge, staring into their eyes and answering their questions, one by one.

Violence, for me, is not something strange and despicable, but just one more way to communicate. Something that is there: within us, with us. I don't see it as something deplorably disgusting. I would say that I understand it. I think that contempt, disdain and silent disregard are worse.

"You decide," Father would tell me when I was a young child and would ask him for permission to do something. If I didn't obey him, I would get silence in exchange. My neighbor friends would get punished if they were caught in mischief. No TV. No dinner. No presents. Not me. There was a time when I used to ask Father to punish me; I used to confess all my wrongdoings to him and if I didn't have any, I would embellish or even make up mischief to deserve his punishment. But Father kept chatting, carelessly, leaving me the entire burden of guilt. Mother, mute. The weight of guilt. No punishment or forgiveness. That is how from one day to the next I began to punish myself: if I thought I did something wrong, I would lock myself in my bedroom, and if a friend called me to go out, I would tell them I wasn't allowed because I was being punished. And I would stay there, completely bored, until I decided that the punishment was over. No punishment, no permission, no prohibition, "You decide."

Violence in person is not the most perverse. Isn't the coercion at a distance more vicious? We witness with indifference the most heartless violence, sitting down and at a low volume. No one speaks of economic exploitation with the same disgust and conviction as people do when speaking about insurgent violence.

The poor are not victims. Poor people can't blame anyone for the mere fact of being poor. No one can reach reconciliation in this division between the rich and the poor. While terrorism is a burden to be eradicated from its roots, the reports that justify economic oppression are written in antiseptic boardrooms. Violence in person is not as evil as they say. In a confrontation, there is always a contact with the adversary; if you are seen by the other's eyes, of necessity, you exist. And I feel fully alive in violent situations, when bodies bump against one another, in the screams, in between pain and justice. I would love to know if four Spanish policemen pulled me out of the car and forcefully took me to the hills, would I show courage or shit my pants; how would the mud and the pigs' breath smell? The impulse for defiance comes from my gut, from the same place I feel my sexual impulses. Challenge the police, fight the pain. Will I endure?

I believe I've been very fortunate. I have always gotten out of bad predicaments. I have often been at risk. I've evaded broken glass, punches, rubber bullets, guns, knives, clubs, rapists. Men have followed me all the way to my house, and I haven't taken off running; when I heard their steps, I stopped, I turned around, I faced them, and closed my door in their faces. And they left. I invited danger, because it felt safer than having danger take me by surprise. I felt a sense of immunity for many years. Until life caught up with me and told me, you're wrong, Nagore, you are not immune.

—

Somosierra. A road cracked by the heat and the cold. On the roadside, a few holm oaks, scattered bushes: heather, rosemary, thorn bushes.

"Nagore."

I pulled my head away from the window and my thoughts.

Karra's eyes in the rearview mirror.

"You're quiet."

It hadn't been two hours since we saw him leaving the Supreme Court. As soon as he stepped onto the street, Irantzu jumped on him before he was able to draw his first breath outside. Karra's reaction frightened me. It was subtle, barely the beginning of a gesture; when his friend came to him I thought I saw him instinctively bringing his arms up to protect himself. He stopped in his tracks and quickly controlled his first, almost unnoticeable impulse to lift his arms. I searched for my friend's eyes from a distance. He smiled at me cordially and nodded. A detail that I didn't know how to interpret: he was missing the laces of his Martens boots. Luka was immortalizing the moment from behind his video camera.

Once he had hugged us all, he looked around.

"They're waiting for you at home."

"They didn't come?"

"Liher is sick with chicken-pox and has had a high fever these last two nights. It worried me to have him make such a long trip, you know how he gets when he's in the car."

"Poor thing."

"We promised him that we'll have you home by lunch time."

Karra rubbed his stomach.

"Would you like to have a cup coffee? Did they feed you?"

I pointed at the Riofrío bar across from the courthouse.

"No way! Let's get out of here now!" he said.

Irantzu grabbed him by the arm.

"I left the car running."

"Whenever you want," said Luka.

We stared at him.

"Weren't you headed to Havana?"

"Who? Me?"

He finished packing the video camera. Karra put his arms around Irantzu's and my shoulders.

"How was the trip?"

I had to endure Irantzu's sideways look.

"I came by myself."

He was searching for an explanation. Karra was confused.

"I believe I missed a chapter."

"I think I have too," said Irantzu.

I looked at Luka. He winked at me. He slung his backpack and camera bag over his shoulder.

"Irantzu, will the four of us be able to fit in your Corsa?"

On the road once again. Cerezo de Abajo. Aldealcorvo. Cantalejo. The journalists on the road: Irantzu the driver, Karra her copilot, Luka and me in the back.

"How did they treat you?" Luka stroked Karra's hair from the back seat.

"I can't complain."

"Was it hard?" Irantzu slowed the car down.

"It's not like going on vacation, but you know…"

"Did they drive you crazy?"

"They wouldn't shut up."

Karra, looking out of the window, went quiet for a while.

"They must've fed you lie after lie, for sure."

"That was the worst of it: even though you try to convince yourself, your mind tries to separate truths from all the lies.

He glared at his watch.

"Turn on the radio."

"We can only get the Catholic Radio Maria."

Karra laughed.

"Separate a truth right there!"

Pardilla. Fuentenebro. Rain-drops.

"Were you calm?"

He asked about our phones by placing his thumb to his ear and his pinky to his mouth. We let him know that he could talk freely.

"Until I appeared in front of the judge, I didn't know I was the only one they arrested. I thought I heard Nagore's voice in the holding cell nearby."

I raised my eyes.

"I was convinced of it until the attorney assured me otherwise."

Luka rubbed my thigh. He noticed I was completely absorbed in my thoughts. I held his hand.

"What's that all about?" Karra turned around at once.

"What?" asked Irantzu.

I let go of his hand, scared.

"No shit. You have been having sex while I was in there!"

Irantzu looked back. The car swerved to the right.

"Look ahead, Irantzu!"

"And I was worried about you!" Karra scolded me.

He addressed Irantzu.

"You knew about this?"

"What are you guys talking about?" Irantzu asked, infuriated.

"We're carrying two traitors back there, in heat."

For the first time in two hours, I opened my mouth.

"It's not what you all think."

Irantzu let go of the steering wheel and lifted her hands in the air.

"You stood me up so he would lick your crotch?" Irantzu exclaimed.

"Shut up, Irantzu," Luka said outraged.

"Stop right there."

Irantzu followed my command and stopped the car at a rest area by the roadside. It was raining. I lit a cigarette without rolling down the window.

"I know this is not the right time to talk about me. You've just come out of prison, but things have taken a turn for the worse for me."

Irantzu stared at me gravely.

"The day of the arrest I went to the hospital to have, what I thought was routine, blood work done."

"What do you have?"

"I have been diagnosed with AIDS."

I observed my friends' faces become disfigured.

"When I told Luka about it, he invited me to come to Madrid and without thinking twice about it, I hopped on the bus. I'm sorry, Irantzu, I couldn't handle the press conference."

The three of them fell silent.

A truck honked at us; we were blocking the road.

"So, it was true…" Karra shook his head.

"What?"

"What the pigs told me."

Karra kept his eyes fixed on me.

"What do you mean?

"They knew it. They kept telling me that you had the *Bug***.** I didn't want to believe it."

"But… there's no way…"

A surreal feeling jarred me. I stared at Luka, scared.

"How did you tell Luka?" Karra asked me.

"Shit," said Luka.

I was completely lost.

"Your telephone, Nagore. It's tapped."

I got out of the car. I needed to breathe.

"Nagore!"

I took off walking and returned quickly, soaking wet.

"What did they tell you exactly?"

"I don't know…"

"Tell me the truth, Karra."

"That the day of the arrest they saw you on your way home and that you looked wasted away…"

I remembered the policeman that I saw when I was carrying my groceries.

"The one that seemed the calmest among them brought it up: '*the poor thing looked like a skeleton*.'"

"What else did he say?"

"'*Sure, you know, the illness the whores and the junkies get…*' or something like that another one said."

"Fucking sons of bitches," Luka was infuriated.

"And what else?"

"That's all."

"Tell me the truth."

"It's nothing but poison."

"I want to hear it."

"*The bitch got what she deserves.*"

"Did they say I would die soon?"

He remained in silence.

"Great. Now you all know it: the doctors, the police, you. Nothing to declare. Let's go home."

We rode the next miles in silence. Quintanilla de la Mata. Villafruela. And further ahead Burgos, Atapuerca. As we were driving by Armiñon, Irantzu tuned in to Euskadi Irratia. We found out during the 1:00pm newscast that, though Karra had been freed, Judge Pablo Ruz had ordered the preemptive closure of Radio Libre.

—

The sky hung low. It was a foggy and humid day in September 1994. I was twelve.

"Shall we go out for a stroll?" Father asked me on the phone.

He took me to Zumaia. The rising tide dragged the sea to the edge of the seawall.

"Shall we go in?"

I didn't feel like getting wet.

"The last swim of summer!" he exclaimed.

All "lasts" were sacred for Father: the last cigarette, the last song, the last chance. He began untying his tennis shoes.

"Lets' go!"

We didn't have our swimsuits. We found an old towel in the trunk of the car. Father crossed the empty beach naked, and I followed him in my underwear. On our way in, the waves slapped our thighs and waist, foamy; the current dragged the sand under our feet, unsettling the ground, and making our feet sink into sand holes. I eyed a tree trunk carried by the river at about twenty yards away from us.

"I dare you to swim all the way there."

I submerged my head under water and I ducked under the wave. Another one. I swam ahead riding the waves that didn't break and sinking under the sudden, white-capped ones. I held on to the trunk. I grabbed it with my hand and when I was about to show it to Father, a big wave caught me unexpectedly from behind and the trunk hit my head. I struggled to keep my head above water, but as soon as I drew a breath, the next wave pulled me under again. Instead of fighting the sea, I decided to remain still under water, to wait until the waves had calmed down. When I surfaced, I realized that I was a few yards farther from the shore than before. The tide was dragging me to the open sea. I called Father. I lost patience and began swimming towards the shore, trying to do powerful strokes. Another wave swallowed me. White. I gasped for air. Sand. Father's head in the distance. White, black and then red. A piece of sky, gray. Far away, the sensation that I was being dragged to the bottom. And suddenly, surrender. Silence. My arms and head powerless under water. The calm swaying of being. The melody of the sea in my entrails. A cradle. Falling asleep.

I woke up in Father's arms, wrapped in the old towel.

"Where were you going, Jenisjoplin?"

I was shivering. He carried me in his arms to the car, like he used to take me at home from the sofa to bed. He covered me with the blanket and turned up the heater. A comforting sound. A kind of interior happiness came over me; the warmth was so gentle and calming, Father's hand resting on my head.

He got dressed.

"Nagore..." he said.

I smiled at him. He held my chin softly.

"Mother and I have decided to separate."

I stared at him in silence. The sea still echoed inside my ears. I began to hear a whistle-like sound.

"It's just a decision like any other."

He paused.

"The same way you have decided to quit music, we have decided to break up."

Nothing but the cackling of the seagulls in the air. Another car parked next to ours, the ruckus of a few boys. I concentrated on the rumbling of the heater. The absurdity of wearing my wet underwear wrapped in a checkered blanket. A heavy feeling of being crippled. A traitor tear slipped away, warm and fat, down my cheek.

"I might start playing the guitar again."

He pushed aside my wet hair from my face.

"For starters, I'm going to move to Madrid. And figure out what to do next."

I felt my body tensing. That zone where the ocean freezes. The first raindrop in the wind. In silence, I tried to review the last months in my head. I couldn't think of my parents kissing or hugging, or fighting either.

The tide was low at Itzurungo beach and dragged the water forcefully to the open ocean. The engine was still running, and the tree trunk I thought I had caught remained there, on the shore, still, in the dark.

—

When my parents separated, we moved for the fourth time. Some former neighbors were putting their place up for rent and gave Mother a good deal, so we returned to Lasalde. Angel helped us with the move. I was thrilled to move from Altzadi back to our neighborhood.

Our new place was on the ground floor, I could get in the house through my window instead of the door. A rude woman named Maritere Kortaberria lived next to us. The rest of the neighbors thought she was crazy because she always wore her robe, lived with a dozen cats, and especially, because she chatted with Pakito, her parakeet.

"How are you able to get your parakeet to speak?" I asked her.

"The most important thing is to place a mirror inside the cage. Parakeets don't speak unless they think they have company. And then, it takes many hours. You have to build a relationship with the bird, you know. The best time for practice is early in the morning, right when you uncover the cage. You have to repeat the words, repeat, repeat, repeat. "P," "t", "k" and "d" are the best sounds. *Pakito*, *Pakito*, *Pakito*. And then, there you go, a piece of celery.

"*Pakito*, *Pakito*!" the parakeet continued screaming.

"Now, this one here is more challenging."

A thickset girl walked by us. She looked a little older than me and came in Maritere's house. She walked across the entryway as if we were not there. Maritere herself had told me once that her daughter was schizophrenic. Apparently, she also had a son but he was in jail.

"Because of some rapes," she said barely changing her facial expression.

She didn't mention her daughter's or son's names. She pointed to a photo in the hallway: a slim man about thirty years old.

I spent quite a few afternoons in Maritere's house, looking after the cats and teaching Pakito new words: *Compote*! *Compote*! *Compote*! One day, word spread in the neighborhood that they let Korta out of jail. The rapist was on the loose; parents and teachers warned girls not to wander alone and to avoid going toward the hills. The boys enjoyed scaring the girls on the playground: "rapist!" they would shout, and the girls would take off running, leaving behind their backpacks, dolls, pebbles, little sticks or whatever they had in hand. When they realized that the boys were teasing them, after grumbling at them, they resumed playing.

I didn't sense any movement in the neighborhood, I told my friends that it was nothing but gossip, not to listen to the rumors. When the boys saw that I stayed put, they counter attacked.

"Look at her fat tits!" I heard a boy called Mikel shout.

When they began measuring us, we began measuring ourselves. In a few months, my breasts had grown noticeably and it wasn't just because I gained some weight. I borrowed a bra from Mother's drawer and confirmed that it was too small. The boys' jokes and teasing went on and so did our disdain toward ourselves. They would tell us to pick a hardcover book, open it in front of our breasts, and try to close it. When we did it, those who had a little flesh, got their breasts squeezed by the covers, and the boys mocked us. For others, the book would completely close and they would laugh at them too. The boys who attended Basque schools referred to girls who did not have breasts yet as "surf boards." In Lasalde they referred to them as "cardboard." They ranked on the classroom blackboard in chalk each girl's breasts by comparing them to mountains. They biggest ones were Everest; the smallest ones Xoxote. They compared us to animals, mountains, objects, food, materials etc.

One day, as I was walking home after school, Mikel came from behind, grabbed my breasts and shook them up and down. I turned around and slapped him with all my might but he continued laughing at me, surrounded by his circle of buddies. I noticed that even the teacher standing near the boys couldn't hide his laughter. I felt a fury rise from my legs, an impulse to punch that teacher but I stayed still, paralyzed. At home, I took off my undershirt and stood in front of the mirror in my bedroom: where the heck did these breasts come from? They didn't feel like they belonged to me. I didn't know them, I didn't know anything about them, they hurt, they swung. The boys stared at them, sized them and compared them. I felt that because of those two pieces of flesh, I was forever expelled from somewhere, but I couldn't tell for sure from where.

I kept spending time with Maritere; at least she let me be. I ran errands for her; she mostly sent me to the store to buy canned goods. I also helped her store jars on the highest shelves, since, by then, I was quite a bit taller than she was.

At school, they asked us to build a musical instrument out of recycled materials; and one afternoon, another classmate and I headed to the dump site across the train tracks, in search of materials. Once on the other side of the tracks, as we walked along a dirt road, I spotted Korta. I was sure it was him. He was coming down the road, staggering.

"It's him," I said.

I sensed that my friend was about to start running, but I grabbed her arm firmly and yanked her to come along. We walked by the man, hardly half a yard from him; we turned back to watch him walk in the other direction. When we arrived at the dump site, she let go of me and pushed me away, infuriated.

"You're nuts!"

A few days later, in the evening, when I was watching TV with Mother, we heard a dull noise. We tensed up on the sofa and when walked up to the window, we saw flames in Maritere's house. We rushed to the entrance hall of the building, there was our neighbor, wearing her usual robe, her hair on fire, screaming. Mother threw a towel over her and the stench of smoke and burned flesh spread around. Her son had broken the window with a rock and then threw a Molotov cocktail inside. All the cats disappeared, Pakito too.

"I opened his cage, otherwise he would have perished—suffocated or burned," Maritere told us.

Then we realized that Maritere's daughter was still inside the house, sitting on the side of the bed, staring at the wall, still. The three of us together had to bring her out, since she did not want to move from her bed.

Mother called the police, but they didn't even spend five minutes with Maritere. Our two neighbors stayed with us that night. A few days later, the cats returned. Pakito did not.

—

When we arrived in Bilbao, we accompanied Karra home. His little boy, covered in red splotches, was crying in his mother's arms. Karra's girlfriend invited us to stay for lunch but we preferred to respect the family's privacy.

She showed us the morning news images on her phone: the door of "*Radio Libre*" sealed off.

"Our mail has also been seized," Irantzu informed me.

"You'll need to start all over again," Karra's girlfriend said.

As we were driving by Atxuri, I saw, through the windshield, the round shape of the back of the Arriaga theater. When we stopped at a red light, Irantzu lifted her arms over her head and stretched backwards. She turned her neck left and right. She must've been tired after the round-trip to Madrid. Now she was unemployed. She would need to begin sending out her resume and start working on collaboration projects for pennies: a commissioned short article for *Argia*, a supplement about gardening for *Berria*… She wrote well, precisely and concisely, but she hadn't had much luck. During her last year in college, she interned at the *Berria* newspaper, on the TV programing and agenda sections, but couldn't really show off her talent. In Areatza they were setting up the street stands for the October book fair. When we reached the round-about in front of city hall, I felt like going for a stroll by the river.

"Stop for a minute," I asked Irantzu.

She parked the car at the taxi stop.

"Should we go for a walk?"

I asked them both, although I was really just looking for Irantzu's company. I hadn't spent time with her since the whirlwind had started. Fortunately, Luka was a very perceptive person.

"You two go, I'll find a good parking spot," he told Irantzu.

The sunrays peering through the black clouds created winking reflections in the waters of the Ibaizabal river. Luka got out of the car and took over the driver's seat. Irantzu and I got out of the way on the sidewalk.

"I'll wait for you at home," he told me.

I enjoyed the echo of the phrase.

"Tell Mother I'm fine."

We started walking along the river, toward Zubizuri bridge.

"What are you going to do now?" she asked me.

"We'll need to get the Radio Station going again."

She looked down, at the ground.

"I don't have the strength. I'm tired of living on the edge, aren't you?"

I never thought that living on the edge could be a personal choice.

"I'm not sure."

We had just sold Ataka in order to by the perfumery and I owed money to the bank and to Father. I was about to start taking a few shifts at the left-wing bar, Somera. Maybe Luka would find a job and could help me with rent. After repairing the radio station a little, I could start again. Thinking of "other things" had a calming effect on me. It was easier than thinking about myself.

"I'm thinking about doing something with this."

"With your diagnosis?"

I nodded.

"Talks?"

"Talks, some research, a documentary… I'm not sure yet."

"There is plenty to talk about."

"I might have an outlet that way."

Father had also mentioned the idea of vindicating my aunt.

"Be careful," Irantzu warned me.

"Why?"

"You have a tendency to save the world instead of yourself."

"You know something? I already know this whole area," I said, pointing to the river bank and the old part of the city.

She began to slow down, but I yanked her arm forward. It was easier to talk while walking.

"I used to come with Grandma to Bilbao as a child. Grandma Rosa participated in the Committee Against AIDS."

I stopped, turned around and pointed at Areatza with my index finger. They held their meetings at the gay and lesbian center, in the old part of the city. Grandma came weekly and I joined her sometimes, especially in summer, when there was no one left in Lasalde. We would come by train to Atxuri and Grandma used to chat with the junkies we met under the bridges.

"In front of you?"

"Yes."

I resumed walking.

"Grandma read during the train ride. I would fall asleep on her lap, on her black skirt with the rocking of the train. She distributed syringes and condoms among heroin addicts, and sometimes she gave them sandwiches too. She held my hand and took me to the meetings at the center. There, she gave me a few sheets of paper and crayons to keep me occupied during the meetings. Afterward, she took me to have hot chocolate with *churros*." I turned around, again, "In that coffee shop."

I remembered Grandma Rosa's smell.

"In 1988, we participated in a Gurutzeta Hospital protest."

"You…"

"Six years old."

I opened my hand and lifted my palm toward the sky.

"Rain?"

Irantzu pulled out a folding umbrella from her backpack, and I pushed my body close against her arm.

"In 1988, they organized a protest in front of Gurutzeta Hospital because its daycare denied admission to a child suspected of being an HIV carrier. The case had a boomerang effect, and other protests took place in Durango, Basauri and Markina schools. Grandma was outraged. Parents made threatening phone calls to school principals, threatening to take their children out of school if the infected children were not dismissed.

"I didn't realize that happened."

"Of course. That would be expected."

"You grew up around all that."

"Grandma and I went out on Saturdays to distribute condoms among young people."

"It must've been difficult."

"I had a great time."

"Fortunately, your grandma didn't live to see this."

"If she were alive I could never forgive myself."

"The same hell twice over."

"I think of her every day."

I began rolling a cigarette under the umbrella.

"You want one?"

She shook her head no.

"She wouldn't believe it."

"I can hear her telling me: '*Sweetheart, with all the condoms I gave you*'."

I exhaled a sigh of smoke.

"Really, it's hard to believe. AIDS, now, in 2010."

"It seems a thing of the past."

"Yes."

"I've always had the feeling of having been born too late."

"Too late? For what?"

"I have an *eighties* spirit."

"That's true."

"You think so too?"

"I'm not prone to believing in superstitions, but, shit, this looks like destiny's dirty trick."

We continued walking in the rain.

"I'm thinking these days about Esther Ferrer's interview in *Argia* magazine. It could have been right here," I told her pointing at the bridge.

Irantzu didn't remember.

"One time, when Ferrer lived close to Pont Neuf, she said that she went out at night and walked around in the rain. It was winter and there was no one else outside. When she made it to the bridge, at the very same instant she was about to place her foot on it, she eyed a man walking from the opposite direction and thought: 'We're going to cross paths.' She did her best so that they would cross paths right in the middle of the bridge: she matched her steps to the man's, she calculated the specific rhythm..."

"And?"

"They crossed paths right in the middle of the bridge. The man, of course, was not aware of anything."

Irantzu stared at the Zubizuri bridge.

"It feels as if we just crossed paths."

"Who has?"

"My aunt and I."

We were getting closer to the stairs to the bridge. We climbed them slowly.

"Irantzu, and what if it was me who was looking forward to meeting her halfway?"

"Don't be fatalistic."

"How come all this is happening? It must mean something."

"Nagore, you have never protected yourself; you have been completely self-sufficient. Maybe the time has come for you to admit weakness."

"So, then, you think this is a life lesson?"

"How many times have you put yourself at risk?"

The Salbe bridge was right in front of us. It burdens me to think of all those I put at risk, more than the risks I took.

"You said you were ready for anything, even to face torture… Are you aware of how many stupid things you've said?"

The glass floor of the Zubizuri bridge was slippery.

"Often, bravery is the result of a lack of attachment to life."

"Whatever you say."

She resumed walking, leaving me behind, with no umbrella to cover me.

"Things are not at all simple," I said.

"I don't know, I want to help you, but it's not easy."

She turned around and took off quickly toward the other side of the river. My arrogance unnerved her. I saw her slip in the rain when she reached the downhill curve at the end of the bridge; she fell flat. I ran to her and helped her get up. The umbrella's small ribs looked completely disfigured.

"Stupid!" she scolded herself.

"You wanted to cross the bridge too quickly," I teased her.

"Go fuck yourself."

She started the sentence loudly but finished it almost in a whisper. She must've thought that the sexual reference of her insult made me feel uncomfortable. I enveloped her shoulders with my arm and kissed her.

"We'll learn something from this too," I assured her.

We stuffed the broken umbrella in a garbage can and, in the rain, on that other side of the river, retraced the steps we had taken earlier.

II

I called him right after we returned from Madrid. I got his number through a common friend and we met half way between each other's towns. I thought he looked even more child-like than he did two months earlier. He arrived with a careless look at the bar where we agreed to meet, carrying a gym bag hanging from his shoulder.

"I don't remember anything from that night."

He pulled a little pouch from his pants pocket.

"This is how I knew you had been at my place."

I opened it and recognized my red necklace. I didn't remember taking it off.

They brought us our coffee.

"I have been diagnosed with AIDS," I told him.

He stared at his hands. They were strong and tanned. I noticed the corners of his nails were covered in magnesium powder and figured that after our meeting, he was headed to Atxarte to do some rock climbing.

"I thought you were going to tell me that you were pregnant."

I couldn't tell by his voice which one he thought was more alarming.

"I believe you're the one who infected me."

He remained silent, looking absent-minded. We stared at each other without a word.

"You should get tested."

It was a five-minute conversation, if that. A few days later, he sent me a text: 'I tested positive.' I tried to get in touch with him but he never answered my calls.

—

In the months following the diagnosis, I wandered through my everyday routine. Though I looked the same in others' eyes, it didn't take much for everything to turn unsteady. The diagnosis brought ripples of emotion especially the feeling of insecurity: the ground stopped being a secure foundation. I was architecture disassembled from the top down, keeping inventory among the debris. Those had been sunny days. In the midst of all those broken cinder blocks, I found unexpected little moments of happiness among a few unidentifiable corpses.

Luka returned to my apartment and we decided to take the master bedroom for us and move Mother to the guest room with no complaints or questions from her.

"It's hard for me to confine Mother to that dungeon."

"You should stop acting like your mother's mother."

In the evenings, the three of us sat together on the sofa to watch TV. We had begun watching the classic *Twin Peaks*. Mother and I would each light a cigarette and Luka, holding a book in his hands, would switch from watching the series to reading the political essay that he already knew by heart. I usually sat between them. It was the second time sharing my apartment with my mother and my partner and it wasn't uncomfortable at all. Sure, I pretended that Mother was annoying. Sometimes, Luka would stroke my calves under my pajamas, discretely, and we would share a complicit smile. But, secretly, I was thankful for Mother's presence, because besides being a buffer to Luka's sexual drive, she also was a sort of extension of my presence which transmitted me strength.

I had two more appointments with Dr. Puertas which filled me with contradictions. A bunch of confusing data piled up on top of the skepticism I already had about the medical establishment. I would share my uneasiness with Luka.

"I don't understand; in my first appointment, he told me I was turning seropositive, but that I already had contracted AIDS. How can it be possible to develop AIDS before becoming seropositive?"

The appointments were short and the doctor's deer-eyes made me too uncomfortable to ask him the questions I had rumbling inside. But when I compared my own experience with the information he shared with me bit by bit, I found many inconsistencies.

The day before my appointments, I wasn't hungry because I felt so nervous and on the days after the appointments, my doubts made me lose my appetite. After I returned home from the doctor's office, I would have a couple of bites of the salad that Luka had prepared for me and I would store the rest in the refrigerator.

"I'll finish it in the evening."

"Nagore, eat it now."

I straightened the crooked Mona Lisa magnet on the refrigerator door.

"The way I got infected does not coincide with what Dr. Puertas says."

"What do you mean?"

I wasn't sure what to share with Luka. I didn't like talking to him about previous relationships, especially about *that* one. I thought it was inappropriate.

"I'm not sure what to think."

Luka didn't ask me to tell him more than what I had told him.

"We did not have intercourse," I shared.

"Are you sure he was the one who infected you?

I hadn't shared his name with Luka.

"It was a guy, right?

"Yes."

"Are you sure? Because you..."

"I what?"

"Nothing."

"I'm sure."

Then Luka said something I didn't expect:

"Maybe, in this case too, the official version is not completely trustworthy."

That sentence shook me. Luka put into words what I had refused to consider. A speck of hope and the fear of feeling it.

"What are you talking about?"

"We always question the official version."

"But this is happening to my body."

"Don't swallow everything."

'Swallow everything.' I felt disgusted by the mere expression.

"There are contrary theories."

He had done his homework. He stood up and walked to the bedroom. He returned holding a book in his hands.

"Christine Maggiore," I read the name of the author.

"She turns everything upside down: she talks about false positives, about the lack of certainty of the testing, she even questions the virus being the cause of AIDS..."

I put the coffee pot on the stove.

"These days I've been considering something, Luka, but I don't want to have empty hopes."

He observed me attentively.

"I don't feel sick."

I stood, opened my arms and took a deep breath.

"You seem to feel much better than a few weeks ago."

When I walked by him on my way to turn down the stove where I had the Italian coffee pot, he patted my bottom.

"You're still missing a little meat but…"

"I'm not taking the medicine and yet my immune system has improved. My last bloodwork showed my count was above 1,000, higher than many healthy people's. When I had the yeast infection, my immune system was at 800. So, it wasn't an opportunistic disease."

"It doesn't make any sense."

"What would've happened if the doctor who wrote me a prescription for my oral thrush hadn't ordered any further testing?"

"But he did."

"What would've happened?"

"I don't know."

"Things would be different now."

"Most likely, yes."

"Right now, my yeast infection would be healed and my white blood cell count would look normal."

"Without a diagnosis."

"There. If I went to see the doctor today rather than two months ago, at most I would be seropositive."

"Maybe not even that."

"They wouldn't even have tested me."

He placed the book on the table.

"You know what? I could devour you."

"You sure haven't lost your appetite."

I stood to remove the coffee pot from the stove. Luka stood up behind me and fondled my breasts under my t-shirt. I felt my nipples harden.

"Let's go to the bedroom."

We lay down on the bed. He stroked me for a long while. I closed my eyes. Since the day of the diagnosis, I couldn't bring myself to initiate sex. The mere act of accepting his caresses without any resistance became a challenge for me. I let him keep going. He kissed my belly. My freckles.

"Cassiopeia," he whispered.

He licked the edges of my panties. I thought maybe I could reach an orgasm. I tried to zero in on the universe between my legs. He moistened the freckles of my inner thighs with his saliva.

"Andromeda."

He licked my vulva over my black panties, slowly, breathing warmth. I ordered my mind to enjoy the pleasure. I held on to my bedsheets.

"I'll be back."

I opened my eyes: I saw Luka standing next to the night table putting a condom on. I closed my eyes and tried to get back to the previous moment. I slid my fingers down to my vulva, for the first time since everything changed. I shed some tears.

I felt Luka next to me. He drank my tears and looked for my mouth with his. I removed my panties. I wanted to signal to him that I was looking for it too. He returned his head to my crotch. He smelled me, kissed me, caressed my vulva up and down from the bottom to the top with his tongue, without my underwear or bedsheet between us, for the first time.

"Careful."

He lay on top of me and devoured my neck and ear. He pulled my hair and kissed me. I felt Luka's penis against me.

"Stop."

"Don't worry."

"I can't."

Suddenly, the muscles in my vagina tensed and the smallest pressure hurt me.

"I'll do it slowly."

He pushed against me.

"I told you to get off me!"

I pushed him away. He got scared. He sat on the edge of the bed, away from me.

"Sorry, Luka."

"It's OK."

"I need time."

"Don't worry."

I knelt behind him and caressed his back.

"Why don't you continue on your own?" I encouraged him.

I kissed the back of his neck, I felt guilty for sabotaging all our attempts at sex.

"No, lie down," he asked me.

"I want to see you enjoy it."

From the time we were together, he worried about my handicapped pleasure.

He on the edge of the bed, me behind him on my knees, I caressed his chest and stomach area. I felt his penis erect once again.

"You do it for me," he asked.

I swallowed. I hadn't touched his penis since the night of the arrest. I rested my ear on his shoulder and, without looking, I began masturbating Luka. His breathing accelerated rapidly. I let it go.

"Keep going!" he begged.

I rushed out of the room, went into the bathroom and locked the door. I bit my lower lip. I wanted to feel pain. While crying, in between my sobs, I heard Luka's short sigh.

—

It used to be quite an adventure on Saturdays for us to go from Lasalde down into town.

"Watch out for the syringes," they would warn us when we went out.

Most girls my age preferred to remain among familiar surroundings, their blossoming bodies inhabited the usual spaces between the train tracks and the river, but I yearned anxiously for Saturdays to go down to town with neighborhood boys who were older than me. The places that were familiar to me, Ataka, the *gaztetxe* building where anti-system youth squatted and the concrete, trashed space between them turned into a battle field once every seven days. The punkies who came to the *gaztetxe* concerts filled the area with Mohawks, leather jackets, drinking glasses and noise. Those bodies that went back and forth between Ataka and that *gaztetxe* moved unlike others, creating different meanings: their way of walking, taking long and heavy strides, the way they sat on the backs of the benches, the way they lined up against the wall to smoke…

The Lasalde boys and girls bought sunflower seeds and sat next to the riverbank, as if ready to kick empty beer glasses left behind. We used to play a guessing game to distinguish the cigarette smell that reached our noses from that of a joint. There were some in the group who were able to differentiate marihuana and hashish joints by the way they smelled. Suddenly we would hear sirens that came from the road behind the *gaztetxe*, and a trash can would catch fire; we used to hear screaming, the police cars' lights blinking against the house façades, young people running in all directions, covering their faces with handkerchiefs. We would quickly get out of the battleground and, by the time the sound of shooting and hitting began, we would take refuge in the rearguard, still chewing gum. Before anyone explained it to me, I knew which side of that war I belonged on, and, thanks to Father's help, and those words that became part of my vocabulary from a very early age, like demonstration, graffiti, roadblock, pigs, I added a few more like Molotov cocktail, nightstick, riot police, rubber bullets, pigs, rabbit coop referring to police vehicles. With each new word I compiled, I experienced the exciting feeling of having conquered a new territory inside my head.

Then Sundays arrived, the slow days that made you wonder if what happened the day before had occurred at all. We referred to them jokingly as the 'Days to kill ourselves.' Suicide wasn't a foreign concept. I remember two or three who threw themselves under the train, one of them had been a woman who, after making lunch for her husband and children, killed herself at 11:23 in the morning; the man who hung himself from the crane at the construction site in front of his house, and whose legs swung at the same height as his wife's balcony; the man found in his car after blowing his brain out with a hunting rifle; the one who jumped from the ninth floor and others who used to become the topic of our conversations during recess the following day.

I remember all those Sundays as a single, big, fat day with one exception. It was the Sunday when I walked into the *gaztetxe* and ordered a glass of water at the counter. On my way to Ataka, I decided to act on something that I had been thinking about for a long time. I changed directions and walked into the building painted red and asked for a glass of water. It was the first time I saw the interior of the *gaztetxe*. I thought it looked brighter than I imagined it, and it surprised me how you could hear the river so clearly. The floor was sticky, and the smell of the place stuck to my nostrils harder than my shoes stuck to the floor. There was no music. There was only a man working the bar. He was slim with long hair. He wore a vest over his bare chest.

"Can I have some water?"

I thought he looked old, though he could hardly have been thirty. Since I didn't know what to say, I drank the water and left quickly. Then I heard behind me:

"Karmen's niece?"

—

I began working at Ataka alongside Mother and Angel when I was fourteen. I used to help Mother make '*pintxos*', finger food, but I preferred working at the bar. I loved lighting a cigarette, playing the music I liked and working to its beat, us behind the bar, and, on the other side, the mediocre world.

It was the first year of high school. Students from different middle schools ended up in the same classroom, students from Urruzuno, from the public school, the girls from the Catholic school, Basque school students, and others who came from neighboring schools. At first glance, I could tell the group of the well behaved from the rebel group and understood at once where I belonged. Within the rebel group, there were two sides: the hooded ones that organized strikes, meetings and demonstrations, who I named ideology-rebels; and the others who wore wide pants and were immersed in the electronic music vibe, the ones who flunked every class, the ones registered in the Spanish module, children of immigrants, the ones I knew from Lasalde, marginal rebels. I soon sensed the antagonism between the two factions, but I was familiar with both and liked them both: I saw them as two versions of the same anger caused by oppression. I met Peru as he was engulfed in smoke. He belonged to the ideological ones. He was the son of a Basque leftist HB party politician.

"You didn't attend the Basque school," he said. "I don't recognize you."

"I'm from Urruzuno."

Peru's parents worked at the left-wing separatist "people's bar" and one afternoon, he invited me to drop in. The first time I walked into that bar, I had my school backpack on. We chatted while having a beer; he introduced me to his parents.

"Do you recognize them?" he asked me, while pointing at a few pictures over the bar.

I felt embarrassed; not so much for not recognizing the pale faces of those men and women but for feeling completely ignorant in front of a classmate who told me about the Basque Country and its armed struggle, and his family.

"My father spent time in clandestine ETA activities and in prison."

"Clandestine activities?"

They stared at me with friendly curiosity, as if I were a strange being. The bar looked strange to me: a yellow flag with a black eagle in the center; stars, axes and the silhouette of a young man wearing glasses who I didn't recognize. My confusion must have amused Peru.

"But where do you live?"

"In Lasalde."

We began cutting class and going to the industrial area behind the school, through a field full of brush. We walked by a bridge underpass where junkies used to hang out. We would look at the goldfish released by the workers to the puddles on the flat factory roofs. We called them the *worker fish*.

While we smoked joints, Peru would give me articles and pamphlets to read, and once again, my vocabulary began to widen. I underlined the articles and asked Peru for clarification. He gave me a pro-amnesty key-shaped pin which I rushed to put on my lapel, next to the antimilitarist '*Mili KK*' pin that Father had given me, next to the feminist '*Egizan*', *the Nuclear Power-No Thanks,* and *Che Guevara* pins. Sometimes, in the afternoons, I went to the library on my own to read about Marxism, the history of ETA, about revolutions in the Basque Country and other places around the world, and about the lives of bearded leaders. I wasn't a disciplined reader: I would jump from one book to another, stitching together my ideological map with patches from here and there; piling up names, places and dates in random order.

I learned about *Jarrai* from Peru. Militancy, the people, the armed struggle, revolution, socialism, dirty-war, clandestine actions, political prisoners, us vs. them, face to face visits…

"My aunt spent time in jail, too" I told him once.

I sensed a sudden interest and curiosity on his face, which soon began fading, as I told him the details of Aunt Karmen's story.

"That's different."

It bothered me.

"Well, I believe that those who you call 'common prisoners' are awfully political, if I may say so. Hasn't your father told you that heroin was introduced with a political purpose?"

Karmen pierced her veins in that very same industrial complex. It was right there where they found the body of the first youth overdose victim.

"Getting drugs here was easier than getting a piece of candy; law enforcement turned a blind eye. The police entertained themselves conducting small operations against hashish while the *horse* ran with no bridle. Father saw members of the Civil Guard police force distributing drugs in Deba. Drugs are not what people think they are. The anti-drug operations are nothing but fallacies. No wonder ETA has killed traffickers. *Ammonal and machineguns, traffickers to the ditch*. They wiped out a whole generation, indeed, the generation who would not buy the story of the transition to democracy. Get informed, dude."

We switched roles. Peru listened to me attentively.

That afternoon, he came to my house to ask me to forgive him. He confessed that it was the first time he had set foot in Lasalde; he had never been in our neighborhood before.

"There is plenty of underground activity here too."

"You're right. I shouldn't have looked down on your aunt."

I shared with him a few photocopied articles I got from Grandma. They denounced the police's behavior related to heroin consumption. I told him about what happened in the U.S. with crack.

"It was a plot to conquer black people. They transformed cocaine and turned it into rock, 15 times cheaper than coke. Poor black people consumed that. Police arrested them. The punishment for having 0.17 ounces of crack or being caught with seventeen ounces of cocaine was the same. Result: jails filled with blacks who consumed crack, while rich, white, cocaine addicts did literally what they pleased."

He looked at me amazed.

"Drug consumption increases in all countries in which the U.S. is involved in a war."

I realized that I succeeded in mesmerizing the guy. I could tell by the way he looked at me that he had upgraded my ranking on his personal scale.

I decided to tell Peru that I was planning to become a member of *Jarrai*. I was excited to work for Basque nationalism and, especially, socialism in my neighborhood. He spoke first.

"I'm in love with you."

I was astounded, holding the latest issue of the *Communist Manifest*o he just had brought me. We had just finished smoking a joint we had shared, and since I didn't say anything, he left. I didn't become a member of *Jarrai*, and it would be a long time before Basque nationalist statements were proclaimed in Lasalde.

—

Irantzu came to get me at the perfumery around mid-morning. She couldn't find a job as a journalist and had started doing some commissioned translations for miserable pay. The positive side: she could set her work schedule and was always available to go for coffee. She chatted with Mother for a while about the new German essence vaporizers, fresh out of the box.

"Next time I'll buy one for home," Irantzu told Mother, "when I calculate how many words I'll have to translate to earn fifty euros."

It would take her many half-cent-per-typed characters to amount to fifty euros, even though she confessed to Mother that she did her best to come up with twisted, long sentences.

"And then people complain that they don't understand Basque translations."

Mother gave me time off until the afternoon.

"Where should we go?"

"To a discreet place."

Lately, the trendy Bilbao bothered me.

"Sanfran?"

I preferred to go toward the Erribera Market Station.

"By cable car?"

We never took the cable car.

"This occasion is worthy of the cable car."

We got off at the Guggenheim stop and took off toward Indautxu. People there were more Spanish-speaking, richer and more urbane.

"What do you think?"

She stared in awe at the Silken Indautxu Hotel building where the Bilbao classic-style palace and the modern shiny glass building merged, following the trend known as "tradition and modernity." A self-aware and sterile, yet marketable style.

"Will they let us go in?"

We pushed the door and walked through the wide marble and wood reception area on our way to the coffee-shop.

"Have you been here before?"

"Courtesy of a long-ago lover."

"I thought you were a socialist in bed too."

We were walking the corridor by the red armchairs and glass tables.

"Usually."

The coffee shop was deserted with the exception of two adulterous-looking couples who must've gotten up too late for the buffet and were sitting at the bar. We picked the table in the corner, next to the outside door.

"Two decaf lattes with cold milk and sweetener, please."

Irantzu muffled a laugh.

"I've always wanted to know what it feels like to utter those words."

"I forgot to order one of them with oat-milk."

They brought our coffees to us at the table.

"You don't have to tell me anything if you don't want to."

"That's why I called you."

She nestled her cup in both hands and listened attentively.

"It happened at the beginning of the summer, not long after I broke up with Kaiet. I didn't think he would forget me so easily."

"Wasn't it you who left him?"

"Hoping that he would come back."

"Don't be a child."

"I know, it's immature of me."

"You know it."

"Being aware of one's highest level of immaturity, demonstrates the highest level of human development."

Following the latest trend of establishing one's femininity without losing it completely, Irantzu had shaved the area above her ear and I pointed at it.

"You viper, you."

"To the point: right after Kaiet left, I called Mizel."

"Who's Mizel?"

"A lover from about ten years ago."

"I remember now, he used to fix breakfast for everyone when he came to the apartment. I heard that he became a father."

"He has a five-year-old daughter."

"So?"

"We had nostalgic sex a couple times. It's great but sick."

"Feeling the heartburn?"

"He told me he wants to be faithful to his wife."

"He's married?"

"They're thinking of the child."

"Did you like him?"

"The peak of my sex life, without question."

As I pronounced the words, I realized that it was the truth. I never desired and wouldn't desire anyone with such intensity and lack of distraction: by pure instinct, with no control, free of guilt, disappointment or boredom.

"You know that my vanity is always proportional to my downfall, right?"

"Exponentially proportional."

"I decided to become a *femme fatale*."

"You have always been a little *femme* and definitely *fatale*…"

"A pure façade. I usually ended up falling in love and, almost always, with friends."

"Or with your friends' friends," Irantzu clarified.

"More or less, with people I loved."

"That time it was the opposite."

The night I got infected was turning into an unpleasant blood clot in my mind.

"You know that in order to open the perfumery we had to sell Ataka at the beginning of the summer. We did it suddenly. At the time, breaking the strongest umbilical cord to my place of birth didn't affect me. Perhaps I didn't realize that I was severing my roots. But soon after, I joined my friends in getting drunk, which I hadn't done for a long time, and I couldn't even decide what to order."

"An identity crisis."

"I thought of what Miren told us right after she quit the radio station and became a mother."

She couldn't remember.

"Apparently, she felt protected when she carried her baby close to her chest. She felt safe in situations where she would have felt uncomfortable before; for example, when attractive young guys looked at her, she felt safe carrying her baby."

"Her bullet proof vest?"

"Even with friends in her group, with those she hadn't seen for a long time. She said she never felt like a stranger when she had her baby with her."

"That's interesting."

"I understand it very well: the same thing happened to me with the bar."

"Being a mother is a common alter ego," she said thoughtfully.

"There are as many alternate personalities as you'd like."

"Ataka is now a bakery-coffee shop franchise. There are old ladies and women with strollers having coffee as we speak."

"Motherly coffee shops."

"It felt as if I'd got a limb amputated. I shared a complete identification with the bar."

"You'll be forever Ataka's daughter."

"Suddenly, I became the boyfriend-less, lover-less and bar-less Nagore, not much of anything."

"It's dangerous to hold on to identities."

It surprised me to hear Irantzu say something like that; I didn't think she thought that of all types of identities. I saw how she held onto the motherland. To the language. To certain leftist ideologies. I continued speaking:

"The town was deserted. Total exodus. There was no one left except old people, crippled people, South American care takers and us, poor families' children."

"Far West."

"We went to the bars by the river shore, the last black holes that are about to disappear."

"The real bars."

"The catacombs."

"The ones that smell like tobacco and caves. Where dirty intimacy is still possible."

"The underground galleries are for us, human worms."

"Lucky us."

To defend late-night bars was to defend myself. I ordered a shot of rum, on the rocks; she brought it to me in a heavy, wide-bottom glass, on top of an elegant coaster.

"I felt at home there; the drunker I was, the more at home I felt. Outside the rickety river exposing its bones, bartenders who survived heroin still drafting beers, traces of speed inside the feminine-hygiene waste bin.

"Right in your habitat."

"And Tina Turner on the loudspeakers: *Rolling on the River*."

"Brutal."

"There were new people on the dance floor: those who were children when we left our town, Generation Z. Us, at the bar counter. I started drinking beer, moved to cocktails and went on to tequila shots. Since I didn't know what to choose, I mixed everything. They played Nacha Pop and I joined the girls on the dance floor. What the hell, they played *La chica de ayer* (Yesterday's Girl), we should've gotten the senior discount. And there he was."

"Is he from town?"

"No."

"A young guy, three or four years younger than me, I had seen him at our bar, he was wasted. A hand stretched toward the ceiling, stumbling while crossing the dance floor. He wasn't particularly handsome, though some might call him attractive. He approached me from behind and we began dancing. When the bars in town closed, we went to a dance club in a nearby town on the coast. I would like to think that we took a taxi, I can't remember. We continued dancing and I believe he kissed me. I don't know how we came back to town when they closed the dance club. I got in the car and told the guy I would drive him home. He didn't live far. I was sure I wasn't going to go to his apartment, I was tired, done for the night. But I went up, who knows why. We began messing around, you know, both of us completely hammered…and as soon as we began having sex, he stopped, the guy fell asleep."

I hardly felt embarrassed about my sexual adventures.

"Just imagine what a blow to my ego."

Irantzu downplayed the situation.

"You guys were completely drunk."

"I wouldn't have felt worse had he spit in my face."

She looked at me in disapproval.

"You punch someone who spits at you, but what the heck do you do to someone who falls asleep on you?"

"You let him be," she answered.

"Well, since I'm an idiot, since I had to challenge myself and since I always need to outdo myself… instead of leaving, I began to kiss him, licking him, slowly downward, thinking that when I reached his penis he would wake up. I kept at it for a long time, thinking that all that sucking would resuscitate the dead. But the dude's penis remained softer than a worm. And for an instant, fuck, I pictured myself: me sucking that guy's penis and him passed out and it happened right then, I was hit with a horrible stench, I felt nauseous and disgusted by that horrible taste.

I remembered that Irantzu once told me she didn't like to suck penises.

"I got out of the room, collected my things and dragged myself out, with an overwhelming inferiority complex."

"Nagore."

"I remember the stench and the taste." I couldn't erase the revulsion I felt from my face.

"I can't explain the decreased self-worth I felt at the time. I've never felt so humiliated."

"Are you crazy? What does his drunkenness have to do with you?"

I signaled her to join me outside to smoke a cigarette. The door of the hotel bar opened onto a bright street corner.

"It affected my ego and self-esteem, and everything else."

"You can't measure your self-worth based on men's desire."

"Too late."

Another coffee shop customer came out behind us; a woman wearing a pencil-skirt, with reddish, recently straightened hair. She smelled like shampoo. She asked us for a light, took two pulls of her mint cigarette and extinguished it.

"The disgusting taste was the key. Soon after that I began with my throat candidiasis."

"Do you think, things started after that encounter?"

"I never have oral sex on one-night stands, I have sex without preambles. It's all about impersonal fucking sessions, I consider oral sex something more intimate…I don't know why I did it. Yes: because he fell asleep. But the smell, it was the smell. As soon as the doctor mentioned the diagnosis, the stench returned, it penetrated all the way to my lungs."

"That's when you got infected?"

"Yes."

"But the guy ejaculated while asleep?"

"I don't think so."

Irantzu looked at me perplexed.

"But the guy is seropositive?"

"Yes."

"How do you know it?"

"He told me."

Irantzu didn't ask me more questions, and I really appreciated it because I was exhausted. I asked the server to bring us the bill.

"I will charge it to your room," she said. "Number?"

"304," I replied.

We came out to the noon sunshine.

—

In the fall of '94, when Father returned to Madrid, we returned to Lasalde and Mother's sadness filled the house. I physically suffered the pressure of her weariness: I walked close to the walls, trying to occupy as little space as possible. I always saw Mother crying, everywhere, at any time, in all situations: standing in the kitchen, sitting on the toilet, lying on the bed, in the hallway on her knees, undone on the floor… There wasn't any room left for my sadness. Father continued calling and I recognized Mother's voice variations: howling, imploring, cursing, dragging, silent. Sometimes, I think that Father used to ask Mother to let him talk with me, but in those instances, I used to lock myself in my room.

My relationship with Mother changed. I tried to get close to her because I pitied and needed her. I confirmed then that I was afraid of her body: afraid of getting close to Mother's flesh and yet afraid of getting away from it.

We began to sleep in the same bed. I left her in bed in the mornings. After fixing and having my breakfast, I would go to school. She returned to work at the end of fall, and I would have dinner ready for her by the time she came home from Ataka. It was good for me to help Mother. It was then that we began smoking together. She was always sad, she didn't accept another state for herself, and I also ended up believing that such was the only alternative for her.

I made the decision during one of those dispirited dinners that we shared: I informed her that I was going to run the Ataka and that we would share the responsibilities. I didn't see that she was able to hold onto anything, she was in a liquid state. She didn't argue with me; just stared at me with her big, blue eyes from a silence that I thought was appreciative, that was all.

From then on, we became a team: we shared the work day at the bar. I took on the responsibility of putting together the crew that would work on Saturdays and busy holidays. By the time I turned fourteen though, without formal authority, yet practically, I was in charge, with Mother, of the bar mortgage, home expenses, placing orders for Ataka, and the workers' salaries.

We both earned the same salary. Mother tiredly followed my steps; I lived propelled by her exhaustion. The fact that she had turned into a liquid state necessarily solidified me.

—

I hired someone we called Piti to gather glasses, I had DJ Santos in the music-booth and Angel, Mother and I worked the upstairs bar. We opened the “Catacombs” for young people, the two most handsome guys in the team were in charge of the bar. They served adolescent customers plenty of peach-liquor to the beat of pop music. On Saturday afternoons, around three, we would meet at bar Sokoa. After drinking a *kalimotxo*, a coke and cheap wine mix, Piti and I would leave to go to the Ataka to prepare the battle-field. We turned off the lights, turned on the spotlights, and would make the amps rumble with techno music that made limbs shake. Progressive, Techno, House. We worked based on the train schedule, at the whim of people who were unloaded in town after lunch and picked up at ten in the evening. Mother would arrive around five, and we would drink White Label whisky shots camouflaged with Coca-Cola while we worked. Joints got passed from hand to hand, we smoked cigarettes like chimneys and snorted the speed lines laid out in the backroom. I didn’t powder my nose. Neither did Mother. We worked diligently. During the first years, we served a variety of smaller types of drinks like zuritos, beers, klarimostos, kalimotxos… and the smell of hashish filled the bar. But, before we knew it, cocktails had replaced the wine and the beer, amphetamine and LSD the hashish, and bills the coins. We sweated adrenaline and alcohol to the point of derangement. We communicated almost wordlessly. I worked tensely, alert and agile with the confidence of someone who knows what she’s doing. I always hid my hands because I bit my nails and my fingers showed raw flesh and because I was afraid they reflected my lack of confidence. My problems exposed, weakness, self-injury, nervousness. No. I wanted them to look me in the eye; mine were inextricable. My way of looking at people indicated to customers and friends what I meant: *I'm coming*; *excuse me*; *I'm busy*; *get away*; *wait your turn*; *I know you like me*; *it better be the last time*; *I'm going to kill you*; *you're not leaving without paying*; *I'm beat*; *you serve them, I can't stand them*; *we're swamped*; *get me a shot*; *pass me a cigarette*... At ten at night, I turned off the techno music and played what I liked. Pause.

As soon as the youngsters left, the crows arrived, the men who clustered around Mother, clumsy, hungry, scavenger crows attempting to peck the thighs of the abandoned, unprotected beautiful lady. A flock of good-for-nothings, the town nocturnal party-goers, some married and others single, those who were not intimidated to go out drinking alone. As soon as we eyed one of them approaching the counter, my co-workers or I would step in front of Mother and ask dryly, "What do you want?" while Mother lit a cigarette in the rearguard. I always gave my verdict on all the men who approached her, which she took to heart, and it wasn't just me; my friends also took the liberty of sharing their impressions and opinions with her. If by chance she hooked up with one of those lost souls and if things went bad, she would walk to me like a wounded lamb saying, "You were so right," in a more liquid state than ever before, mushy.

Fights became part of the weekly agenda. The decrease in political street-fighting and the increase in bar fights happened simultaneously. At the end of the 90's, violence decided to change locations. At the bar, we managed the impulses that religion used to manage: desire, rage and fear. All three increased as the evening advanced. The peripheral children of immigrants fought against each other; the Ikastola youth and those from Urruzuno didn't touch each other just in case; the guys fought "to defend their girls;" groups of girls would form circular walls, turning their backs to the world; the bikers who came from the outskirts scratched the BMW's of the rich Basque kids who had parked their cars close to the bar. With the night partying as an excuse, each defended or attacked from their vantage point the other's social class, homeland, sex and other territories as they galvanized in the name of social class, homeland and sex, their own rage against those around them. That dynamic infuriated me. I felt my own anger pulsing in my veins, tensing my muscles and sharpening my eyes. Each week the pushing, punching and kicking became more violent. Glasses flew everywhere and customers threatened each other with broken bottles. When fights broke out, I brought the workers to the back room, turned off the music, turned the lights on, and came out from behind the bar to separate those who were kicking each other. I did it without thinking twice: I came in between the bodies fighting, pushed them away and dragged them out of the bar by their t-shirt collars. Once, after saying goodbye to my co-workers and when I was about to close Ataka, a guy threatened me with a knife, and why? because, apparently, I didn't play the type of music he requested. I came out from behind the bar, held his wrist, made him drop the knife and pushed him out of the bar, with the same determination as shooing a fly. I was fearless then; I had that mechanism completely deactivated. Physically I was in good shape though I didn't work out. I was tall and big boned by then, and had strong arms from carrying cases of soda and liquor.

The hardest episode happened with the neighborhood hair dresser's husband, Errasti. He was a mountain of a guy, Errasti, a disgusting, slimy guy. He had trouble with many girls in town; he touched them, and when some dared to confront him, he hit them. I hated him, and he returned the hatred.

The couple got drunk every weekend: Errasti himself, the one two-hundred-and-twenty-pound gorilla, and the hair-dresser, Mirari, barely a lemur, a tiny withered woman. We closed Ataka at four in the morning for customers and stayed inside having a good time and dancing until morning. Those were the best times ever.

Once, while the bar was already closed, Errasti forced opened the shuttered doors, broke in and demanded I have a drink with him.

"We're closed," I replied.

He burst into laughter, "C'mon." I said no. Mirari looked at me, embarrassed. I told them that they had to leave. And the jerk said no, that they were going nowhere.

"You're as retarded as your mother," he mumbled.

OK. Enough. I came out of the back-room crazy, infuriated. Angel held me by my shoulder.

"Where are you going?"

"I'm going to kill him."

I truly believed that I was going to kill him. And in the meantime, he kept staring at me, cursing and laughing from the dance floor. I begged Angel to let me go, let me be, that he insulted Mother and that I had to finish him. Finally, he let go of me. By then Errasti was leaving the bar, but I chased him and slapped him with all my might. Silly of me. I didn't close my hand. Angel and our friends separated us and Errasti called the police, threatening to report me. Some undercover police came in and one asked me what was going on, and all I kept saying was, "I'm going to kill him." The policeman laughed at me too. As soon as I was able to get past the officer, I began running after Errasti once again, got on a bench and when I was about to jump on his back, Angel overcame me and pushed me to the ground. Had he let me, I would have kept biting him to death.

Angel took me to the back room. I was shivering, pumped up with adrenaline. When I calmed down, I passed out.

The word about that episode spread quickly in town. Other bar owners in the area came to congratulate me. Apparently, it wasn't just me who was fed up with that jerk. From then on, I sat on the bar sink, staring at the door, just in case, and every time he walked by the bar, the fool pretended to slit his throat while looking at me.

As soon as Father found out that I hit Errasti, he called the bar:

"Shit, you finally gave him the beating I should've given him long ago."

—

One evening, I heard the doorbell ring while I was doing my homework. I went to the window; my friends always waited for me there, but I didn't see anyone. Someone was knocking at the door. I put my notebook on the table and rushed to open the door. I stumbled upon a giant bear, a big, fat brown teddy bear, as tall as me.

"Do you remember me?" Father asked me while mimicking a deep voice, hiding behind the bear.

I was about to shut the door in his face but I didn't. I hadn't heard from him for two years.

"Does Mother know you are here?"

"Yes."

"Are you here to stay?"

"I have to go back to Madrid, but I'll come back soon, I have tons of things to tell you."

He approached to kiss me, I stepped back.

"You've grown."

I went to the kitchen and for the first time, lit a cigarette in front of Father. He walked behind me and lit his. We smoked in silence.

"How's school going?"

"I'm not an intellectual but I'm no dummy either."

He explained that he came to see us and to make sure that we were running Ataka OK.

"We manage just fine without you: at home and at the bar."

He carried on about stupid stuff, as if we had been hanging out the day before.

"What did you come for?"

After a long silence, he spoke while staring through the window.

"It's Angel."

"What about him?"

I had been with him the day before and hadn't noticed anything different.

"He felt some lumps under his arm. He's been diagnosed with a serious AIDS-induced cancer."

I took each word like punches to my stomach. Lumps. Aids. Cancer. Serious. I stood abruptly from the chair and pushed Father.

"Mother and you knew Angel had AIDS, right?"

It was obvious.

—

I first learned about Christine Maggiore through a book Luka brought me. I opened the cover that showed the words AIDS and WRONG in big letters, and after a long list of thank yous, I read the section "Message from the Author." Next to the first paragraph, a photo of Maggiore herself, sitting in the co-pilot seat of a red car holding her two-year-old son on her lap, the door open, her legs stretched outside, wearing a dark sleeveless t-shirt. I connected the following confession to this smiling, sharp-eyed, brunette woman:

"My journey began in 1992, when I took what is commonly referred to as an AIDS test. I had no symptoms of illness, no particular risks or fears, just a new doctor that insisted that the test should be part of a routine medical exam. My visit turned from routine to life-altering when the test came back positive.

I was referred to an AIDS specialist who declared that my test was not positive–no enough to be considered conclusive, anyway.

He had me take it over again and, at the same time, ordered lab work on everything from my cholesterol level to my T-cell count. I left his office frightened and confused but hopeful, and spent the days before my next appointment alternating between frantic affirmations of wellness and bottomless despair."

The result of the second test was indisputably positive. According to the specialist, my progression from somewhat positive to really positive indicated a recent infection, even though the concept of a new infection conflicted with the circumstances of my life.

He told me that I was exceptionally healthy, that I was fortunate to have detected the condition early, but that there was nothing I could do to prevent devastating disease and eventual death from AIDS. He warned me about wasting money on vitamins and other foolish attempts to save my immune system, advising that I simply wait to become sick and then take AZT, a drug with severe side effects that would make me sicker. I was given five to seven years to live. I went directly from his office to a health food store. The following day, I began a search for a new AIDS specialist.

Life as I had lived, planned and hoped came to a grinding halt. I lost interest in my business, I dropped out of the university program I had been attending, and I bought myself a wedding ring to ward off potential suitors. Wanting to keep my tragedy a secret, I stopped spending time with my family and all but a few close friends. Instead, I attended AIDS seminars and joined a support group for HIV positive women, where once a week, we were encouraged to compare notes on our fears and frustrations, mention any potential symptoms, and cry about the lousy deal we'd all been handed.

I was asked to join their public speaker's bureau. Almost immediately, I was touring local high schools and colleges as the person that HIV should have never happened to. I made the audiences laugh, cry, and scared—I appeared as the embodiment of the slogan that everyone is at risk for AIDS.

A year into my diagnosis and public service, and after interviewing half a dozen AIDS doctors whose recommendations ranged from immediate drug therapy to world travel, I found an anomaly among AIDS specialists—a doctor who didn't routinely fill people with toxic pharmaceuticals and lethal predictions. She treated me as an individual rather than an impending statistic and, in doing so, noticed my good health. She told me that I didn't fit the profile of an AIDS patient and urged me to take another test. Afraid to raise my hopes, at first, I refused. When I finally found the courage to retest, the result was inconclusive. Further testing produced a series of unsettling contradictory diagnoses: a positive followed by a negative and another positive.

Confused by a personal situation that defied all the rules I'd been so passionately preaching as a public speaker, I turned to the AIDS groups where I worked for help. Instead of finding answers, I found my questions were dismissed and that persisting with my line of inquiry resulted only in meaningless explanations and the distinct impression that I was ruining morale.

My search for information led me outside of the confines of the AIDS establishment and into a body of scientific, medical and epidemiological data that defied everything I had been taught about AIDS, and everything that I had been teaching others. The more I read, the more I became convinced that AIDS research had jumped on a bandwagon that was headed in the wrong direction.

Since it was clear that the information I had found, however life-affirming, was not welcome among the AIDS organization I belonged to, I decided to start my own. In 1995, together with a few friends gathered from various support groups and other places along the way, I started an organization that shares vital facts about HIV and AIDS that are unavailable from mainstream venues.

In the seven years since I received my life sentence, I have gone from frightened victim to AIDS activist to HIV dissident to spokesperson for new views about HIV and AIDS. Although my HIV status has been decidedly positive for the past five years, I enjoy abundant good health and live without pharmaceutical treatments or fear of AIDS.

In 1996, I met a wonderful man I plan to marry as soon as I take a day off. We have a beautiful, healthy little boy who, at age two, has never had so much as an ear infection.

For most people, the surprising thing about my story is the fact that it is not unusual—I know hundreds of HIV positives who are alive and naturally well years after receiving their own dire prognosis."[1]

Father returned after Angel died, but didn't stay in town to live, he moved to Bilbao instead. Ataka stayed under Mother's name. Father couldn't bring himself to work at the bar again and found a job as a longshoreman at the Bilbao port.

We went through some changes in Lasalde too. Unexpectedly, we went from being two at home to being three. One evening when Mother and I were working in Ataka, an unfamiliar, soap-smelling young woman walked into the bar.

"I was Angel's friend."

She told us her name was Maria, that she was from Madrid, a friend of Angel and Father. I calculated she must've been barely twenty years old.

"We got initiated with them, with Angel and other wonderful scoundrels."

When she uttered the word 'wonderful' it seemed to me that she turned her eyes upward and tried to hold back her tears. Angel had called her a couple months earlier. The last time they got together in Madrid, during a wild night of drinking, she told him that she was unemployed. When she received his call, he asked her if she was still unemployed. With some astonishment, she replied, yes.

1 Translator's note: When Nagore Vargas mentions books, TV series, YouTube documentaries, Wikipedia and Leonard Cohen's "Chelsea Hotel" song, the references have been excerpted from the original texts in English.

"He told me that there was a position open at his bar in the Basque Country."

Mother and I looked at each other astounded.

"A little later, I found out he had died," Maria said.

We realized that Angel had sent us his replacement, *post mortem*. A pale nymph, who looked like Angel's younger sister.

By the suitcase she left outside the bar door, we concluded she had nowhere to go.

She came into my bedroom, spreading her soap fragrance. Mother asked me to empty half of the closet for her. She hung her few clothing items delicately. She looked like a child who had just taken a bath, she looked so spotless, soft.

After the unexpected arrival, there were three of us, young women, sharing an apartment: Mother, thirty-seven; Maria, twenty-three and me, fifteen. The communal living didn't last long, but it turned out to be essential to the way I developed relationships with women. The older sister that I often had imagined in silence, now had turned into flesh and blood, though she did not resemble how I had imagined her at all. My pretend sister had always been a kind of extension of myself: brunette, with piercing eyes, smart, rebellious, an arguer. Maria, on the other hand, was blonde and calm, with a soft voice.

Soon after Maria's arrival, we lived like three sisters: we worked side by side at the bar, and we shared more than our home life, we also shared long conversations, getting drunk, cigarettes and all the expenses and earnings of the bar. We created perfect choreographies behind the bar. Me, with a cigarette in my lips and a defiant gaze, I worked as if I were angry, holding liquor and soda bottles in twos and threes and serving drinks over my head with the sound of gushing liquids, clinking ice cubes and the splashing of lemon juice. On the other hand, Maria took each step carefully, with no rush or flair, pouring the liquids delicately, picking up ice cubes slowly with a calm continuity, with her baby fragrance and swinging her golden hair with a cadence that was so her. Mother, like a reptile dragging the beauty of sadness, served loser's charm in iced glasses. That's how we were behind the bar and outside of it.

I noticed immediately that Mother was charmed by Maria. By the time she had been with us two weeks, Mother had begun to openly imitate her movements and mannerisms. Maria was an esthetician and dreamed of opening an all-natural perfumery. She tempted Mother with the idea of opening a business like that between the two of them in the future. She used lavender or cardamom-essence fragrances, depending on the day. Mother softened her way of smoking, slowed her walking pace, gathered back her black mane and bought light colored clothing.

Some nights, during the week, Maria and Mother began going out to dance and left me at home because I had to go to school the following day. I saw them from my bedroom combing their hair and putting on make-up. Maria dabbed a few drops from her fragrance flask on Mother's neck. Mother couldn't hide a dumb smile that exposed her gums, similar to the one she gets when she drinks too much. I stayed awake waiting for them; they arrived home after having squeezed the night to its max, smelling like smoke and giggling. I heard them whispering in the kitchen. Then Maria would walk into the bedroom and proceed to undress slowly. I tried to see her breasts, but I could only catch a peek at them, when she turned toward the window, a quick glimpse, evasive and white, and below them her flat stomach reflected by the streetlight, and a hint of perfume that attracted me as much as it frightened me.

During one of those evenings, while Maria was in the shower, I called Mother to my bedroom and though she didn't ask me, I examined her from head to toe and gave her my opinion:

"You're still a meek farmer."

—

Stillness is an overwhelming feeling for someone who has never kept still.

Before my diagnosis, I lived dominated by passion; moderate emotions depressed me. Whenever I looked for extreme emotions and didn't find them, I would make them up: I had to be in love head over heels, completely convinced by ideas, stimulated by projects, completely passionate about each task, hot in bed, contradicting all contradictions. The more on the fringe, the closer to the truth.

If not lived passionately, it wasn't worth living. I needed intensity to justify life, and anxiety resembled pleasure. Unrest was the guarantee of anything real, to be a radical was the only way to be. In a life with no middle ground, it was impossible to retract your opinions, desires, and commitments. I had to love against the clock and fight against comfort. Eat while standing up and sleep while alert. Have hard core sex. Be ready for anything.

Stillness and silence were one and the same. Before, I couldn't stand silence. People who didn't speak made me nervous. For a period of time, I felt words defying words in my throat, stepping on each other, pushing each other, competing for expression. They stole my breath away. They were alive in my tongue. They filled my head with saliva and teeth. They would come out even if I covered my mouth with my hand; there was no way to stop them. Words, words, words. Hungry birds that lunged at the ground full of bread crumbs. Nervous birds. Ugly. Words carried me around by the lapel of my shirt, a foot off the ground, wherever they wanted.

I used to run away from the eyes of those who loved me slowly and softly. Tenderness became the mirror of my weakness. When passions calmed down, my sadness would surface, with the subtle violence of the child who succeeds in attracting everyone's attention, so discretely, that no one saw it coming.

The fall of 2010, I quit men like one quits drugs. Though I lived with Luka, I had quit men as a concept. I stopped being inside their eyes. I abandoned the hypothetical fascination of a bird of prey: the times when those who I hunted or could hunt me defined who I was, those days were over. The fatigue made me walk slower and sleep more. The diagnosis suffocated sex and shot my inner hunter. Without fanfare, I stepped away from bars and crowded get-togethers. I quit drinking. My boisterous friends gradually left me alone; Thursday, Fridays and Saturdays lost their names. Along with closing down the radio station, I stepped aside from the militant community and I quit being a mover in Bilbao's trendy circles. Gradually fewer people were interested in what I thought, beginning with myself. I stopped paying my dues to the Stock Market of the "us circle." My value didn't fluctuate any longer depending on what I said or did. I removed myself from the market, and people I cared about did not care as much as I wish they did.

I spent a lot of time without leaving the house, bent inward and, when I went back outside, I realized that I was fearful of being with people. For the very first time in my life, socializing became a problem for me. I, who before only existed in relation to others, now withdrew like a scared, wild animal, when I saw a human figure. I avoided crowded places and public transportation. I stopped hanging out in the old part of town, afraid of meeting people I knew. I began shopping online.

The diagnosis made me peel off my disguise, and I didn't know how to behave among people without it. My own gestures seemed alien to me: I couldn't measure the right sized smile or how wide to open my eyes. How to modulate my voice, its volume, rhythm… there were too many decisions to be made before opening my mouth.

One afternoon that Luka convinced me to go out shopping, he found me crying in front of the mirror.

"I don't know what to wear!" I told him in desperation.

I had forgotten the acts of getting dressed, speaking, and being. I needed to reinvent myself.

The buzzing of the intercom interrupted my reading.

"Stop what you're doing and come, quickly!"

It was Father from downstairs. We had shared a couple calls after the fateful sunrise of the day of the diagnosis, but we hadn't seen each other since then. I put on a coat over what I was wearing at home and came downstairs. He was accompanied by another man.

"What're you doing here?"

He was supposed to be working at the port at that time of the day.

"Can't I visit my daughter?"

"Good morning!" the man greeted me politely.

The unfamiliar man's eyebrow was trickling a fine thread of blood. Father took a step back from me, stretched out his arm, and "showed me off" from top to bottom.

"See? What did I tell you? Is she pretty or what?"

A dealer trying to sell a mare wouldn't have done a better job.

"If you two don't mind, I have tons of things to do."

"Wait a minute, Jenisjoplin! We want to talk with you."

I didn't want to step outside. It was cold.

"What're you waiting for? Let's go!"

Unfortunately, I had chronically missed Father for a long time, and against my pride and comfort, I needed to be with him, preferably alone, but, apparently, that wasn't going to be possible.

"Half-an-hour. Then I need to go to work."

"To work?" he asked, upset. "Are you serious?"

I stared at him looking for an explanation.

"Today is January 27, a general strike day. Have you changed so much?"

I hadn't watched the news for days. I had swallowed documentaries: *The Science of Panic* and *House of Numbers*, I had bought books about dissident theories from Amazon, and had spent the last days and nights immersed in them. I hadn't paid any attention to the strike.

"What happened to you?" I asked Father's friend while pointing at his eyebrow.

"The 'pigs' attacked the picket line."

I fixed my hair in the building doorway and stepped outside.

"Where do you want to go?" I asked.

Father never took me to his place; the bars were closed and it was cold outside.

"We can go to the association," proposed Father's friend. "I brought the keys."

It wasn't easy to be alone with Father. He always found a way to bring something or someone that would impede our privacy. He loved to be my father in public; in private, he preferred to act as my buddy. He used to invite me to hang out with his friends, for drinks, dinners, parties, though he knew I didn't like crowded places.

We walked across the Merced bridge to cross the river and took Nasa street all the way to Father's friend's association.

"Right there," he said when we entered Bailen street.

I recognized the blue façade of the gay bar *Balcón de la Lola*, right under the train tracks. I hadn't been there for a long time, but the sunrise had caught me right on that street corner more than once. Father's friend could be one of the owners of the place. He did have the look of a Bilbao gay man. Instead, he walked toward the adjoining entry, to an office-looking place with stained glass.

“Welcome.”

As soon as I walked through the door, I saw the *BizkaiSida* organization’s logo: a closed hand, with the thumb extended, covered with a condom. They had brought me to the headquarters of the citizens’ committee against AIDS.

“Wait a minute.”

He walked to the restroom and washed the blood off his eyebrow.

“This is our home,” he said while showing us around. “I haven’t introduced myself yet.” “My name is Kike,” he told me.

There were all kinds of posters on the walls, most of them with the multi-colored rainbow referring to homosexual men. There were two big desks in the room, one on the left side and the other on the right. A leafy plant and a pile of cardboard boxes against the stained-glass window. Two doors inside. Father placed his hand on my shoulder.

“You could be of great help here.”

Kike nodded, while looking at me with gratitude.

“Your father told me you’re a journalist, and that you are prepared to speak out. We need young people like you to work with teenagers; we just started a school program. Most AIDS militants are grown men like me, who have grown old without realizing. It is important that young girls have some references they can identify with. They can learn a lot from your experience. Your father told me that you are good at using social media: we have a void in that area.”

Father sold me; as usual, instead of respecting my journey, he had to walk the path ahead of me. Father told the so-called Kike about my diagnosis without my permission, and I’m sure he wasn’t the only person my father had told about my condition.

“We’ll see,” was all I could say at the time.

“You’ll feel better once you let everyone know,” Father slapped me on the back. “It’s asphyxiating staying in the closet, isn’t it?”

He directed the question to Kike. I felt like punching Father because he was capable of forcing people out of the closet by dragging them out even if they were naked, always in the name of liberation, without realizing that it was someone else's vulnerabilities that were getting exposed, not his.

"Enough," I told him under my breath.

Kike sensed my discomfort.

"Don't put your daughter on the spot," Kike told Father softly, and then to me, "I'll get you some reading material. You can take a look at it at home calmly."

Information about the illness, prevention advice, support-groups brochures... He put a few souvenirs inside a cloth bag: posters against stigma, stickers and colorful pins.

"I'm going home," I said.

"Nagore!" Father stopped me.

Whenever he was angry, he called me by my name.

"Leave me alone!"

I left the building infuriated. I walked down by the river bank, my mouth shut tight. I kicked a street light and cursed my father.

When I arrived at Abando, the sound of an explosion brought me out of myself. I stopped abruptly. I quickly recognized the sound of rubber bullets being fired: three or four dry gunshots. I followed the Abando round-about, straight to where the ruckus was coming from. I heard screaming, whistling, clapping and clamor. I felt drawn to the crowd. There was a big group of people gathered by the Corte Inglés department store. Facing them, more than thirty 'gorillas,' outfitted with helmets, clubs and shields. At that very moment, two additional police vans arrived blasting their sirens, and more than a dozen riot police came out of them, holding their rubber bullet shotguns. I pushed my way through the crowd and placed myself in the first row. I joined the screaming picket line and assumed its collective rage.

I began cursing the big department stores and the 'pigs.' I felt my insides boiling.

"Bastards!"

An older man, standing next to me, left the group and approached one of the hooded policemen to ask for explanations. The police reacted violently. The man fell backwards, and five of six of us charged the 'pigs,' shoving them. A big group behind us supported us by yelling at them. Then, I heard shotguns go off, and before I knew it, I felt a club-blow against my back, and then more, on my ribcage and legs. I protected my head the best I could and continued deriding the police. I can't remember how I got out of there; someone yanked me away.

The group of strikers began to disseminate little by little. I was sweating and unzipped my coat; all I was wearing underneath was my pajama top. I decided to return home. As I crossed the Areatza bridge, I felt calmer. A strange, seldom felt happiness tried to surface. My body ached, but my breathing was calming down.

"You're bleeding!" Luka jumped off the sofa.

I asked him not to touch me.

"I'm going to clean you up."

He followed me to the bathroom. I covered the wound on my chin with gauze. I disinfected the scrapes on my elbows.

"What the hell happened to you?"

"I joined the demonstration."

A sharp pain made me bring my hands to my waist when I bent to sit down on the sofa. I piled up a few pillows and lay down. I linked my hands behind my head. I felt ecstatic.

"I needed a little action. Action and fighting, that's it!"

"Will you please do your best to adjust your emotions to the situation?

I threw a pillow at him, playfully.

"Adjust my emotions to the situation? Where did you get that from?"

He fell silent.

"And you? What have you done today besides managing moderate emotions?"

"I went out to get some footage," he said noticeably annoyed. "I told you this morning."

I took a drag on my cigarette.

"I didn't realize."

"Yeah."

I pretended I was holding the video camera in my hand and that the scene was happening on the ceiling, I pointed the camera there.

"You should've come to the Corte Inglés to film: there was quite a ruckus there. The 'pigs' went crazy, you should've seen them. There were at least four police vans; by the time I arrived, the riot had started; the demonstration was going strong."

"What made you go out? You haven't left the house for more than a month."

I continued telling him passionately about the confrontation.

"I hadn't felt this burst of adrenaline in a long time, it was amazing!"

"You don't even answer you friends' phone calls."

"What do you want me to say?" I became angry.

"The truth."

I sighed.

"Father came."

"What for?"

I forcefully stubbed out my cigarette in the ashtray.

"For once I'm happy, you're going to screw it up for me, really?"

I stood up at once.

"Shit!" I yelled, enraged and in pain.

The pain made me bend; a sharp pain on my side. I had to drop to all fours. I felt like crying. Luka placed his hand on my shoulder.

"Show me your back."

He pulled up my t-shirt.

"Fuck, Nagore, they beat you up!"

I turned to face Luka.

"Father is telling everyone I have AIDS."

He made me sit on the sofa and, while putting ointment on my bruises, he asked me to tell him what happened. I wanted to speak without drama but I couldn't manage it.

"Why don't you let me be weak, eh?"

I regretted my childishness.

"You must call him right now."

"What for?"

"To demand that he respect your privacy."

"You know what? Sometimes, like Father, I would tell the whole world about it. I would go out on the street and tell everyone, one by one, that I have AIDS. Or I would hold a press conference. Or I would send a text to all my phone contacts. I would write a group e-mail. Tell everyone and be done with it. Sometimes I think it would be a huge relief."

"You and your kamikaze impulses."

"Don't analyze me."

He sat next to me.

"But my intuition tells me not to tell anyone," I continued.

His glance proved my intuition to be true.

"I'm a coward."

"So, what if you are."

"Besides, now I'm not certain about anything. I read all those books. Sometimes I feel that it's the diagnosis itself which is going to sicken me."

"You wouldn't be the first."

"I haven't read anything official about AIDS except all these dissident theories. I haven't asked doctors about my fate, nor have I tried to find information on my own… In a moment of temptation, I might have searched the internet for "AIDS today" or if I typed something like that, I read the first two lines and shut the laptop."

"Does it frighten you?"

"It infuriates me!"

"Why feel fear if you can get mad instead?" he teased me.

It amazed me that Luka knew me so well. He always deactivated the traps I set for myself.

"I feel like I should protect myself from the information they want to program me with."

"And what are you going to do?"

"I'm going to stop going to my appointments."

"We could look for an alternative therapy."

"I don't want to," I interrupted him. "I don't want to know anything."

I pulled my pants down and showed him my leg.

"You're going to have a huge bruise there."

I spoke to him with as much confidence as I could.

"I find it dangerous to believe that I'm sick. If I admit a fate, feel fear, or a symptom… I'm doomed. I don't want to be predisposed to a set of symptoms, to a specific fate…"

He listened to me in silence.

"You don't understand it, do you? I don't want to beg anyone for my salvation in fear."

"We'll find something natural."

"To feel chemically scared will subjugate me as much as feeling naturally scared."

My mind was on a roll; I had too many ideas circling in it.

"It's like eating organic. What does it mean to eat organic in a capitalist system? A beautiful deception. You'll spend money, the same people will become rich… Perhaps, you might feel healthier for a while… I don't want to be a medicine vegan."

"I'll bring you the electric blanket."

"I don't know if AIDS exists any more, and if it does, what is the truth about it? What does it mean to have AIDS?"

"I don't know."

"Neither do I. But I know that living in fear is going to make me sick. My main problems now are the conflicts the diagnosis stirred up within me."

He sat on the arm of the sofa and caressed my hair.

"I can't shake off my guilt."

"Nagore."

"I fucked up everything, damn it!"

"You are too hard on yourself."

"Father lost his sister and best friend to this fucking monster."

"That doesn't make you guilty of it."

"I live in a constant state of anxiety: I'm going to lose it. AIDS might not kill me but it's going to make me go crazy."

"You need to calm down."

"With the sexual block I have, it wouldn't surprise me if I developed uterine cancer."

"You're being dramatic."

"I harbor a monster between my legs."

"Nagore, look at me!" he ordered me. "Don't go there."

"What?"

"Do you hear yourself? 'I'm harboring a monster between my legs.'"

He drew a light smile from me.

"*Vagina dentata*," I joked.

Then I got serious.

"This sucks. No pun intended; this is impossible to keep straight."

I felt calmer now.

"Apparently AIDS could trigger any illness: pneumonia, cancer, depression, craziness... Remember what Dr. Puertas told me four months ago: 'Stay alert, it could attack anything, at any time.' Once diagnosed, once labeled, they'll read any symptom or sensation, any lack of energy, whim, shiver, cough... or smallest intention from a diagnostic perspective. And what will be worse, if I'm not careful, I will do the same."

I was finally speaking without melodrama.

"If you suffer from pneumonia, depression or gastroenteritis, that's what you'll have and that's what you'll be treated for. You won't worry any more than necessary. I, on the other hand, will always have AIDS. I won't go through a fucking toothache without provoking pity."

"The diagnosis is still new; you're in a state of shock."

He brought a few chocolate and orange cookies.

"If I lose weight, it will be because I have AIDS; if I get the flu, it will be because I have AIDS; if I get cancer, it will be AIDS induced..."

"An ant will always be worried about having an elephant behind it."

"You've got quite a graphic perspective."

"Professional bias..." he joked.

"But it's the truth; in my case, those who know that I've been diagnosed won't pay attention to the size of the ant; they'll all stare at the elephant. And it makes a difference whether you're carrying along an ant or an elephant on your back."

"You must regain confidence in your health."

He bit into another cookie and hit the bull's eye.

"They're really tasty; do you want one?"

I shook my head.

"That's it! Doctors don't help me trust my own health. I always leave Dr. Puertas's office out of sorts with my own body. In his reports, my blood is not what gives me life but instead a source of infection; it's the poison that is killing me, and could poison others too. He orders me again and again to take anti-retroviral medicine; he does, indeed, trust those. I find myself at an impasse. I need to decide."

"Between...?"

"Between the tranquility that being submissive brings and trusting my own body."

I thought I sensed a certain skepticism in his eyes.

"Between medicine and fate?"

"Between control and freedom, order and chaos, concern and complete trust... What the heck do I know: it's a philosophical matter."

"I suspect that you have already made up your mind."

"With all its consequences."

"You can always go back."

I shifted on the sofa. I clenched my jaw in pain.

"I don't know how to be tame," I concluded.

I writhed on the sofa: it was hard to breath.

"That's why my ribcage aches."

"I'll bring you a painkiller."

Father came into Ataka during Mother's break, when it was just Maria and me at the bar. He greeted Maria tenderly, pushing her hair from her face and kissing her on the cheek. They obviously knew each other. I served him a beer. He presented me his proposal while passing me a half-smoked joint.

"A friend is getting married in Bilbao. I don't want to go alone."

From the day he left home, this was the first time he was inviting me to 'his terrain.' I agreed to go.

Father waited for me at the Bilbao bus station. He was wearing black jeans and a white shirt, a gray sport coat over his shoulders, his arms out of the coat, foggy glasses and his hair gelled back. Against Maria's advice, I wore a pair of boot-legged pants, a Ramones gray t-shirt and a leather coat.

"That's the way to embody rock."

He held my arm and pointed at a motorcycle, with pride.

"Is that yours?"

It wasn't an expensive model, but it was a good-looking bike. He put a helmet on me, and I sat on the back.

The celebration was at a pub in the outskirts of town where its name began to fade. The newlyweds completed the paperwork in court and invited their friends to that location. They placed food on the tables and bottles on the bar, apparently, so people could serve themselves as much as they wanted. They made an odd couple. The bride, a tall white-haired, robust woman who wore her silver hair half way down her back on top of a wine-colored shawl. The groom was younger, short and brown-haired.

"Rafa!" they greeted Father.

I sensed them looking at me, wondering who I was.

"His girlfriend, probably," the woman said.

Father laughed.

"My daughter," he clarified.

The pub began to get crowded. The guests looked like escapees from an Almodóvar film: women exaggeratedly made-up, wearing cheap jewelry, serious men who kissed each other, women with fluffy hair, city scoundrels, a psychiatrist here and there with their own complexes, dandies in hats, freckled girls, a limping patriarch…

"And what are you, the tamer?" I asked Father.

He introduced me to a friend of his, a handsome man, about his age. When Father called out to him, the man left the cocaine trail he was fixing on the bar and greeted him with open arms.

"Long time no see!" The man hugged Father.

"This is my daughter," Father told him. "Nagore, Markos."

I walked over to him to give him the traditional two kisses and Markos held me lightly around my waist.

"He's a psychologist's assistant," Father introduced him.

Markos snorted the line and started laughing, using his thumb to push in the dust stuck onto his nasal lining.

"With no degree, I have to add," the friend made sure to clarify.

"Markos liberates women. He's an artist at it."

"I work with men, too."

I poured myself a vodka-cola.

“There are lots of people sexually stuck,” Father tried to loosen his tongue.

Markos didn’t seem to feel like talking about work.

“They go to therapy,” Father continued, stubbornly. “But the couch doesn’t provoke orgasms. That’s where he comes in.”

I concluded that he worked in prostitution. I wasn’t that mistaken; he was an out-of-the-ordinary sex-worker.

“I assist a psychologist; she refers cases to me.”

When he said ‘she,’ he pointed at the bride.

“Lidia is the psychologist.”

Truly, that big woman inspired trust. Markos explained that every week they got together at Lidia’s office and that, after studying each patient’s file, they designed the appropriate intervention for each person. The patients, of course, were not aware of that maneuver.

“I’m like the hitchhiker that you see on the road.”

I grabbed a second vodka-cola when Father and Markos started talking about harmful sexual consequences during the armed struggle.

“We act as if we could live without pleasure,” I heard Markos say. “We’ve suppressed our libido for the adrenaline created by the struggle. When ETA stops, the psychologist visits are going to skyrocket, you’ll see.”

They toasted.

“But you shouldn’t talk about that yet.”

Lidia served me a rum shot and we toasted the shipwreck.

Later, at an undetermined time, the lights went off, and the music of the 70’s took me from one drink to another. I got lost among the random bodies and finally, hardly able to support myself, ended up in Father’s arms.

“Time to go to sleep,” I heard him say.

We left the party around three in the morning to go home on the motorcycle. I threw up twice on the way. Father lived in an apartment in Txurdinaga's subsidized housing complex. He parked in front of a brick apartment building. He opened the door, turned on all the lights and started showing me the hallway and the living room. It smelled like paint.

"And that cat?" I asked him when I saw the hairy animal that ran away down the hallway.

He threw open the door on the right. There was a girl in her underwear on the bed, fast asleep.

"Her name is Josune. The cat is hers."

—

A year later I lived in Bilbao, at Father's place.

It was Monday, three in the afternoon, coffee time. October 13, 1997. A white Ford Transit crossed Iparragirre Street. Right in front, the new museum, the huge titanium ship, shiny under the autumn sun. They had just finished the final decorations on sculptor Jeff Koon's British puppy. From then on, Puppy was to guard Frank Gehry's little house. The World Cycling Championship was going on in Donostia and, in a few days, the Bilbao Guggenheim Museum was about to open its doors. All surrounding hotels were full of cultural types and art curators, and the attendance of the Monarchs of Spain was expected for the following Saturday. '*Ven y Cuéntalo*' (Come and Tell Others.) was the motto of the campaign created by the Basque Government. Basque president Jose Antonio Ardanza and Spanish president José María Aznar were going to deliver a few remarks during the opening ceremony. If only for a few minutes, the eyes of the world were looking on this place full of complexes.

The van stopped by the Museum. The sign, '*Garden Igorre*,' on the white body. Two workers, one of them dressed in green coveralls, the other one wearing a dark windbreaker, began unloading planters: ficus, philodendron, fern. They looked heavy.

A stone-like structure with many pounds of soil inside. In front, the City of Bilbao coat of arms displaying the San Antón Church and bridge with its images of laurel, crown and wolves.

The mother of one of the gardeners had carefully chosen the plants, thinking that they were to be used to decorate the entry to her son's farmhouse. Ficus, symbolizing strength, shrubs with strong perennial leaves, so they could stand the heat of the full sun as well as strong winds. Philodendrons, with heart-shaped leaves, for her oldest son. Fern, a beloved native plant.

On paper, it looked like the perfect attack: inside the planters, buried under the ficus and philodendrons, they hid 12 anti-tank grenades wrapped in plastic, which would get activated next Saturday timed with the arrival of Spanish monarchs Juan Carlos de Borbón and Sofia of Greece, specifically, when one of the gardeners made the sign and, from 75 yards away, by the gas station, his colleague would pull the trigger.

But no explosion happened. A small detail alerted the guards in charge of watching over the museum 24/7, and they suspected the flower shop workers; the license plate didn't match the type of vehicle. In a few seconds, two dry shots. The fern shivered ever so unperceptively. A Basque police force agent was shot and down on the ground. Two young men on the run. They arrested one a few yards from the museum. The other one, gun in hand, hijacked a car on Henao Street. A woman and a child got out of the vehicle and the car continued, toward Sarriko. At that very moment, one of the art curators had an appointment at the hair salon, red was the trendy color. Sirens on Iparragirre Street. An ambulance. Police cars. The young man in the jumpsuit abandoned the vehicle next to the San Ignazio market and hijacked another one, a blue Fiat Marea, which he drove to Ibarrekolanda. At 6:30 in the evening, a man reported a hijack: a guy who identified himself as a member of ETA, at the Galdakao Hospital parking lot, ordered him to give him his car. That's where they would lose his trail.

That summer, I decided that my childhood and adolescence were over, as if such a decision were in one's hands, that's it, enough, done, with the same relief that one closes a book that will not be read again.

'Sons of bitches,' I heard a woman tell another one, on my way home from the institute.

I had gone to Bilbao to stay with Father at the end of August for the Aste Nagusia festivals. I convinced him to let me stay there for the school year that was about to start. I argued with Mother that our town was becoming too small for me, and, as expected, she answered me with her usual silence. Maria had just left us, disappeared with no explanation whatsoever, leaving behind her a trail of the bitter perfume of abandonment. Nevertheless, Mother didn't dare try to convince me to stay at home with her.

Even though the enrollment period had already closed, Father was able to enroll me in the Txurdinaga Institute, on the condition that I spend weekends with Mother and continue working at Ataka.

"But you must leave Adrian," he dealt the last card of the negotiation.

He didn't say it in a menacing tone; it was more like revealing a piece of evidence that he was certain about. I had been going out with a guy from town for more than a year, and that, in Father's opinion, was too long.

"You need to try new things, experiment, take risks."

"You're crazy."

Father's house was Josune's too. She had been nice to me from the very beginning, especially when Father was around. When I first arrived, she fixed up the guest room for me and left me some pads and tampons neatly arranged in a small pink basket on the nightstand; the tampons wrapped in yellow plastic in the middle and the white pads forming a circle around them, the hygienic arrangement formed a daisy. Though younger, Josune was uglier than Mother, and, to tell the truth, she looked dim-witted. Any time I imitated his girlfriend's moronic expression, Father said she had a 'serene look' about her.

"Since when are you interested in serenity?"

That is when I realized that Father intentionally chose girlfriends who were obviously younger than him, so that in contrast with their naiveté, they would cast a little brightness on Father's plain intelligence.

Josune held on to the sugary redemption, and tried to trap me in her net by bringing me all kinds of sweet treats: bollicaos, doughnuts, chocolate palmiers… I wondered if she wanted me to gain weight. Father disliked fat women, 'more than fatness, what I don't like is how they neglect themselves,' and I thought that she wanted to push me away by stuffing me. She weighed 110 pounds; she rode the stationary bicycle at the gym for twenty minutes, lifted weights for ten minutes, and completed three sets of abdominal crunches. No more, no less. She did everything with determination and precision, systematically, without any passion. She was one of those women who love filling out questionnaires. No wonder she worked as a bank teller.

Any time we were at home alone, Josune's attitude toward me became harsher. Her constant smile would tense up and her usual dumb expression would look a bit sharper, enough for me to notice the change. She didn't attack me directly, there wasn't a face-to-face confrontation, but she would parade herself in front of me holding the last of the yogurts I used to have for breakfast, or she would decide to wash the dishes with hot water right when I was in the shower.

That stupid competition served as entertainment for me during the first weeks, since I felt quite lonely in that unfamiliar city. Father spent all day at the port, and Mother, ridden with jealousy, wouldn't even call me. It was good for me to have someone around who would piss me off, because that domestic opponent at least reminded me that I existed for someone. I didn't take that competition seriously, I didn't feel like wasting my time with Father's latest fling, and the failed attack on the

Guggenheim reinforced that feeling. It was a kind of revelation for me, a war-like metaphor, the call to step into life's front lines. Grudgingly, I began to realize that I had to agree with Father, because, once again, he came up with the key word: risk. Put on your coveralls and get dirty. All the way to your knees. The story with my boyfriend was too comfortable. The competition with Josune, too easy. The compassion toward Mother, too old. As always, there he was, Rafa Vargas, a few yards from his daughter, ready to push the detonator's button. The rest was a matter of time. The count down.

—

Mother came home in the middle of the afternoon. Luka was editing the morning's images on his computer, hoping to sell them to a media outlet. I was still stretched out, lying down on the sofa, trying to find a comfortable position so I could bear the pain in my kidneys. Mother didn't sit next to me nor did she light a cigarette, her usual invitation to conversation. She said a quick hi from the hallway and walked into her bedroom. I raised my voice:

"Did you know that today is a strike day?"

She didn't answer me. I could hear pacing coming from her room.

"Luka, please, tell Mother to come out here."

Without taking his eyes off the screen, he made a gesture, signaling for me to wait.

"Don't expect to sell those images easily. All unemployed journalists are doing freelance work."

I lit a cigarette.

"Will someone bring me a glass of water?"

Mother left her room and walked by me. She took off her shoes by pushing the heel with her toes. She got in the shower. As soon as the water started running, I thought I heard her trying to sing something resembling Amy Winehouse's *Back to Black*. I turned on the TV and closed my eyes.

I must've fallen asleep because when I opened my eyes Mother's hair was dry and she was wearing a black dress I had never seen her wear before.

"You finally woke up!"

Mother sat next to me and asked Luka to join us.

"Diorissimo?"

The smallest bottle of Diorissimo perfume cost 60 euros. She touched her neck.

"I met a man. It's been four or five months already."

I closed my eyes once again. Luka shoved my thigh with his knee. It was the first time Mother had started a relationship without me knowing. Whenever she met anyone, she always asked me for my opinion, because she was unable to read someone else's intentions.

"Another thug, for sure."

"He's the owner of a small hotel. He doesn't like to go out at night."

"You said it's been four months?"

Mother's adventure must've started around the time I was diagnosed.

"And where did you meet him?"

"Through the Meetic site."

I sat up on the sofa.

"I created a profile in summer. I wasn't very hopeful… But, look!"

Luka stood up, and, laughing, he hugged her tight. He acted as euphoric as a soccer player celebrating a goal.

"That's great! Congratulations, Arantza!"

She pointed to the two suitcases she had in the hallway.

"He has a small apartment right at the hotel, an attic; he asked me to go live with him. Can you believe it! No need to pay rent, and a daily breakfast buffet!"

"What a bargain!"

"I think this is the first time I'm involved with someone who doesn't have money trouble."

She packed her toiletries, a hair-dryer and a small radio in a wicker tote.

"The house is all yours. I won't bother you anymore. I'll miss you, for sure."

I stood up and let out an involuntary sigh of pain.

"What's wrong?"

"It's nothing."

"Are you sure?"

She rested her hand on my shoulder.

"So, you're leaving," I said.

"Yes."

"OK."

"Won't you wish me good luck?"

She grabbed a suitcase in each hand.

"Good luck, Mother."

She shut the door behind her. Luka and I stayed staring at the door.

"Congratulations," he said. "Your mom has become independent."

"She'll be back soon. Give her a week."

I went to the kitchen to get another painkiller; because now I had just added a headache to my side ache. Luka's telephone rang.

"She did leave her birth home once," Luka pointed out when he hung up. "Don't underestimate her."

"She'll be back."

"That's what you'd like?"

He jumped and pointed at me with his index finger.

"Pick a color!"

"What?"

"A color, whichever one you want."

"Black."

"OK. We'll cook a black dinner to celebrate."

"What're we celebrating?"

"That your mother has a boyfriend and that I sold my story."

He gave me a peck.

"Produced by Luka Moretti."

He patted his own back.

"Congratulations."

He took a beer from the refrigerator and returned to the computer to adapt his footage to the format the buyer requested.

I whispered:

"*Diorissimo.*"

—

On October 14, 1997, the Spanish language teacher asked us to hold a minute of silence for the policeman killed the day before. I had been at the Txurdinaga Institute for about a month; I hardly knew my classmates, at least not enough to know definitely how they positioned themselves politically. I tried to get a sense of it: a couple classmates buried their heads in their books. Most of them grew quiet, but without solemnity, winking and continuing to throw spit balls at each other. To one side a little murmuring.

Then, the sound of a dragged chair, of someone who stood up all at once. I turned around. It was a boy whose name I hadn't learned yet.

"Where are you going?" the teacher asked him.

He didn't answer. He grabbed his backpack and headed toward the door. I followed him.

"Nagore Vargas!" the teacher scolded me.

I crossed the classroom quickly. I shut the door behind me and introduced myself to the boy who was waiting for me in the hallway.

"Jokin," he replied.

We left the playground and walked away. After sharing a few light brush strokes about my life, where I was from, why I was in Bilbao, how I liked the city, we went over what happened the day before, talking over each other, competing over who could give more details. I told him about the type of vehicles used in the flight. I didn't know more than what I learned in the news. He talked about the cell members' clothing color, and the two of us listed the inventory of grenades and other weapons seized. Jokin spoke about the consequences that the "boys" would suffer: torture, isolation, dispersion, prison.

"The van belonged to my cousin."

He took me off guard.

"He was arrested."

"I'm sorry," I said, but, truly, I was more jealous than sorry. I felt jealousy due to the authority he had, and stripped me of, resulting from the connection he shared with the arrested person, instead of the solidarity I felt toward his cousin whom I didn't know. Though I owned the leftist discourse and was ready for rebellion, the pure-blood Basque nationalists, inadvertently, reminded me time after time, with their ancestral surnames, with their imprisoned family members, that I wasn't one of them, not completely, not fully. More than lacking the feeling of collaboration, I lacked the right to be angry and the charm that being persecuted gave them. There was always a blood connection, some lost subordination umbilical cord that didn't connect me, that would always leave me outside their dazzling circle.

We were sitting on the grass, in Europa Park. The city at our feet.

"What a pair of eyes you have," he told me.

I kissed him, the Txurdinaga block apartment buildings as backdrop. Risk it. He brought me toward him, and I sat astride him. I felt like someone else. The thrill of an alter ego. He caressed my breast over my t-shirt, for a long time, completely focused, without budging to slide his hands under my clothing or touching me elsewhere. A shiver. The detonator. Father was right. I had a city waiting to be discovered, a few revolutions to identify, and a body to take a stand in the square between violence and eroticism.

—

I didn't break up with Adrian but continued spending time with Jokin. Like in many other facets of my life, I kept accumulating, keeping and combining, to the detriment of replacing. I acted similarly with frustrations, alcoholic beverages and house knickknacks. Through Jokin, I met Haritz, and through Haritz, Karra. For a while I was involved with the four of them. Out of the four, Adrian was the only one who thought we were in a monogamous relationship. For me, Bilbao and my town were two different worlds; I acted in one as if the other didn't exist. I didn't lie but set aside explanations that I wasn't asked for. Jokin knew about Adrian. I didn't tell him about Haritz and Karra, but he suspected something. Haritz and Karra knew that I slept with both. Each had their place, and perhaps, their function.

I used to end Saturday nights with Adrian: we closed Ataka, went to the hangout, undressed on the sofa we rescued from the trash, and helped to stem the adrenaline accumulated at the bar, the alcohol we consumed, and the rest. We were parachutists who were too afraid to land alone in the outskirts of town, like the street cleaners' truck, thrown at an inconvenient time by the night into the daylight, like cigarettes still releasing smoke, surrendered to survive the inertia in a tamed and dirty state. After closing the bar, we used to need about three or four hours to begin to feel sleepy, but finally, heavy and dark, exhaustion would come.

The affair with Jokin was limited to time between classes. Besides writing communiqués and making photocopies with other amateur political analysts like us, we made rounds visiting all of the classrooms to let everyone know about the protests organized by the *Ikasle Abertzaleak* (Basque Nationalist Students). We painted banners in the art classroom and dreamed about creating a fanzine. But as soon as we were alone, we desperately looked for each other's bodies, regressing from the sapiens species to smelling, licking and rubbing. We kissed each other in a corner of the school playground, under the eaves of an apartment building close to school or at Europa Park until our lips swelled and our chins were raw. We touched each other over our clothes or in the gaps between layers, until our underwear felt wet. I acted like a shy adolescent with Jokin; I enjoyed the boundaries that shyness set and that I had lost long ago: hesitant touching, measured caressing, body parts touched inadvertently, offered and requested indirectly, looking for something new in uncomfortable positions and movements. We did what people our age did, no more; we closed our eyes and allowed one another to search, nervously and clumsily, for our own hidden body parts and unknown thrills. Feeling the liberation of surrendering yourself to someone else. Playing for the wonder of it. Only that, and yet, all that. We didn't undress in front of each other and would never do so; our bodies had to be like ones that exploded unintentionally, scattered on the ground accidentally, smelling like sweat, deodorant and sex.

Haritz was older, a man, in my eyes. He had a job, was a full-time union representative, lived in an apartment he shared with other three people, and owned a car. He was a serious and cautious guy; the glasses over the bridge of his sharp nose gave him the appearance of a perpetual student. By then, he had already obtained his political science degree and was becoming quite known in the small world of article writers. He carefully read the international news sections and leftist periodicals. Quiet, hard-working, a little stiff, elegant in an anti-capitalistic way, intelligent. He almost always kept his eyes half-closed; I couldn't tell if it was due to being nearsighted or skeptical by nature. He was one of those people difficult to imagine having sex, not at all organic, not at all basic and, therefore, a provocateur. Jokin introduced me to him after we had had a few ideological discussions. I had some disagreements with Jokin; we argued about terminology: *conflict, issues, dispute, problem*… due to the simplistic way he had of referring to the conflict: he spoke about Spaniards with disdain, without making any distinction among them; I had to remind him of Grandma Rosa, Grandpa Manuel and all of their ancestors and, in my opinion, he was too forgiving of the Basques that he put all together in the same bag. I thought his was a very poor debate tactic, childish.

"And what do you have to say about our own oligarchy? You should think of the places where different types of repression cross paths."

I told him to get lost, ideologically. Sexually, we kept touching each other over our clothes.

Fed up with my discourse and my tendency to continuously question his, Jokin left me in Haritz's hands. He gave me away:

"She's one of you," he said verbatim.

Haritz and I spent the whole evening bar hopping on Somera Street, and the very same day I met him, I stripped him of his t-shirt which bore the motto, "*Ni guerra entre pueblos, ni paz entre clases*," (No War Between Nations, No Peace Between Classes) at the 'revolutionaries' apartment.' That was how I baptized the apartment that Haritz shared with Karra and two other long haired, rebellious roommates. He remained as serious and concentrated while having sex as when we chatted between beers. On some occasions, I missed Jokin's clumsy natural ways, but I liked Haritz's careful way of pausing at each of my words and forgotten nooks of my body. Quiet and precise, he could get lost in a fold of skin of my underarm like he did looking for the right word for one of his articles, and he stayed there, searching for the mere sensation, at someone else's service yet lost within himself. On that first night, when he turned on the light, I couldn't control my laughter when I saw a line of shoes organized against the wall from biggest to smallest in his hyper-organized bedroom: hiking boots, running shoes, tennis shoes, rock-climbing shoes, slippers, flip-flops.

"With this organization, we'll fix the world in no time."

I broadened my horizon of the struggle for freedom with Haritz—Nicaragua, Venezuela, Mexico, Bolivia, Palestine, Brazil, Kurdistan—and also crossed a few body-cartography borders, at night and clandestinely. Our way.

At night and clandestinely, it's how I ended up in bed with Karra, Haritz's roommate as I started the tangled and fruitful trend of getting involved with my lover's best friends. Karra was a hybrid like me, the son of immigrants and a new Basque language speaker, with a happy, carefree personality. I was in their apartment sitting on an armchair, not able to sleep, when Karra arrived at four in the morning from a meeting.

"From a meeting, at this hour?"

We closed the deal without uttering a single word: I would get into his bed, and he would open the doors of Bilbao for me. If I got to know the Left Bank area of Bilbao with Haritz, it was Karra who made room for me there and who included me in his group of friends. A few weeks after I got involved with Karra, I was well-known on Somera. As I walked along the street, people from all over greeted me, bought me beers. Sex with him was quite lame, with no special spark. He didn't try to give pleasure, he had a lazy libido, but he made plans for me in the city, invited me to meetings, introduced the leftist pro-independence youth organization known as *Segi*, women, Irantzu among them, and after a few months, I moved to her apartment.

So, I can say that, thanks to sex, I left loneliness behind and I regained my lost adolescence and that what happened under the sheets opened the doors of militancy for me, allowed me into a group, the city and autonomy. I am truly indebted to sex.

—

The black dinner promised by Luka got delayed almost six months. On a summer evening, when I arrived home from the perfumery, I found him sitting at a candlelit table.

"Go to the bedroom."

A sleeveless black dress on the bed. I put it on. I returned to the kitchen barefoot, since I didn't have shoes that matched the dress.

"Madame," he offered me a chair.

A napkin draped on his forearm, he recited the menu in French.

"Unfortunately, I'm not a polyglot like you."

"Unfortunately, I'm not as elegant as you."

He looked like an orchestra singer wearing a black shirt that was too big for him.

"Where did you get it?"

"I'm not telling."

He cleared his throat:

"For starters, a black lettuce salad with beets, hijiki seaweed, olives and Modena reduction; potato salad tartlets covered with black fish eggs and huitlacoche quesadillas. Followed by calamari cooked in its own ink and, to finish, a chocolate and blackberry tart. Accompanied by Rioja wine. Coffee and a Fernet spirit for after dinner."

"It looks as nice as your French sounded."

He served me the salad.

"To us."

"It looks like our future will be quite dark."

"You chose the color."

"It's elegant."

"It's the color of silence, winter, darkness, the infinite, mystery and passive feminine energy," he said.

"Passive feminine energy?"

"I have it more developed than you."

"Death is black too," I said.

"There are 50 shades of black," he added.

"We'll toast to the lightest hue," I proposed.

He stood up:

"Here, to light black and almost dark blue!"

We toasted.

"We'll go to Paris when we can and retake the test."

Maggiore's book said that the Western Blot tests used to detect HIV, in addition to being inaccurate, were not standardized. There was no nationally or internationally accepted criteria to define a positive result. Standards also varied from lab. to lab. within the same country or state, and could even differ from day to day at the same lab. As HIV test kit manufacturers acknowledged. 'At present, there is no recognized standard for establishing the presence or absence of antibodies to HIV-1 and HIV-2 in human blood'. Therefore, it was possible for a person to be HIV positive in one country and HIV negative in the neighboring one. The result depended on its interpretation: an indecisive result could become an unquestionable positive depending on one's sexual preference, health history or zip-code.

"What kind of fish eggs are these?"

I bit half of a tartelette.

"They're known as poor people's caviar."

"Just right for us, then."

"Mullet eggs."

I spit out what I had in my mouth into a napkin.

"You're kidding!"

"Why?"

"Disgusting!"

"They're highly valued in Asia. They exchange them as gifts at New Year's; they represent wealth and prosperity."

"You haven't seen the mullets here; they feed on garbage and swim up the river, fat as can be, with the high tide."

He served me some wine.

"What do you think about Paris?"

Maggiore affirmed that AIDS wasn't an illness but a classification. In the United States,the CDC had expanded the definition of AIDS three times since 1981. After the change of its definition, in 1993, if a person's T-cell count was below 200, a symptomless individual could also have AIDS. Consequently, based on this new definition, 21,000 more cases were added overnight, out of which, more than 20,000 had no symptoms.

"I don't want to daydream."

"If you tested negative, we would forget about everything and start from scratch."

He brought the squid cooked in a clay pot.

"Caught with fish hooks. I spent all afternoon cleaning them."

"I don't believe you."

"And you're right not to."

"Very good. Whose recipe?"

"I stole it from Irantzu's grandma from Getaria."

The physical conditions listed under the AIDS label varied from country to country.

Canada's Laboratory Centre for Disease Control (LCDC), for example, didn't recognize the American T-cell count standards, therefore, 182,200 American AIDS patients, more than 25%of all people in the US ever diagnosed with AIDS, would not have AIDS in Canada.

"It can't be that easy: going to Paris to confirm that everything has been nothing but a nightmare, with the Eiffel Tower as a backdrop."

"It'd be like the end of a romantic movie: we would have ice-cream at the Montmartre gardens."

"Too much sugar."

"I'll come up with a healthier ending."

"You should change the city."

"Barcelona?"

"Barcelona is in our same country, for now, anyway."

"London?"

"They haven't used the Western Blot test since 1992, because they don't consider it reliable enough."

"Do you believe that the situation in Africa is true?"

"You mean, the way they diagnose it?"

"Yes."

"It wouldn't surprise me."

The documentary *House of Numbers* explained that the World Health Organization used two completely different definitions for AIDS in Africa and that neither of them corresponded to the

U.S. or European criteria. The most frequently used diagnosis in Africa didn't require an HIV test; it was enough if the patient, together with general body-wide itching and swollen glands, showed one of the three following major clinical symptoms; weight-loss, fever or coughing.

"Black Africa."

Luka cleared the table and sliced two pieces of chocolate blackberry tart.

"Did you read what happened to that child in Málaga?

"No."

"They tested a child born in Malaga for HIV, at the hospital, without permission, illegally, and the result turned out to be positive. Yet the father and the mother tested negative. When a friend of the couple, who was familiar with the critical theories, informed them that the interpretation criteria varied from one country to another, the parents decided to repeat the test in an English hospital in Gibraltar. This time the result was negative. The hospital in Málaga considered the testing invalid, because it wasn't conducted in Spanish territory, precisely.

Fortunately, the child is healthy."

I emptied the remaining wine.

"Bordeaux?"

"What?"

"The city could be Bordeaux."

"When do you want to go?"

"Give me some time."

He finished clearing the table and put some music on.

"Miles Davis?"

"*Kind of Blue*. Any coffee?"

"I'll go straight to Fernet."

He served two shots. We gulped down the liquor.

"Cheers to Bordeaux."

I stood up and held him from his waist.

"Shall we dance?"

Daydreams, caviar of the poor.

"Hey, Luka."

"What?"

"What if I had chosen blue instead of black?"

"We would've had your eyes for dinner."

—

On October 20th, 2011 at seven in the evening, I had just said goodbye to a customer after giving her a facial. The newscast started on the radio station I had playing at the store. They announced that ETA had decided to permanently cease fire. A female ETA member broke the news. It surprised me, yet it didn't; the idea of ceasing fire connected with femininity. I felt the impulse to call Father first and, later, to call Mother, Irantzu, Luka and Karra. But finally, I decided not to, based on the experiences I shared with each one in relation to the armed struggle. Me-ETA-Father; Me-ETA-Mother; Me-ETA-Irantzu … each threesome formed a world of its own. The political struggle fully loaded with passion, pain and contradictions had penetrated the core of our intimacy. Passionately and uncomfortably, it had seared certain scenes and had adopted a different code in the development of each relationship: the uncovered and silenced emotions, the truths and lies we told one another. I imagined how each one would respond if I asked them about the news. Who would be overtaken with happiness, who with nostalgia, who with excitement, who with concern, who with weariness, who with boredom. Who would speak with caution and in a lower voice, who would laugh without holding back. Each one's reaction would echo differently within me, colliding with the original doubt or mingling with it, like the ripples created by throwing the first pebbles into the pool of collective stories.

I closed the store and sat down. I let the news resonate within me with no interference. I was grateful that the moment caught me with no witnesses; there is news that requires solitude.

The lightness of releasing an old tension helped me to breathe deeply. I felt exhaustion deep within my lungs. The wounds and the blurred feeling of guilt, the burden of action and the lack of action. The hardened anatomy of having held and carried tension for a long time. I was overcome by the similar emotion one feels when finding out about a friend's or an enemy's death, though announced: it was too late for many things, too early for others. What to say, who to call, how to organize the images coming to me all at once?

Ours had been a childhood and adolescence pierced by the armed struggle almost as naturally as the wind. Innocence and violence couldn't be discerned: we were children who read graffiti aloud condemning torture as soon as we learned how to put letters together; children who were scolded for bringing to the tip of our tongue what we saw in front of our eyes. I was told what a car bomb was in the playground; in the same playground someone told my aunt what a fix was. The initiation wound I got when I imagined a person could kill another one lurked right under my skin, pulsing, covered by a thick scab, resulting from the constant violence near and far.

Inside of me dwelled the embarrassment of being of Spanish descent and the pride of being a leftist; the hate I felt toward the police, first intuitively and later justifiably; the day when I wrote *GORA ETA* (m), (LONG LIVE ETA) on the flyleaf of my history book; the need to know, yet the shame of asking someone what the 'm' in parenthesis meant; the girl who cried at the park and screamed that ETA killed her uncle; my conversations with Peru; clandestine stickers; the day we started referring to bomb attacks as actions; '*Someone should pull the trigger...ETA, ETA, ETA, ETA*!; the shared smell of sweat; the sense of belonging to a group; the condescending love toward Spaniard friends; the day before and after they assassinated Miguel Angel Blanco; the mistrust toward pure nationalists and the pity and embarrassment felt for leftist Spaniards; the same hypocrisy when singing, at the end of each demonstration, *Eusko gudariak gara* (We Are Basque Soldiers).

The agitated atmosphere of the 80's and 90's perfectly matched my emotional framework: the passion for justice, the predisposition to violence, the stance against authority, the overwhelming hate, the life or death defense of territory, the obligation to avenge our ancestors, the social homage to courage. It was so natural in my case to feel personally conflicted, because the harmony resulting from the inner and outside impulses provided me with a feeling of normality that almost felt cozy.

"We all need to give something so a few need not give everything." In my youth, I believed that to be self-evident. Still, in order to justify the effort demanded by the hardest sector, even if it was delayed, even after seeing the claws of the strategy of hyper-culpability, seated on the recliner at the perfumery, I held myself accountable.

One of the axes that divided our world had just disappeared. The tension and comfort of having to label yourself or having others label you was over. No more biting your tongue. The hostility-induced adrenaline; the cradle of belonging. All the muted "GORA ETA's (Long live ETA's)" provoked the same hoarseness in my throat as the ones I had yelled. The consciousness of suffering was long, wide and multifaceted. The time to start rebuilding identities began at 7:00 that evening. The images of country, identity, and solidarity remained blurry, and we would all need to start refocusing individually, in twos, threes or en masse. Looking for a new truth. Searching for updated lies adapted to a new reasoning and new morals. Our vocabulary, point of view, and attitudes would need to be regulated. We would adjust the opinions that, over decades, had been hyped-up or aborted; they already started adjusting within me. I recognized a hint of sadness: it wasn't nostalgia, but mourning. And I wondered if the feeling of becoming an orphan was more pronounced among those who were in favor of ETA or those who were against. I wasn't sure.

When I stood up, my vision grew blurry. I lost my center, dizzy, the softening of my identity, lost muscle mass. Sclerosis. I felt old and alone, part of history. Entangled with old events, weariness, suffering and fears. For the first time in my life, separated from future generations. At that very moment, the last generation whose every layer of consciousness had been pierced by the acronym, ETA, was redefined.

A chain reaction soon followed: variations of "It was too late a long time ago." Voices of men, that sounded too confident, began expounding with prepared statements. Masculine commentary ratifying the ETA spokeswoman's announcement of surrender filled the airwaves. Violence against violence. Female remorse. Male resentment.

What is the extent of a people's right to defend their territory? By what means, and until what point?

The rhythms set by ETA, the density of the air, the cycles, the pauses. The systolic-diastolic collective emotions directed by ETA grew silent. The body was still warm. Around us widows, friends, enemies, heirs, mourners, vultures. Happiness wasn't clean. Sadness was dirty.

When should fighting stop?

It was dark outside.

Who knows when the right time is?

A silent prayer on the way home, agnostic.

—

One morning, the following spring, while I was having breakfast at the table, someone knocked at the door. I left what I was eating, and the reflex to consider the option of running away kicked in. After a couple of seconds of feeling paralyzed, a skeptic rage took over in me: why the hell would I be arrested? I hurried to open the door, exercising my free will.

Father came in like an enraged wolf. After kicking and punching the door, he stopped abruptly in the hallway, his eyes reddened by rage. He rested his hands on his thighs.

"You, you, you…" It looked like his anger wouldn't let him go on.

"What's the matter?"

"When did you quit going to your appointments"

"Have you been spying on me?

"What kind of game are you playing? It's been a year since you last went to the hospital."

"I can't believe it."

I turned around but he grabbed me by my t-shirt and made me stop in my tracks.

"I don't know why it surprises me," I told him infuriated: "You've been policing me. Very nice, yes sir!"

"Don't go there."

"What about a patient's right to privacy? Who the hell do you think you are?"

He let me go.

"Your father, and I'll tell you something: if you don't go to your appointments, forget about me."

"Suit yourself."

He was beside himself, to the point that I thought he would hit me.

"Give me a reason! A fucking reason! Why the hell don't you go?"

I walked from the hallway to the living room and from there to the kitchen. I spoke to him as calmly as I could:

"I'm a dissident."

It was the first time I defined myself that way. Father followed me. He let out a hysterical, shrieking laugh. He came up to me and with his chin against my parietal bone, asked me with disdain:

"A dissident. A dissident of what?"

I didn't answer.

"Do you know how many people die because they don't have the chance to receive antiretroviral treatments? Are you going to start lecturing me from the privilege of a rich and spoiled European child?"

I placed the palm of my hand on his chest and, barely applying any strength, I pushed him away from me.

"Respect my space."

It frightened me to ask Father for something that I had never asked of him before.

And what I most feared happened: he fell silent. He took a deep breath, turned around and with no threat, no door slamming, disappeared.

—

It took a while to finally make the trip to Bordeaux. I bought train tickets twice, and both times I let them expire at the last minute. I had such a need to be right, because the fear of not being right had possessed me. So, what if science confirmed, for a second time, that I was sick? With no checkups and without having done new testing, all I had as a measuring instrument was my own body. If the diagnosis were confirmed, I would need to accept it, accept the defeat and obey the path of submission. Or would it be possible to run away once again? It would have to be in another direction this time.

Finally, on July 2013, we boarded a train to Bordeaux. We left Hendaye on a Saturday morning and would return midday on Monday. We made an appointment through one of Luka's friends, at a private clinic, for Monday morning, to be tested for AIDS but decided not to talk about it during the entire weekend.

As soon as we stepped off the train, I got a good feeling about Bordeaux. The weather was beautiful, a nice breeze making the midday sun enjoyable; I could almost feel the salt in the air because, as a port city, it had the right to claim its portion of the sea.

It had been about three or four months since Luka had been hired by a television production company and, with his first paycheck, he rented a neat apartment in the old part of the city. We rode the light-rail to Porte de Bourgogne and walked to Camille-Jullian square. The surroundings were sprinkled with street musicians.

Close to St. Pierre Church and lured by a group playing gypsy music, we joined a circle of people that had formed around them. It was a group of eight young men and women: guitar, ukulele, sax, violin, castanets, drums, rhythm box, voice… I thought they looked offensively young. Barefoot, with a well calculated, neglected shameless look, something between new hippies and hipsters: just shampooed messy hair, second-hand clothing and instruments, leaf tobacco to roll and, almost certainly, though not obvious, I could smell a university scholarship for each one, which allowed them to live quite carefree. The way they harmonized seemed improvised and anarchical, but most likely had been as calculated as their messy ponytails. They displayed a cool and rowdy energy that announced, I am not sure why, that as soon as they finished their concert, they would go off to have sex with each other.

"Who do you like best?"

The group's sexual aura had caught Luka's attention too.

"The sax player."

"They must've put him there for his good looks because…"

Luka knew more about music than I did.

"Is he bad?"

"Between you and me," he whispered in my ear while we applauded their last song: "He sounds like an elephant with a cold."

I laughed.

"The rhythm box and the voice carry the weight; the rest are decorative."

"Are you jealous or is it what you really believe?"

For part of our way home, he mimicked a duck's walk and imitated the fat sound of, more than a saxophone, an old euphonium.

His attic was located on a fourth floor, with no elevator. I reached the top of the stairway sweating and out of breath, but the effort had been worthwhile. The light hue of the wood radiated warmth when the 2:00 p.m. sun came in through the skylight, and the bed, made up in white, invited you to lie down. We put down my stuff and played soft music on my phone and, without undoing the bed, lay on it and covered our half naked bodies with a light shawl.

We fell into a sweet sleep for almost two hours. When we woke up, the bed was now shaded. I took a shower and dressed nicely: I had bought a pair of wedged espadrilles that laced up around my ankles to wear with the dress that Luka gave me for the black dinner. I puffed my hair and gathered it loosely at the nape of my neck. To my astonishment, Luka wasn't far behind: he stood waiting for me in the bedroom, wearing a pair of mustard-colored, ankle-length pants, a white linen shirt and a dark sport coat. On our way out, he put on a straw hat.

He proposed having coffee at the Utopia Café Cinema which was located at the Camille-Jullian plaza. The old but newly-remodeled former church served as a cinema that showed indie film series and had a restaurant, coffee shop and cultural exchange center. We sat outside and ordered coffee. Then we got lost in the nearby streets: we had a gin and tonic at the Parliament Plaza and identified a couple possible places for dinner on Fernand

Philippart Street. After strolling around, we finally chose a winery next to the Cailhau Gate. Setting aside my Spanish comments about French dining times, I appreciated being able to sit down for dinner at seven. We were hungry. The place wasn't cheap, but their local wines, and cheese and cold-meat platters were reasonably priced. We weren't accustomed to indulging ourselves in such luxuries, but we had agreed to loosen our wallets a little along with our convictions.

"If worse comes to worst, we can always sing a few Basque songs on a street corner."

"Wearing a straw hat?"

They served us each a Cremant.

"Nevertheless, St. Pierre musicians don't seem to lack money."

"And how do you know that?" He wondered.

"When people build their look based on poverty, it means it's not real. Those who are poor don't sing barefoot. There's a kind of rejoicing in their 'poor-look,' as if they were celebrating something."

Luka snapped his fingers.

"It happens to Irantzu too," I added.

"How?"

"I say it with all my love, but, poverty and an ascetic look are nothing but a personal whim in her case."

"An ideological choice?"

"Ideological, esthetic… a temporary situation."

He burst out laughing.

"Don't you know? Irantzu's mother's farmhouse has its own coat of arms; she's a descendant of an aristocratic lineage, and an only child."

"I've never heard her say anything about it."

"It embarrasses her; that's why she lives as if she were the child of a working-class family. Every time she has a chance, she'll tell you she lives in a shared, rented apartment and that she hardly makes a thousand euros a month. She never says a word to anyone about her vacation home in Getaria. When she graduated from the university, her father wanted to buy her a brand-new Vectra, but she preferred to buy a third-hand Corsa; she had to decide if she wanted to adapt the car to her life style or her life style to the car."

"Nevertheless, she's nice."

"Adorable."

Along with the cold-meat platter, they served us each a glass of a red wine from a local chateau.

"The same thing used to happen with the machos who used to shout, 'long live ETA;' none had ever even touched a gun."

"Post-revolutionaries?"

"Why do you say post?"

"Like those who offer their help to clean the kitchen when the dishes have been already washed: post-involved, post-generous, post-ies."

We took a sip of the wine.

"These are hyper-guilt-feeling people: there's always guilt hiding behind arrogance: the guilt of being a child of a bourgeois family, the embarrassment of being too big of a coward to hold a gun; the gut-eroding feeling of having had your friends arrested and you getting off scot-free…"

I asked the server to bring us some more bread to accompany the cold-meats.

"There!"

"What?"

"A real bourgeois wouldn't order more bread," Luka clarified.

"Not even if she were hungry?"

I put a thin slice of sausage in my mouth and the last piece of bread.

"In your opinion, do you think that it's obvious that we live on a budget?"

"No question: one has to be rich to notice the difference."

"It's amazing everything one inherits along with class. It wasn't just because of class, the times were such too, but I inherited chaos, a lack of punctuality and a chronic lack of discipline, and even though I might have money in my wallet, I can't control these flaws: I always have a small outstanding debt, always a job left to be done later… the exhausting feeling of always having to patch holes and ask for forgiveness. You're not like that."

"We were nomads, not poor."

The waiter came with the cheese platter.

"Even if one tries, it's hard to disguise one's cradle. Has living with your mother all over the place marked you?"

"Obviously it has."

"For example?"

"I don't accumulate useless stuff, and if I'm in good company, I don't care what time I have dinner."

"It must've left some deeper marks too."

"Deeper than that? I don't think so."

We quickly took care of the cheese platter and the rest of the wine. We walked out to the warm night that was becoming lively.

"Are we expected to leave a tip?"

We were about twenty yards from the wine-shop by then.

"Did you leave one?"

"No."

He gestured not to worry about it. We decided to cross the Place de Bourse and stroll along the Garonne river. The stock market building seemed to float, reflected in the river's mirror.

Down the Garonne, the unpretentiously lit Pont de Pierre. We headed in that direction.

"We never walk around holding hands in Bilbao," Luka pointed out.

We walked by a group of adolescents, sitting on the ground playing music on their phones connected to small speakers.

"I feel like dancing," I said.

We walked a little more and headed back toward the old part of town once again. Not far from the Parliament plaza, we came across a pub that played Cuban music.

"It looks authentic."

The bar counter of the narrow establishment, lit by neon lights and a few spotlights, had glasses already lined up with fresh mint leaves, buckets full of sliced lemons and bottles of rum. On the back shelves, more rum and a few bottles of whisky. The bar was packed. Further inside, in an indoor patio, a terrace full of flowers. We sat at the only free table.

"I'll order the drinks; you hold on to the table."

"It's packed."

The old graffiti-covered walls displayed posters, mirrors, old photographs and small flags on top of each other. Fidel, Che, Cienfuegos, July 26, Russian cars, palm trees and a complete postcard collection. It was hot. On the back shelves two fans whirred on. I grabbed a stool and sat down.

"Want to dance?"

I didn't notice him approach. He stood in front of me. I recognized him even without the sax. A thick beard, long hair in a ponytail, wearing what must've been a second-hand shirt. He held my hand and, I'm not sure why, I stood. I couldn't help but look at his feet: he was wearing sandals. He murmured something that I didn't understand into my ear and made the flesh of my arms and thighs crawl. That forgotten tremor, the memory of pleasure. I confirmed through my sense of smell that, yes, he must've been the recipient of a scholarship and, perhaps, also a parent-supported checking account. Who cared? He caressed the nape of my neck. There was barely any room on the dance floor; the crowd made our bodies press against each other. I looked toward the patio. A song. A dance and I would return to get my mojito. I held him around his waist and smiled at him. He twirled me around, making my dress puff up with hot air. He rested his hand on my shoulder. We gazed into each other's eyes. He squinted when he smiled. Under the dim neon lights, he very slowly traced with his finger the inside of my arms and palms, and once again twirled me full circle. When I placed my hand on his waist in order to keep my balance, I touched his warm skin under his half-opened shirt. With my fingertips, I caressed his abdomen, on the border between his waist and pants. We continued dancing. He whispered something else into my earlobe. With my shoulders supported against the wall, I kissed him gently, moist. I felt my entire body waking up, melting and going mad, with an intensity that I hadn't felt since my adolescent years. When the song came to an end, I opened my eyes, I rested my head on the guy's chest for a moment, and I left.

I returned to the terrace holding my mojito.

"You're sweating."

I took a long sip of my mojito. The atmosphere at the terrace slowly became livelier: suddenly, four men appeared dressed in white from head to toe, carrying a trumpet, maracas, a guitar and a Cuban tres guitar. We didn't notice the microphone placed at a corner of the terrace. As soon as the musicians began playing the first notes, a Cuban couple, that we wagered had been hired by the bar, came out onto the dance floor and put on quite a show. After three or four more songs, the bravest locals dared to join them. The Cubans offered to switch partners, in order to create Caribbean-continental asymmetric dancing pairs.

"Shall we join them?"

We took to a corner of the terrace, next to our table, and, clumsily following Luka's steps, we began dancing to the rhythm of Cuban melodies.

"Forget the steps, let yourself go."

We sang together:

"*Cuando Juanica y Chan Chan en el mar cernían arena, como sacudía el jibe, a Chan Chan le daba pena…*"

When I felt embarrassed, I held on to my mojito. Luka in his straw hat and skillfully dancing, looked like a real Cuban.

"I didn't know you danced so well."

"You all kept me completely repressed."

We danced until the musicians stopped playing. Our feet ached when we left the dance floor, our arms around each other's waists, singing, "*píntate los labios, María*!

The next day, I woke up late, full of energy and ready to take on the new day, no matter how much my muscles and head ached. I showered, got dressed and made two cups of coffee in the apartment's coffeemaker. I sat astride Luka who still lay asleep in bed and woke him up singing at his ear:

"*De Alto Cedro voy para Marcané…*"

I brought him the coffee and a clean towel.

When Luka got ready, we decided to head toward Saint-Michel. The architecture, similar to that of the area, Saint-Eloi and Saint-Pierre, made the neighborhood look more real. The façades that had started to deteriorate, the kebabs, the Arabic food stores, the fruit stalls, and the Sunday market gave a soulful and cosmopolitan touch to the area. At the very end of Claire Street, we stumbled upon a huge, noisy market. We got lost among the stores in the Marché des Capucins. Luka found a stall where they offered half a dozen oysters and a glass of white wine for seven euros.

"Two," Luka ordered.

We began slurping the flavorful oysters while surveying the crowd.

"Cheese, wine, mojitos, oysters… what a life!"

"You even lost your fear of crowds: think of the power that luxury has."

Luka slurped a meaty oyster.

"I'm not sure if I'm sick or not," I brought up the topic for the first time while in Bordeaux, "but this would sure cure anyone."

Luka, with the way he looked at me, reminded me that I had broken our pact of silence, but followed my lead.

"I'm certain that Christine Maggiore eats oysters in England too."

"She's a Yankee. Chicago."

"Are you sure?"

"Look it up if you want to."

He took out his phone and waited for the result. Suddenly he turned pale.

"Are you OK?"

He had a delicate stomach; I wondered if the oysters weren't sitting well with him. He exhaled and brought his hand to his forehead.

"It can't be."

I grabbed his phone from his hands. That's when I read it on the Wikipedia page: "Christine Joy Maggiore (Chicago, July 25, 1956 – Los Angeles, December 27, 2008)."

—

To find out that the dissident leader whom I had chosen as a model had died was a humiliating blow. I had placed my hope to live on someone's fight against death, unaware that she had already died. The fact that she had died gravely sabotaged her dissident ideas. It was enough to take a quick look at Wikipedia to realize how social media had judged her: guilty. It looked like in addition to accusing her of bringing her own life to an end, they accused her of endangering many other people's lives. They stated that the president of South Africa, Thabo Mbeki, following Maggiore's ideas, blocked the funding assigned to seropositive pregnant women, and that while that AZT treatment support for mothers was stalled, 330,000 people died as result of new AIDS-related infections. Nevertheless, the strongest accusation against her was having caused her own daughter's death. Social media declared that Maggiore's daughter, Eliza Jane Scovill, died of a special pneumonia caused by HIV, when she was just three years old. Her mother refused to take medication while pregnant to decrease the risk of having her daughter contract HIV and she never had her daughter tested, while she was alive.

The judgment directed toward a bad mother was at least as bad, if not harsher, than the one directed against Maggiore as a dissident woman: leading a daughter to death could not be justified under any circumstances; it was nothing but an abomination. The section about 'Eliza Jane' was not far from being a moral judgment.

"Christine Maggiore chose not to take antiretroviral drugs or other measures which reduce the risk of mother-to-child transmission of HIV during her pregnancies. Maggiore also breastfed her children, despite evidence that breastfeeding can also transmit HIV from mother to child. Her youngest daughter, Eliza Jane, was never tested for HIV, nor did she or her older brother Charlie receive any of the recommended childhood vaccines."

"In April 2005, Eliza Jane became ill with a runny nose. She was seen by two physicians, one of whom reportedly knew of Maggiore's HIV status. Eliza Jane was not tested for HIV and was diagnosed with pneumonia. When Eliza Jane failed to improve, Maggiore took her to see Philip Incao, a holistic practitioner and board member of Maggiore's organization Alive & Well AIDS Alternatives, who described Eliza Jane as only mildly ill and prescribed her amoxicillin for a presumed ear infection. On May 16, 2005, Eliza Jane collapsed and stopped breathing. She was rushed to Valley Presbyterian Hospital in Van Nuys, California, where, after failed attempts to revive her, she was pronounced dead. An autopsy revealed that Eliza Jane was markedly underweight and under height, consistent with a chronic illness and that she had pronounced atrophy of her thymus and other lymphatic organs, and died of pneumonia caused by *Pneumocystis jirovecii*, a common opportunistic pathogen in people with AIDS and the leading cause of pediatric AIDS deaths. The coroner concluded that Eliza Jane had died of *Pneumocystis* pneumonia in the setting of advanced AIDS."

"Maggiore rejected the coroner's conclusion and had the autopsy reviewed by Mohammed Al-Bayati, a veterinary pathologist who is neither a medical doctor nor board-certified in human pathology. Al-Bayati argued that Eliza Jane had died from an allergic reaction to amoxicillin, a conclusion Maggiore embraced."

A false water mirror, Bordeaux.

III

The shrieking of the seagulls woke me. The book Irantzu had been reading lay open, face down on her deserted towel. I caught sight of her walking in the distance, by the shore, naked, wearing her yellow wide-brimmed sun hat. I got up and walked toward her unhurried. The high clouds of dawn were vanishing in the sky. For a while, I followed the footprints Irantzu left on the wet sand. She had broad shoulders and a narrow waist, muscular thighs and glutes. Unlike many, she was more beautiful naked than dressed.

"From here the horizon appears to be round," she told me when I caught up with her.

I didn't think so.

"The island is so small that if you stand on somewhat higher ground, nothing interrupts the line between the sky and the sea."

We were almost alone on the beach, in the last days of September. It was still early; the seagulls had only just begun to reclaim the sea shore.

"I wonder what time it is."

We found a series of dark mud puddles behind a rocky mound. Irantzu bent over and scooped a handful to spread over her chest and then her stomach and thighs. I smeared the mud down her back and she proceeded to do the same to me.

"Now the head."

We stood facing each other and covered each other's hair with the lead-gray mud.

We lay in the sun to dry. As the mud dried, it wrinkled and cracked our skin. I held her hand.

"I could stay here forever."

A daring, small crab climbed over Irantzu's arm.

"It's the nature of vacation, to end."

We walked into the water to renew our skin. I enjoyed plunging into it; it had been a long time since I last swam naked. I submerged my head. I wrapped all my senses around that pleasurable act: the swaying of my hair, my ears turned into sea snails. A fleeting illusion of leaving the world behind. I swam under water until I ran out of breath as the mud on my body washed away. I floated on my back on the surface of the water. The murmuring of the sea and the glare of the sun pulsing on my eyelids. I felt the soft waves under my arms and between my thighs.

The 'dead man's float,' that's what we called it as kids. A fish brushed my calf.

"Should we get back?"

By the time we walked up to our towels, we were dry, our skin covered with little salt scales.

"Lie face down."

We were surrounded by round rocks that the waves had rolled onto the beach. Irantzu used them to create a puzzle on my back. Little by little, she completely covered my back and arms with various-sized rocks. A heavy, new warm skin.

"Close your eyes; see if you can guess when I remove the last one."

She began lifting each rock, one-by-one. I felt lighter each time she lifted a big rock; the smaller ones felt like the touch of a feather.

"Now," I said, when I thought she had removed the last one.

"One, two, three…"

She counted twelve rocks that I did not feel on my back.

Irantzu brought me to Formentera because of the movie *Sex and Lucia,* because of the light in that film, specifically. Our initial intention was to sleep outdoors on such an expensive island and we would have done so had the police not awakened us on our first night and rudely kicked us off the beach. Fortunately, a woman took pity on us and let us use a couple of hammocks she had in her patio, and that is where we spent the remaining nights. She let us use her outside grill so we could cook, and a garden hose so we could shower. During the day, the sun warmed the hose and we could count on having warm water in the evening.

We rented the same type of motorcycle Lucia rented in the film.

We put sundresses over our naked bodies, grabbed our towels and headed toward Calo de Sant Augusti. It was thrilling and stimulating to ride our motorcycle without any underwear. The wind lifted our dresses and hair, and the rumbling of the motorcycle reaffirmed our sexuality.

Calo de Sant Augusti is a small fishing port, great for snorkeling. We sat under an empty old-fashioned wharf shelter made out of juniper wood and ate chunks of watermelon. We saw an old fisherman dragging a small boat down the rails of the boat launch all the way to the water.

“Do you sell your fish?”

“It depends on how much I catch.”

We agreed to meet him in the evening.

“I can’t promise you anything.”

We grabbed our rubber sandals, goggles and snorkels and walked all the way to the water. We draped our dresses on a boulder. The sea bed was rocky. In such shallow waters, the sun intensified the shape and color of the rocks. A few tiny, black fish swam nervously away from me. Sea urchins hid in rock crevices. An octopus that I did not see frightened me when it stirred the sand and moved away. Further ahead, the sea floor was covered in tall, waving vegetation. Irantzu was swimming over it as if in slow motion. I saw bream and red mullet and other fish that I did not recognize. A few yards from me, close to the surface, I saw something resembling a balloon, a yellowish bubble that had dark spots underneath: a jellyfish or some kind of odd algae species, perhaps. I swam away. I looked for Irantzu. She was swimming among rocks. When she sensed my presence, she came close to me and placed an orange star fish in my hand. It made me cringe. I let go of it instinctively. It sank slowly.

Once on land, I told Irantzu, “The underwater world both frightens and attracts me. There are so many creatures that I don’t know!”

“I feel safe,” she said.

She had spent her childhood summers in the coastal town of Getaria, and told me how she would go out to sea to catch squid with her grandfather, and how they would swim the width of the small boat under water.

"You get to see the dark side of things, you feel the thrill, a feeling similar to vertigo. Our common sense tells us to leave, but the key is to go against common sense."

We found a nice spot to have lunch, a wooden table above a cove. We brought out the sandwiches and beer. Below, on the sand, two young men were sunbathing.

"This island makes me want to have sex," Irantzu said looking at the cove.

Not long ago, I would have already been down there, ahead of Irantzu. In a way, having taken myself out of the game meant that I no longer had to carry that burden.

"Go," I encouraged her.

"Not now."

We counted three sailboats in the distance. They sailed and anchored in hidden coves that were inaccessible to us by land.

I brought two cups of coffee that I got from an ice-cream truck parked on the side of the road, about a hundred yards from where we were.

"I'll be back in a jiffy."

She headed toward the cove, down a rocky path, wearing her linen dress that exposed her back. She walked up to the men. They sat up and placed their hands against their foreheads in an attempt to shade their eyes. Irantzu said something; she touched the arm of one of them. I heard laughter. They said their goodbyes and she returned.

"Let's go," she told me.

We chose a cove on the southern side of the island to spend the afternoon: Calo des Mort. The 'Cove of the dead.' It was impossible to get there by motorcycle. We went on the main road for a bit and then took a dirt side-road, to the right. When that road came to an end, we parked the motorcycle and walked along trails all the way to the cliff. We found a rope where the footpath ended. We held on to it and went down the stairs carved into the cliff.

The small, half-moon shaped, white sand cove was surrounded by flat, dark rocks. We lay on them. The sky grew more and more menacing. The seagulls stopped flying in circles and rested on rocks. We decided to read while we waited for the rain with no fear of the sun burning our backs. Slowly, the small cove emptied and we were left alone. The turquoise-colored tongue of water turned into a lead bay. We sheltered our books under the towels.

We got into the water as soon as we felt the first raindrops. When the water was up to my neck, I closed my eyes. The subtle sound I heard was similar to leaves murmuring, barely a whisper. The coastal smell, the smell of the moss and the cooling rocks. It started pouring. When I opened my eyes, I saw fat raindrops drilling the sea surface. A thousand drops like pellets stirring the flat surface of the sea. The water felt warm. I submerged myself. I listened to the whispering of the downpour from under the water, as if I were on the other side of a window. Once again, I lay on my back, the rain on my face, abdomen, thighs. I opened my mouth.

We stayed in the water until it stopped raining.

"It will clear up soon."

The first rays poked through the clouds. The hues on the sand were much warmer than those at dawn. The afternoon was advancing. Again, we took the trail that brought us to our motorcycle. The fragrance of rosemary and thyme drying in the sun. White thorny thistle.

We made it back to Calo de Sant Augusti by the appointed time. There was the fisherman, at the wharf, sitting on a small barrel and smoking a cigarette while holding a wicker basket between his feet. When he saw us walk toward him, he opened the lid.

"Lobster?"

He told us that it was prohibited to catch them, but he smuggled one in thinking of us.

"Do you have a grill?"

There was one at the house but we would need to ask for permission to use it.

"Make an incision from top to bottom, without cutting it through. Put it belly up and squeeze a lemon on it. Salt and then onto the grill. In five minutes, it's ready. Take the basket, you can bring it back tomorrow."

He charged ten euros for the lobster, enough for him to break even.

"I've been going out to sea since I was a young boy. I don't do it for the money."

We thanked him and when we turned around, he spoke in a soft voice, as if he were talking to himself.

"Careful with snakes."

We had already heard the story: apparently, Formentera has been known throughout history as the land of poisonous snakes. In the adjacent island, called Ibiza, they did not have such reptiles. If you went to the small island, you had to be alert not to get bitten. Locals said that if you kept a fistful of Ibiza soil in your pocket, you were safe.

"We'll walk carefully," I replied.

On our way home, the lobster antennae peeked out from the lid of the basket that hung from my folded arm; the lobster was moving. I asked Irantzu to stop the motorcycle.

"Put the basket between your feet, Irantzu, or I might get too attached to it."

We bought a couple of lemons, ice-cream and a bottle of white wine in San Ferrat.

The owner of the house had no problem letting us use the grill. When Irantzu had the coals ready, she asked for a big knife, held the lobster from its backside and, pow, she plunged the knife into the lobster's stomach. It continued moving its antennae and legs. She placed it on the grill, belly down.

We took the fisherman's advice, followed his recipe to prepare the lobster and placed it on the small table together with our wine glasses by the hammocks.

"To our friends" we toasted.

The lobster was wonderful.

"I have a date on the Llevant Cove tonight."

I nodded.

"Don't you want to join me?"

I slurped a lobster's leg.

"No."

We finished off the lemon and sea-flavored delicacy by licking our fingers and saved the last of the wine for a cigarette.

"Any ice-cream?"

We ate it directly from the carton, each with our own spoon. It had started getting dark.

"Go," I told her.

She put on a light sweater and left. I heard the sound of the motorcycle departing.

After I cleared the table, I decided to take a shower. I washed away the salt from my body and hair. I dried myself with a towel and rubbed some almond oil on my skin. I lay down on the hammock.

The sky was full of stars. I looked for the constellations I knew: Andromeda, Cassiopeia, Ursa Major, Orion. It made me think of a poem: "Think of a constellation / the one you like best / all are good / lower it a little bit / leave me alone..." Parts of Alfonsina Storni's last poem, the one she left behind before she drowned at sea. I fell asleep.

I woke up with the first light of dawn, curled up in the hammock, the towel on my shoulder. The temperature had cooled down over night. I couldn't remember getting up to get the towel.

Irantzu was nowhere to be found. I got up and went to the entrance of the house in my bare feet. The motorcycle wasn't there either. I was just about to go check behind the house; I heard the familiar vroom-vroom of the motorcycle. She was coming down the road.

"I was worried," I said.

She took her helmet off and kissed me.

"Good morning."

Her skin was covered with grains of sand and in her tangled hair she had pieces of reddish algae.

"You guys spent the night on the beach?"

She grabbed me by the arm and we walked to the patio.

"Want some tea?"

She said yes. I heated enough water for both of us. When it began boiling, I added the tea bags. I let it cool down a bit, poured it into two cups and brought it to her in the hammock.

She had fallen asleep. I covered her with the towel.

She woke up two hours later, reenergized.

"Sorry for making you wait."

I reheated her cup of tea and she toasted the leftover bread from the day before.

"I'm hungry."

Once she finished having breakfast, she undressed to take a shower. The hose had cooled down during the night and she let out a little scream when the water touched her belly. I could see the goosebumps on her skin. She rubbed her arms and legs vigorously and placed her head under the water stream, breathing loudly.

"I feel like new."

We took off down a straight road, Irantzu driving. I rested my head on her back. The wind and the whine of the motorcycle kept me from hearing anything else. We were south bound. We rode by a sign indicating an archeological site and kept riding ahead on that road.

"Look!" Irantzu yelled.

The lighthouse at the end of the straight road. We rode all the way there.

We parked the motorcycle and instead of heading to the lighthouse, Irantzu turned right.

"Where are you going?"

She didn't hear me. I followed her. She pointed at a hole in the ground about fifty yards from the lighthouse and the edge of the cliff. It must've been about a yard in circumference and looked deep. She bent down, stuck her head in and then sat on the edge of the opening.

"Be careful."

By the time I realized it, she had disappeared. I found an old wooden ladder against the wall of the cave. I went down.

"There are hundreds of holes like this one."

We walked in the dark cave until we reached a sort of balcony open to the sea.

"There's where the sun sets."

She signaled a point on the horizon. We remained seated on the edge of the cliff for a while. Seagulls flying high. The sun wasn't hot enough yet and it was nippy. We retraced our steps and came out of the cave. We headed toward the lighthouse.

The wind was blowing on the cape and it forced us to speak loudly.

"Go all the way to the cliff and see!"

Once there, I followed the line where the dark blue of the sea and the light of the sky came together.

"You're right! The edge of the sky is round!"

I turned in a complete circle.

"Wait, let me take a picture."

I opened my arms to the wind.

—

At the beginning of October, not long after returning from Formentera, my hair began to fall out. If I tightened my hair in a ponytail, I ended up with a fist full of it. Every morning I checked my pillow in fear. Seeing the fading, henna dyed, reddish-black curly hair terrified me. That sudden, painless, quiet loss felt like a dark omen to me. I lost a lot of weight and, feeling exhausted, I only left the house to go to work. I soon began feeling short of breath and on November 6, I had to quit smoking because no oxygen could reach my lungs. On November 24, I ran a fever and felt worse each day. I took sick leave.

Luka phoned Father against my wishes. He came to the house three or four times in an attempt to convince me to go see the doctor. Each time I refused. I told him to let the fever run its course, that all I needed was rest. Mother would visit me after work and would place a wet towel on my forehead. She stayed by my side, holding my hand until I fell asleep.

On December 2, I argued with Father while running a temperature of one hundred and four. I could hardly breath. I refused, once again, to go to the doctor.

"I'm not going to just watch you waste away."

He stood up from my side and left the room. Between coughs and gasps for breath, I began calling for him. I did not have the strength to get up on my own.

"Father, don't go."

I thought that he had left for good. But he came back.

"Take me wherever you want," I gave in; "but, please, don't be mad at me."

He took me to the hospital. I was barely able to walk without running out of breath. A doctor received us and, panting, I told him the symptoms I had recently experienced with as much detail as I could. He quickly sent me to have X-rays done and, on my way back, sitting in the waiting room, I noticed Father's serious face.

"Why didn't you tell him that you're seropositive?"

I didn't think it was necessary.

"I just want him to cure the illness I have now: I told him all my symptoms."

The doctor called us in.

"The X-ray doesn't show anything serious."

He wrote a prescription for a common antibiotic.

"I left something out earlier. I'm seropositive."

He became infuriated and scolded me.

"Are you making fun of me?"

Enraged, he sent me home.

But he was right: I had *pneumocystis jirovecii* pneumonia which cannot be detected in regular X-rays. The very type of pneumonia that killed Maggiore's daughter.

I spent four days at home delirious and on December 6, Father took me to the hospital again. As soon as we walked in, I told the attending doctor everything.

"I'm seropositive."

He patted me on the shoulder.

"I'm not going to ask you anything else."

He placed an identification bracelet around my wrist and assigned me to an observation room.

—

I went through two long hospitalizations: the first one from December 6th to the 30th in 2013, and the second one from January 3rd to the 28th in 2014. The first hospital stay, the one falling on the same day as the Day of the Spanish Constitution, was like a jail sentence. They did not let Father accompany me to the observation room: two nurses undressed me and put on my hospital gown; once in bed, they connected me to oxygen. Without wasting a second, they began delivering intravenous cortisone and antibiotics to fight the pneumonia. I didn't have the strength to speak. Soon after checking into the hospital, I contracted another infection, the result of a megalovirus, and they administered an additional antibiotic. The first medication to fight the pneumonia meant trouble: I had an allergic reaction to the first antibiotic; the second one gave me mouth and esophageal ulcers, the third one serious anemia... They gave me a total of seven antibiotics. By the time I was hospitalized, I had run a fever for more than ten days and I was completely without strength. I scarcely recall the first days in the hospital. I only remember the desperation I felt at not being able to sleep.

I became obsessed with resting. To the point of lunacy. Overflowing with cortisone, annoyed by insomnia and poked by all those tubes, it became almost impossible for me to close my eyes. But the worst was to be awakened as soon as I had finally fallen asleep. I thought that they did it on purpose. The auxiliary nurse, the main nurse, the janitor, the doctor, the aide bringing a snack, my roommate's family members... It was impossible to rest. In the mornings and evenings, they gave me the corticoids, then every four hours the medicine for the pneumonia, and every six hours the medicine to fight the cytomegalovirus. All of them intravenously. Each bag lasted about an hour and as soon as it became empty, an alarm would start beeping. The door kept opening. Voices constantly, all kinds of creaking noises, needles, window blinds closing and opening, doors being slammed. They kept calling my name. Every time I wanted to take a nap, they would come in to change the IV bags. When I finally fell asleep, they came to change my bed sheets. “Please don’t open the door,” I would implore while curled up in bed. Each time the door opened, I cried.

“Shut the door!” I screamed.

They cut, interrupted, chopped, grinded my sleep into a thousand pieces. I believed that if I did not sleep, I would die.

“You’re going to kill me,” I screamed over and over.

I felt a complete physical and psychological desperation. At night, in addition to the usual sounds, I could hear the screaming of other patients on my floor. An old man called for his mother for four straight days. I heard screams of pain from patients lost in their delirium. The temperature was suffocating. Even at the beginning of winter, the thermostat was set at 86 degrees. They did not let me open the window because they were afraid that the old woman in the next bed, covered all the way up to her neck with a blanket, would catch cold.

Luka spent the first ten nights, the worst nights, at my side. I felt him standing by the bed. I wanted to cry but I couldn’t because of my swollen mouth, full of herpes, wounds and ulcers. Each time I moaned, my lips would crack and begin to bleed.

“Don’t cry,” Luka would say.

I begged them to give me something to sleep. I couldn’t understand why, after pumping me so full of drugs, they couldn’t just give me one more pill to sleep?

On the fifth or sixth day, a doctor in charge of the AIDS cases came to see me. He caught me sitting in the visitors’ chair, because if I lay down, the asphyxiating feeling became overwhelming. I was at the worst moment of my decline, so skinny that I could grab my full arm with the opposite hand, no sleep, feverish, with a swollen mouth, disfigured with scabs. Since I could not speak,

I communicated by writing messages on a notebook. I was a mess. "Give me something: I need to sleep," I wrote.

He took the pad from my hands and began yelling at me:

"You are in this situation because you didn't come to the hospital sooner, because you refused to take any medication. I will say it clearly: because you were stupid, irresponsible and arrogant."

I tried to get my notebook back.

"Look at me!" he demanded. "I don't know if I'll be able to keep you alive: 40% of people in your situation die."

With my bones scattered on the chair, with my eyes closed, I continued moaning.

"Your blood work results are very bad; your platelets are very low; you'll need a blood transfusion."

"No!" I refused.

"It's not your decision."

I was about to faint.

"I'll be back later and bring you a sleeping pill."

A nurse rested her hand on my shoulder.

But no one brought me the pill. The nurse who took pity on me finally went to get the doctor. It was one thirty, and he finished his shift at two. She returned holding her head down.

"He left."

I began screaming and waving my arms in the air. I disconnected the tubes and oxygen line. The wounds on my lips cracked open. I believe they gave me something to calm me down, which made me feel dazed but did not make me fall asleep.

—

They did not touch me. Not Luka, nor Father nor Mother. During the first two weeks, I refused to see anyone. Luka stayed overnight with me and left for work early in the morning. Father took vacation days and came every morning by nine. Mother came to see me at noon, after closing the perfumery for lunch break. But none of the three came close to me, at least not close enough for me to feel them. They sat close by, at an unreachable distance for me.

Father was angry because I refused treatment.

"You won't survive this without antiretroviral medicine."

I limited myself to shaking my head no. I heard him curse in the hallway but he didn't leave. He didn't say a single word to me and turned his back to me, but he stayed in the hospital until noon.

I was defenseless inside my body. I thought of my aunt Karmen, how she used to ask us, when she was about to die, to embrace her more tightly. That is when I understood her desperate effort to bring Grandma and me inside her body. She wanted us inside her bed, because she could not get us inside her skin.

I thought that Mother and Luka acted as if nothing were the matter. They read the newspaper beside me, played music, watched a TV show, worked on their job assignments. Mother even put on lipstick to go see her boyfriend.

"Do you need anything?" They asked. "Are you comfortable? Would you like another pillow behind your back?"

They stroked my thinning hair. They kissed my sweaty forehead.

Nothing was enough. I asked them for the impossible: to hold me up from within my skin.

"You know that I can't feel your pain, right?" Father warned me long ago.

The impotence of not being able to eat combined with the bewilderment of insomnia. They brought me my meal trays but I could not eat anything. I could not even drink water. No one explained how I could nourish my body with a mouth like mine. I had to do my best however I could. I asked them to bring me two big syringes; I filled one with water and the other with mashed food and introduced them slowly into my mouth.

I was trying to eat yogurt through the syringe when the auxiliary nurse walked into the room.

"The tray!"

She also scolded the old lady in the other bed for eating slowly.

"I have seen faster ones!"

Before she handed the tray to the auxiliary nurse with a trembling hand, the lady hid her dessert, an apple, under her bed sheets.

That night I thought Luka seemed sad. Like every evening, he kissed me when he came into the room, and went to the bathroom to take off his street clothes and change into his shorts. He came to my side.

"It's raining outside."

My roommate had the curtain closed and I couldn't see the window from my bed.

Every evening, Luka sat next to me and told me about his day. He would tell me things and share his thoughts, mingled with little stories.

"I guess the future belongs to the crows too," he said.

He showed me a page in the newspaper with that headline.

"It's scientific news that I wouldn't read if not for such a poetic introduction."

He spoke well, not rushing, beautifully. I don't think that I had ever been able to listen to Luka as I should have until I was forced to keep my mouth shut. That evening, he glued the dark mood of his spirit to his words.

"They've been experimenting with crows: they confirmed that crows can, based on their experiences, plan for the future."

He got quiet. He caressed my wrist.

"After Hitchcock, I'm afraid of crows."

To me, right then, the idea of the future was more troubling than the crows themselves.

"They lured them with food: they gave them the choice to get a little food or a token that would offer them much better food in the future, and the crows chose the token."

I thought of Father and of people that, like him, had that corvid type of presence.

A thin thread of breath, heavy eyelids.

"I've had a strange feeling today," Luka said. "I've been cleaning closets. I hardly have a single t-shirt without a protest slogan. I had them piled up in the closet; I took them out, placed them on the bed and folded them one by one: it was like taking inventory of defeats… It was difficult to see them all together, lost causes, from here and abroad, demolished intentions, forbidden words, people, ideas… I'm not sure that it's good to always keep holding on to happiness."

It reminded me of my hair on the pillow, the landscape of loss at dawn.

"You don't look good either," Luka said.

I asked him to hold my hand.

"I love you very much," I told him.

His chin quivered with fear.

"You're so weak."

When I stared at his eyes, I saw the reality; I was on the verge of dying. A quick gleam, a black bird, a hint of a dark possibility in Luka's eyes.

"I'll do it," I said.

I surprised him.

"You'll take the antiretroviral treatment?"

This hadn't been a deliberate decision; the spontaneous concession had surprised me too.

"I've had enough."

"You can still resist," my thoughts protested.

"That's for the best."

I realized that he was crying: when I gave in, he gave himself permission to give in too. He looked exhausted.

He hugged me tightly: Luka's breathing, skin, warmth. The crying of defeat came gently, with no pain.

"Call Father."

He held me by my shoulders.

"I realized that you can't go on having your Father against you."

He pressed my head against his chest. It moved me to hear Luka's heart beating.

"The concepts of victory and defeat are relative," he explained.

Luka handed me the phone.

"What happened?" Father asked.

"I decided to accept treatment."

He did not say anything. He remained silent without hanging up the phone. Exhausted, I rested on his breathing. And I slept. For once, I slept.

—

When I was eighteen, I decided to study journalism because I knew that it would allow me enough free time for work at the bar, for militancy and sex.

In 2003, during the summer of my third year, I went to Venezuela as a member of Peace Brigades International, a non-governmental organization. My dream was to learn about the Bolivarian revolution by joining the international freedom organization, but my pockets were empty so I had to stay and wait to receive a cooperation grant. Haritz put me in touch with the director of the political section of the *Gara* newspaper, who gave me some contacts. He suggested I interview a couple of Basque refugees living there and promised me that if I did good work, he would publish them.

I recognized the Petare neighborhood while flying over it: part of Caracas, a rough looking hill surrounded by roads, covered in brick shacks piled on top of each other.

A Jeep left me at the bottom of the hill and I walked to the home of the nun who offered me a place to stay. Up the hill, children, playing soccer next to garbage bags piled up by the road, pointed at me. I advanced along the narrow road and paths as fast as the weight of the backpack allowed me, pretending to be confident. In the rundown houses, clothes hung drying, parabolic antennas at the windows, large buckets on the roofs to collect water, power poles leaning, burdened with cables, shacks covered with plastic or asbestos, caught under landslides. An amalgam of surrender. The poverty in Petare was violent, built and maintained in rage.

Petare. I read in a guide that the name of the place was formed by the Caribbean words "pet" for face and "are" for river. Built facing the Guaire river to keep the marginal people of the city piled up. It was the first time that I was far away from the Basque Country, and I stumbled upon the Lasalde of the Antipodes.

When I arrived at the address, I was welcomed by two Dobermans. I heard them barking in the distance and I saw one of them leave the house in a hurry but, in the middle of the road, the pig suddenly stopped, quit barking, lowered its head and went back inside, as if I did not seem interesting enough. Behind walked the nun, a tallish, wrinkled woman in her sixties.

Instead of the habit I had imagined, she wore pants and a blue shirt.

"He doesn't bark at white people."

The Yanomami nun's name was Gabriela. There were quite a few indigenous people indoctrinated into Catholicism. She likely had her indigenous name changed, surely, to remove her Amazonian savage-complex and to appear more civilized. She lived with two foster children: Alejandra, a nine-year-old and Nandú, who was my age.

As soon as I walked into the house and placed my backpack on the floor, the nun examined me from head to toe and sighed in sadness, without trying to hide it. She disappeared for a minute and returned with a few long-sleeved t-shirts.

"Here you can't show any tattoos. They will think you are a delinquent."

Alejandra stared at the piercings I had in my lips and nose.

"You'll need to remove those."

I covered the three stars I had on my arms with one of the t-shirts the nun brought me and I put on.

"What do they mean?" Alejandra asked me.

"They symbolize those I've lost."

Gabriela dished out some rice for me from a pot.

"Nandú, bring her some water."

He returned quickly holding a pitcher and Gabriela signaled him to sit at the table. She informed me about the work I would need to do in the 'neighborhood' of 800,000 people.

"We have a big problem with young girls getting pregnant. Many of them are raped in their own homes by their fathers, uncles, cousins. Others are abandoned by their boyfriends as soon as they start showing."

The girls that suffered sexual abuse, the ones desperate with their newborns, those who hid or wanted to terminate their pregnancies came to Gabriela looking for help, and I had been assigned to assist her with those cases.

"Nandú will accompany you."

That very night I heard the first shooting. At first, I didn't recognize the sound. It was the first time I had heard real shots and they sounded fake, like toy guns. They didn't sound like the gunfire in films. I fell asleep as if in a delirium, mixing in my dreams the noise in the neighborhood and the rumbling of the radio that Gabriela always had on. The meowing of a kitten woke me up a few times, but I soon surrendered to the exhaustion of the trip.

I got up before daybreak, around six in the morning, I went to the kitchen to make some coffee. Gabriela was already there. I saw her from behind, holding a bundle in her arms. When she felt my presence, she turned around and I saw that she was cradling a newborn baby.

"They left her last night."

The baby was asleep. Gabriela asked me to hold her for a moment.

"We must disinfect her umbilical cord."

I nervously held the baby covered in a blanket; she barely weighed anything. Her hair looked greasy and wet. Puffy eyes. She gave off an animal smell. I figured she must've been a few hours old. An unpleasant pinch tightened my throat. I brought my little finger close to her hand, and she held it, instinctively. She had long nails. The light began to shine on the other side of the window. The baby, asleep, made a little face, sort of smiled.

Those were hard weeks. Almost daily, I took young girls to the small health shack-clinics organized by the Misión Barrio Adentro (Inner Neighborhood Mission) Campaign. They were run by Cuban doctors. Some of the girls held on tightly to me believing that I could somehow help them; many had a lifeless gaze and tense bodies on their way to the health center. I felt guilty about my skin color and embarrassed at having offered them my assistance, ashamed at observing violence from atop the ladder of privilege. One day, a fourteen-year-old girl knocked on the door, and as soon as Gabriela left and I was left alone her, she asked me to help her with an abortion.

"Take it away!" she screamed repeatedly.

I lived that whole episode in anguish, I cried as never before and, at the same time, I felt the need for laughter more than ever. Thankfully, I always had Nandú around. He knew how to see humor in all that misfortune; he had a special talent for it, a long practice in that survival chain, and I always thanked him for it.

"You thought you came here to save people?" he teased me.

He talked to me mercifully. It hurt me to have him poke fun at my contradictions, to expose my arrogance disguised as solidarity, but instead of feeling intimidated by my anger, he made a fist, stretched his arm and began running on the patio in front of the house, pretending to be Superman.

"Stop it, you fool!"

But he continued, going around and around, jumping up and down and screaming "Suuuuuper-Nagore!" He made the dog nervous with his theatrics. He did not stop until I burst into laughter.

"Silly," I said, cracking up.

We shared a love story, a quite beautiful one, in the middle of the harshness of Petare. At night, after Gabriela went to bed, I sneaked into Nandú's bedroom, and we had sex nightly, slowly and tenderly. Lying in bed, we listened to Gabriela's slow snoring and Alejandra's calm breathing. The nights were warm and we left the window wide open. We would sit on the mattress and smoke the rolling tobacco I brought from the Basque Country. Outside we could hear the shootings and the yelling of the neighbors, and we held on to each other. Naked next to each other, my white legs entangled with his black legs.

Irantzu came to visit me at the hospital mid-December. I called her after the worst was over; I told her that I had another bad episode but that I was feeling better now.

"You're wasted away!"

Diplomacy had never been one of Irantzu's virtues.

She had attended the Durango Book Fair and brought me a copy of Joxe Azurmendi's book, *Barkamena, kondena, tortura* (Forgiveness, Sentencing, Torture) as a gift.

"I'm not sure it's the most appropriate…"

"You don't have a sense of pity."

By then my mouth sores had almost healed, and I could breathe on my own. Irantzu lifted my bed sheets and exposed my legs.

"Why didn't you call me sooner?"

"So many things happened."

"What do you have?"

"Pneumonia… and a few small complications."

She began pacing the room. She took her coat off and put her hair in a ponytail.

"But this," she lowered her voice, "is it related to your AIDS diagnosis?"

She pushed aside the curl that had stuck to my forehead.

"You know that the answer to that question is complicated for me."

She pushed the curtain and made sure the old lady in the next bed was asleep before she spoke.

"Look, Nagore, I think that you have gone too far with that dissidence issue. You told us three years ago that you had AIDS, and from one day to the next, that AIDS did not exist. And that was it. You acted as if nothing happened, and we played your game."

She held the IV dispenser.

"What is this?

"Antibiotics, I think."

"That's the easy way out! You don't have anything, right? Everyone's happy!"

She opened her eyes exaggeratedly.

"Do you really believe that AIDS doesn't exist?

She looked at the old lady out of the corner of her eyes.

"Don't worry, she sleeps all day long."

"I think that this time you're not right."

I laughed.

"What is it?

"You dare to antagonize me?"

"Someone needs to."

"Not many people do."

I held her hand.

"Because you're so arrogant."

"I accepted treatment."

"With antiretroviral medication?

"I surrendered: I'll start the treatment on January first, as soon as I'm over this pneumonia."

"I suppose that the chance to become sick will decrease quite a bit by taking the medication."

"Who knows."

"You're not convinced?"

"I don't believe in that shit; besides, it scares me; everyone who took AZT is six feet under. But I must pretend to be grateful. The conflict of resisting all of you is worse than pretending in this charade.

"Surrendering is not the same as knowing when to quit."

"I don't see a difference. No question I gave in, because I couldn't do anything else.

When I decided to take the retroviral medication, I didn't think 'this way I will get better,' but rather, 'this way I'll stop fighting.' What makes me feel better is not hope but being able to rest. The struggle between my beliefs and authority would've killed me. It took too much out of me."

"You've accepted your limitations."

"Illness has its own voice."

"Are you referring to the symbolism of illnesses?

"I hate people who, when you have an earache, ask you, 'what is it that you don't want to hear?' They diminish the authority of doctors, so we all become pseudo-doctors. Kidney stones? A sign that you are afraid of something. Strep throat? You're having trouble accepting something. It's impressive how many psychoanalysts and doctors have graduated without ever stepping into a university!"

"In my opinion, they're right… Let's accept that the illness exits, but there are additional factors. You don't talk about the emotional toll in all illnesses, especially in the case of AIDS, the connection is total. But that's beside the point now."

"You've become a member of that sect?" she grumbled. "Tell me, what does pneumonia mean?"

"The fear of death."

"And AIDS?"

"The lack of defenses and protection as consequence of an overwhelming resistance, a harsh de-valorization conflict, the hyper development of psychological defense to the detriment of the immunological protection, sexual guilt, repressed love…"

"You have it all rehearsed. So then, what about the virus?"

"Let's assume that the virus exists. I don't believe that just by being in contact with it, we get infected, but rather because we had an adversarial contact."

"Sure, and how do you figure out what an adversarial contact is?"

"Forget it. It isn't important. If I have understood anything, it's this: that I can't control what happens in my body with my mind. In a contrarian way, I wanted to be right. It's not like being right will save us from death! Reasoning seems to be a dirty activity. I prefer to accept that I will take drugs and neutralize the battle."

"I'm not sure what to tell you."

"Emotionally, I'm not capable of surviving in dissidence."

"It doesn't surprise me."

"But I can't stand the infantile submissiveness people display in the presence of doctors."

"If they didn't have the power to make you feel like a child, they wouldn't be able to cure you. It's like what happens with parents: they must position themselves above their children; to do the contrary results in their quitting being parents."

I thought of Mother.

"Who is your ideal savior?"

The question sounded ridiculous.

"I feel the need to grow old, to taste the pleasure of giving up."

The IV dispenser's alarm went off.

"I've never heard you speak that way before."

"It's impossible to grow old without giving in. Have you ever thought about that? Perhaps it's the opposite: can one give in without growing old?"

Irantzu intentionally hit her forehead with Azurmendi's book.

"Are you sure that the IV is not dispensing *ayahuasca*?"

We laughed.

"Your crazy spell has had a positive side: for once, you ignored militancy, men, family, work and the whole gamut to look within yourself."

A nurse walked in to replace the antibiotic bag.

"Have they checked your temperature?"

"No."

She took it. "98.6. Good."

"Azurmendi says that triumph and defeat are relative concepts."

"Luka told me the same thing."

She handed me the book.

"After all, it might not be such a bad choice."

I opened it randomly.

"He who seeks victory, seeks war," I read. "He who seeks peace, cannot seek victory."

"Azurmendi agrees with you!"

We burst out laughing. I stopped short of choking.

"Careful, though," Irantzu warned me. "It's fashionable to distract attention and spin defeat as victory."

"It's the loser's last move. It works sometimes."

—

The insomnia persisted, but I had evolved from desperation to acceptance. When I began feeling better, Luka started going home after having dinner with me. The nights with me on the infectious disease floor wiped him out. I spent most of the night awake. I was not able to lie comfortably and read leisurely under the effect of the medication. They resembled nights under the effect of speed. I got hooked on the series *Utopia* released in January. I watched the superb, exponentially dramatic, political paranoiac-thriller using a set of earphones with the iPad Father lent me. I read that the director said, 'I would like the experience of watching *Utopia* to resemble eating jellybeans: sweet, full of color… yet making you vomit.'

Before dawn, around six, I showered and waited for the first shift of nurses while sitting in the visitor's chair. They kept track of my temperature and blood pressure.

"You shouldn't take a shower alone: with this blood pressure, you could faint at any time."

At seven, I would receive Father's text message asking me how I slept. I would send him the report: "Two hours and no fever."

He came by nine, holding the *El País* newspaper under his arm. We got into the habit of doing the crossword puzzle. Once he started giving up, I purposely let him fill in more boxes than I did. For once, I enjoyed playing to lose; it got easier each time.

Father made me walk the long hallway: every morning a little loop, a few meters more than the previous day. I left the room unwillingly. The first few times, the lack of oxygen was harder to endure than my feebleness. Every few meters I had to sit down. It embarrassed me to have other patients and their relatives see me so skinny.

"What do you have, child? Anorexia?" an old crone wearing a night gown asked me while I was walking holding onto Father's arm. "When food was scarce, everyone was hungry, and now that there's plenty, some refuse to eat…"

Father yanked me forward.

It was the first time in my life that he placed any kind of demand on me, and, once at it, he was relentless.

"Tomorrow, all the way over there," he would declare.

We used to argue, always moving between seduction and dueling.

"I regret having abandoned Karmen toward the end," he confessed." I ran away and left you with her. I couldn't handle seeing my sister die, and delegated to you the responsibility of helping her until the very end."

Father's 'deep moments' never lasted more than two minutes.

We played for each other funny videos and songs that we liked. He was crazy about Amy Winehouse: he was a fan of women who died at 27.

After watching a video of a ridiculous fall, he asked me to give him the iPad.

"I'm going to play you a song."

I recognized Antonio Molina's voice. The music reminded Father of the past he shared with Mother and that he so dearly cherished. With no introduction or fanfare, he played the sorrowful song "La hija de Juan Simón," accompanied by a scratchy guitar.

After I served my sentence
I lived lonely and lost
She died of sorrow and I
Who brought her to it, know she died being good
She died of sorrow and I
Who brought her to it, know she died being good

They buried her in the afternoon
The daughter of Juan Simón
And it was Simón
And it was Simón, ay
The only gravedigger in town.

He carried his own daughter
To the cemetery
And dug her grave,
And dug her grave while murmuring a prayer.
And as he held the shovel in his hand
And the hoe on his shoulder

His friends and the people in town
asked him, ay
Where are you coming from, Juan Simón?

I am a gravedigger and come from
I am a gravedigger and come from
I am a gravedigger and come, ay
From burying my Heart.

"She died of sorrow and I, who brought her to it, know she died being good." I was out of breath. I buried my head in Father's chest, and stayed there for the rest of the song.

When I finally got my sobbing under control, I lifted my head from Father's chest and he rested his hand on my shoulder.

"The drugs make you all slippery, Jenisjoplin."

—

In Petare I made friends with a young woman named Gina. She lived in the shack next to ours. I spent the idle hours of the day with her. She was a little bit older than me, twenty-four, and she made dolls out of pieces of cloth and sold them at the nearby market.

"It's too bad that you're a girl," she told me one afternoon. "If you were a guy, I would ask you to get me pregnant."

She wanted to improve her race. Gina was jet black and Gabriela's Doberman would not leave her alone. The dog would start barking as soon as it smelled her. I thought she was joking, but she was absolutely serious about the racial thing. I asked her not to pull my leg.

"Will you let me smell your skin?"

She brought her flat nose next to my skin and began to smell me.

"See?"

She was convinced that my smell was better than hers.

"I thought that you all disliked the smell of white people's sweat."

"I prefer the smell of whites."

"It must be because of the soap."

She looked at me with incredulity. I went home and brought her my body wash.

"For you."

She began jumping up and down like a child. But it didn't last long. The next day she walked to me downcast holding the body wash bottle in her hand. She had just taken a shower.

"It's not the same. I still stink like a black."

During Holy Week, before I returned to the Basque Country, I had been invited to go to Choroní. A few Basque refugees lived there and I had planned to stay over with them. I encouraged Gina to join me. I knew what she would tell me that she didn't even have the money to buy a pair of panties but I assured her that they would host us for free and that I would take care of any other expenses.

She nervously boarded the bus and spent the whole trip looking out the window. It was the first time she had ever left the neighborhood where she was born. When we arrived at Choroní, I decided to buy a gift for the hosts who were going to host us in their home, but realized that the one hundred dollars I had in my backpack were gone.

"It wasn't me."

Gina lift her hands.

"I know," I said angrily.

We knocked on the door of my compatriots with empty hands. It was an elegant home, with a garden at the entrance. Alma and Ramon, probably not his real name, welcomed us with open arms. I told them what happened with my money. Nodding their heads and waving their hands in front of their faces, they told me not to worry, to forget about it.

“Here you don’t need any money.”

Gina was perplexed. She did not understand how that couple had welcomed us, complete strangers, into their home, for as long as we wanted without asking us for anything in return.

“Yours is sure a peculiar country.”

The four of us had lunch together: fish stew and *cachapas*, Venezuelan fresh corn tortillas. They also served wine. I took advantage of the opportunity to ask them a few questions and take a few notes.

“I don’t drink,” Gina turned down Ramon’s offer.

Another Basque man, younger than Ramon, called Fernan, joined us for coffee. He invited us to go to the beach with him. He worked as a bartender at a beachside bar and he praised its lively nightlife.

“You have to come dance a little.”

Two days later, we made plans to go to the bar. In the early evening, Gina and I both showered with my soap and got ready to party. I lent her a white dress.

“Isn’t it too short?”

When I wore it, it covered my knees but in Gina’s case it came to her mid-thigh.

“No way!” I encouraged her.

I braided her hair and gathered it on top of her head.

The bar was located right on the beach, on a wide boardwalk. On one side was the bar, straight ahead, a patio, surrounded by little hanging lights. On one side of the patio there were people sitting at tables drinking daiquiris and typical Venezuelan eggnog. On the opposite side, the dance floor. When we arrived, there were only two couples dancing. Ramon ushered us to one of the tables. Fernan joined us too. Our host ordered a bottle of rum and they brought us glasses. Gina looked around everywhere, in awe. They asked her what she would like to drink.

"Well, just this once!"

Finally, she accepted some chicha. Meanwhile, as the bottle of rum was getting emptied, Ramon, Fernan and I talked about the political situation in the Basque Country. In that context, the words we strung together sounded ridiculous: agreement, negotiation, process, solution… Fernan opened a second bottle, the words stuck to our tongues: staging, peace agreement…

Although it seemed that time flew by, we must have spent two or three hours chatting non-stop. I realized that Gina was getting fed up.

"Is this how you have fun?"

Although she asked me under her breath, they all heard her and burst out laughing. Alma shared Gina's opinion and explained to her that yes, that *that was* how we had fun. Fernan stopped talking and pulled Gina onto the dance floor. Ramon and Alma said it was time for them to go home.

"You guys stay longer. Have a good time."

We decided to stretch the night out a little longer. Fernan returned to work and Gina took pity on me and came back from the dance floor to the table. A guy behind the bar caught my eye.

"Do you see him?

He was a muscled, wide-shouldered guy, brown skinned. His long, messy hair gave him a wild air. Feeling a little emboldened, I signaled him to join us. Gina kicked me under the table.

"Would you like to have a drink with us?" I invited him.

He said yes to a shot of rum and sat next to me.

"Alex," he introduced himself.

Gina looked embarrassed and that tickled me. Another guy joined us. I assumed he must have been Alex's friend. He sat next to Gina and began talking to her. Gina seemed comfortable. I also felt somehow bewitched under the spell of the rum and the company of the beautiful, young man sitting closer to me by the minute. When the guy next to Gina turned his back to me as he whispered something in her ear, I noticed a swastika tattooed on his back.

"What's that?" I asked him abruptly.

He made a regretful face.

"My younger days, you know..."

I wanted to believe him. The children in Petare drew swastikas on the ground and walls. I often approached them and asked what the heck they were doing, and realized that they had no clue what they were drawing. "Calm down, Nagore," I told myself, "relax..." I was exhausted by my need to have everything under control. Always on edge, always alert. The weather too, hot and humid, pushed me to ease up; and it goes without saying, so did the smell of rum. Enjoy and let others enjoy. Gina's new friend invited us to his place. I made eye contact with Gina and she nodded.

That place was paradise. It was close to the shore, close enough to hear the waves break. On the patio, coconut trees; hammocks hanging between trees. We carried on drinking and laughing. Alex kissed me. I called him Mowgly. Tarzan. His breath was warm and tasted like fruit. He split a fallen coconut with a machete and handed it to me to drink from it. Suddenly Gina pull me aside.

"I'm a virgin."

I held her arms and told her not to worry, that we could leave as soon as she wanted, right then if she preferred. I reassured her that she did not need to do anything she did not want to.

"I'm fine," she said.

Alex and I were hotter by the second. He poured coconut milk in my navel and began drinking from it. Sticky. Sugar under my skin. My muscles limp. Honey. Gina walked up to me once again.

"I'm going with him."

The host was waiting for her.

"Are you sure?" I asked her.

She nodded. I felt Alex's tongue in my navel. They left.

Alex asked me if I wanted to go into the house too. I hesitated, attracted by the idea of having sex under the night sky, right there in the hammock, naked, but ended up telling him yes, in favor of comfort. I was quite drunk, and it would be better to lie down on a bed. We heard the first screams and thumps through the stairwell. I sprinted in the direction of the screams, stumbling, completely ignoring Alex. The screaming came from a room on the first floor. The door was locked.

"Son of a bitch! Open up!"

I began kicking the door; Gina continued screaming. Alex joined me and forcefully knocked the door down. Gina stood in front of the broken wood plank on the floor. She was bleeding. She held her right hand with her left one. The stream of blood was soiling her white dress. She looked at me. I held her. The guy still held the knife in his hand. Alex motioned toward the young man, who aimed a gun at him. Gina and I ran down the stairs; Alex followed us. We went out to the patio; the house gate was closed. We could not leave unless the owner opened it. I tried to climb the fence; it was too high; Gina couldn't use her hand. I was half-naked, my limbs tensed with rage and fear. I saw Gina's attacker next to the gate, holding the knife in one hand and the gun in the other.

"Open the gate!" I yelled at him.

Contrary to all my expectations, the gate began to open.

I grabbed Gina's arm. We left the place running, aimlessly. Alex told me to turn right, ahead to the left. There was no clinic there.

"Leave us alone!"

He stopped in the middle of the road, bare chested. His well-toned arms hanging at his sides. We walked on. I had to find something, a hospital, an aid station, a convent, a police station, something. Luckily, we ran into a small clinic.

Gina had lost a lot of blood; she was about to faint and looked ashen. They stitched the wound in her palm from side to side. It was a deep gash. When the guy threatened her with his knife, in an effort to defend herself, she grabbed the blade, instinctively.

The following day, we returned to Petare. I decided not to write the article about the Basque refugees. I would not mention my visit to Choroní to anyone. On the bus ride back, Gina and I agreed that we would say we had been mugged and that Gina had been injured while trying to defend me, and so we did. Crippled, she would be unable to sew her dolls for months and would have to go without her sole source of income. Gina knew how to protect herself; in twenty-four years, no one had raped her nor hit her. My white paternalism was responsible for lowering her self-esteem one notch and magnifying her poverty. The following day, I boarded a flight back home.

—

I asked a nice nurse on the morning shift if she could bring me the newspaper. As usual, I did the crossword first, I nearly completed it, missed two words.

December 15 was a Sunday. Luka had been in Madrid with his mother since the previous day. They both signed up to attend a lecture by James C. Scott on his book *Domination and the Arts of Resistance*; they were thrilled. They stayed at their friends' house and after the talk, they were having dinner at a Thai restaurant they liked. My parents also had plans: they both called me to let me know that they could break their commitments, but I told them not to.

I debated if I should get up and go to the hallway for my walk, but with no coach to lean on, I decided to watch the fifth episode of *Utopia*. With the lights dimmed, the few first notes of the soundtrack set me on edge.

A dark room: slivers of light coming through uncovered cracks of the boarded windows, and, silhouetted against the light, one of the leaders of the conspiracy. A whistling melody settled in my brain.

"We've now passed seven billion on this planet. When I was born, it was a little over two.

Food prices rising, oil is ending. When our resources end in twenty years, given everything that we know about our species, do you really think we're going to just share?"

Wilson, Becky and Ian are in the room. Becky is doing the asking:

"So, your answer to that is some kind of genocide?"

"No, it is not, it is not genocide. Our answer to this is Janus."

The shot is zooming in.

"Janus consists of a protein and an amino acid. Independently of each other they're harmless. But when they're brought together in the subject, they act as a genetic trigger that prevents chromosomal division. The cell targeted can no longer replicate itself and is thereby rendered useless. The change is permanent. And hereditary."

"And which cells are targeted?"

"Those that control fertility, Becky. The purpose of Janus is to sterilize the entire human race."

The scene changes. The façade of the house is in the sun. The voice continues:

"Janus affects 90 to 95% of the population, leaving only one in twenty fertile."

Inside again: the detained sitting down, against the light. Standing up, facing him, the other three.

"We predict the population will plateau at 500 million in just under a hundred years. By then, normal breeding rates should resume but on a planet that will feel empty."

"You're fucking insane."

"Do you know the person who had the greatest positive impact on the environment of this planet? Genghis Khan because he massacred forty million people. There was no one to farm the land, forests grew back, carbon was dragged out of the atmosphere. And had this 'monster' not existed, there'd be another billion of us today jostling for space on this dying planet."

Doctor Puertas walked into the room.

"I need to talk to you."

I paused the program.

"You need a blood transfusion, Nagore."

"No," I stood my ground.

"It's necessary. You're anemic."

"I don't want any transfusions. I told you already."

I didn't know how to explain it rationally; I wasn't ready to accept someone else's blood. Having lost all the other battles, I stubbornly decided I wouldn't let them in my veins. Not in my blood. All my convictions crushed, my ideas shattered and my body full of foreign medication, I identified with my blood. I felt like they wanted to squeeze the very last drop out of me. They wanted to strip me of everything that was mine. Holding on to my blood was defending the last free territory in a conquered land. Almost a spiritual act. My last little fight.

He stared at the screen.

"You watch too many paranoia shows."

"Please, wait until tomorrow. See if the results improve."

He walked to the window. He observed the old lady lying asleep and said, with his back turned to me:

"Janus doesn't exist."

I looked at my iPad. The hollow-eyed face of Conran, the villain.

"We'll wait until tomorrow. If the results don't improve, you won't have a choice."

I had convinced him, miraculously.

When he left, the woman in the next bed, now awake, began talking to me.

"Poor thing, are you afraid of transfusions?" Her feet were sticking out of her covers. "Me too. The risk of contracting something… Imagine if they give you blood from someone with AIDS!"

"You probably shouldn't mind at this point in your life," I thought.

I tried to control my fury by turning the pages of the newspaper.

I stumbled onto some unexpected news. The Basque Country bertsolari, improvisational poetry, final competition was being held that very day, just a few miles from my hospital room. I felt thrilled. I wasn't crazy about improvisational poetry; I guess I didn't check all the boxes of a Basque nationalist but I could not think of a better plan for such an anesthetized hospital Sunday. They were going to broadcast it on Basque television.

I called Irantzu at noon.

"Are you at the BEC?"

I heard the singing in the background. She hung up on me.

I began thinking about sterilization. The idea of the existence of a conspiracy to deliberately sterilize people provoked an unexpected confusion within me. I knew that this type of forced sterilization had been conducted often; in Germany, Hitler sterilized schizophrenic, epileptic, blind, deaf and alcoholic people; in Sweden gypsies were the target and in Peru it was indigenous women. In the United States of America, besides targeting those with a physical or mental "disability," they targeted the fertility of Native Americans as well as African American women. Obviously, they didn't make it easy for prison inmates and mental patients to have children.

I became curious and wondered if people sick with HIV had been forcibly sterilized. It did not take me long to confirm my suspicion: many women in Mexico who were seropositive protested that they had been forced to endure tubal ligation procedures. In Honduras, El Salvador and Nicaragua too, they impeded fertility or severely restricted those who carried the virus.

The list of nations that followed this type of practice was extensive and astonishing; Australia, Norway, Finland, Estonia, Iceland, Switzerland, United Kingdom, Rumania, Russia…

I turned off the iPad.

I had never wanted to be a mother. It had never crossed my mind. But that data had just defined me as human garbage, as a member of a group that should be kept from procreating. After my diagnosis, no one would advise me to become pregnant, and if possible, they would prevent me from procreating. From the time I was diagnosed as HIV positive, all the endless problems that I had to suffer in my genitalia and my ovaries amounted to a symbolic sterilization.

I decided to shower a second time in the same day.

After lunch, I got up from bed, walked to the closet and put on my coat over my pajamas.

"Are you being discharged?" the old woman asked me.

I felt compassion. She did not have much time left.

"No, I'm going to the cafeteria. Do you want me to bring you something?"

"If they have chocolate muffins…"

I walked up to the elevator without any problem. I held on to the wall on my way to the cafeteria. I arrived out of breath. I bought muffins, potato chips, candy and some alcohol-free beer.

"Do you have room service?" I teased the server.

She must have thought I looked weak because she volunteered to accompany me to my room.

"Just to the elevator." I accepted her help.

She grabbed the bag and offered me her other arm so I could hold on to her.

"What are you here for?"

"Pneumonia."

We slowly advanced to the elevators. She handed me the bag of smuggled goods. It was too heavy for me.

"I'll go with you all the way to your room."

"OK"

"What's the big occasion?"

"The Championship."

She looked surprised, but I did not offer any additional explanation.

"May the best one win," she said.

She put the bag inside the closet.

"I hope you feel better soon."

My roommate was snoring. I left her muffin on her nightstand. Exhausted, I lay down too. I closed my eyes and waited for my breathing to slow down.

I realized that I had fallen asleep when the nurse woke me up to give me my antibiotic.

"What time is it?"

"Seven."

By then, it was dark outside.

"Why didn't you wake me sooner?"

She looked at me with contempt.

I turned on the television. The face-to-face challenge was about to start. I opened one of the alcohol-free beers and the potato chips. The salt burned my throat. I threw them in the trash bin. The camera zoomed in on Lujanbio's face, frowning in concentration.

"Who'll win?" the old woman asked me.

I offered her another muffin.

At nine, before they named the winner, the nurse made me turn off the TV, alleging that the old woman was getting nervous with all that action on TV.

Soon after that, the door opened again.

"What now?" I complained, annoyed.

"Nagore, are you awake?"

I sat up.

"What are you doing here?"

Irantzu walked in quietly.

"The hospital is on my way home and I decided to swing by to wish you a good night."

I though she looked like she had had a few.

"Who won?"

"Amets."

"Was it fun?"

"It was great. Rome loves heroes."

She kissed me on the forehead and left.

—

With the diagnosis, they neutered my sexuality, erotic desire, and seduction all at once. In 2010, right at the very moment when Doctor Puertas gave me the news, I understood that sex was over for me. I could, perhaps, if I went after it, trying hard, mechanically reach an orgasm, but I would no longer be able to enjoy the old playfulness, carelessness and, especially, spontaneity. Gone were the times when naturally, one thing leading to another, the opportunity to have sex would present itself almost accidentally. A naughty look would no longer work on me. I wouldn't be lascivious with people I knew, even less with friends; for those who knew about my diagnosis, I was no longer a potential bedmate. The pity they felt for me would kill their arousal. The wild passion to rub skin against skin became a thing of the past. I would no longer be able to use sex in search of love, acceptance, self-esteem, complicity, adventure, and fun. Sex would need to be planned, carefully executed, limited and problematic.

The fear that no one would desire me overwhelmed me. For those who knew about my situation, I would become one of the non-erotic, nice friends in that dull group, and I would not be able to respond with desire to those who desired me.

If I wanted to enjoy the passionate gaze of strangers that conveyed the primitive purpose of arousal, I would need to hide my condition. If anything, I could only limit myself to the seduction of someone with no intention of having sex with them. As long as those around me did not know anything, I could keep playing, not experiencing frivolity but feigning carelessness. I would be able to stroll in the battlefields of attractive women in my night-wear as long as my situation was a secret. Otherwise, I would lose that territory. If the diagnosis meant partial neutering, making it public meant complete neutering.

The second blow was the realization that I did not know how to socialize aside from sex. In my relationships with others there was always something sexual. I experienced tenderness through my skin; I felt close to someone and even connected intellectually with them. I felt it when I walked into bars, when I showed up at meetings where there were men, during futile face-to-face conversations. With my sexual drive extinguished, I did not know how to act. That is why I became estranged from myself and closed myself off. I created a small world with Luka where, through problematic sex, the exchange of love and intimacy was possible.

Unexpectedly, my new situation opened me up to other women. The over-the-top regard I had for the attention of men, men's opinions, their presence and the drive I had for their acceptance prevented me from practicing any level of sisterhood. With my focus necessarily switched, where I once saw competitors or barely acknowledged presences, now I began discovering accomplices. But I had trouble getting close to those whom I had completely ignored for so many years.

As a result of the spaying, the time I once dedicated to the hunt I now devoted to myself. Now that I set aside the effort to bewitch men, I had enough energy left for the life and death struggle facing my own body. I felt free from always having to be on guard. I was rid of the burden of a predator's continuous alert and, unlike before, I dared to nurture a rather stable, monogamous relationship. I got to feel the unreal security of faithfulness, the balance of interdependency and the protection of a companion encouraging me to forge ahead in this journey.

As life went on, I tried to celebrate having freed myself from androphilia, slowing down, embracing serenity and feeling calm. Nevertheless, when I least expected it, under my skin, pulsing, clawing, out of habit, I felt the she-wolf I carried inside me.

At six in the morning, before I showered, I ate everything I could get hold of, hoping that my blood work results would improve. I asked Mother to bring me vitamins and energy-bars; I had them for breakfast with a banana and an avocado. They drew blood from me every day to check the platelet count.

Dr. Puertas was quite skeptical.

"They look a little better. Still very low."

Irantzu came once again on December 20. I told her I had won the transfusion war, raising my fist.

"Your battle skills are limitless!" she sounded disturbed.

"How did you make it home?"

"I hung out on Somera Street to have a drink with other fans. You know, sharing opinions about the competition and... by the time I realized it, was five in the morning."

"How was the competition?

"Do you really want to hear about it?"

"I watched the final on television. You mentioned something about heroes when you were here.

She gave me a package she pulled from her purse. A beautiful hardcover book, *The Tree of My Secrets.* I kissed her.

"We're still tied to the epic culture. The police, prisoners, Sarri, the perfect mother... We need our own heroes and villains. The inertia of the old epic still endures in this "New Era." I got a little confused by Maialen's performance: at first, I thought she lacked the desire to attack, not enough rage, but then again, I wonder if she was avoiding that epic I mentioned. She didn't handle the topics she was given as if they were heroic events. Instead she addressed them as commonplace. But that's the general tendency, right? Not only in this improvisational poetry competition. Isn't the issue of epic culture interesting? How during these last decade, the war-hungry point of view has been diluted? Not long ago, anyone who didn't address the epic narrative was seen as weak. Now, on the contrary, we think of them as lazy or even worse, corny, purpura. Look at the musicians. But when the moment of truth come, at funerals for example, we look for epics. We reject the romantic and war narratives, but it's getting difficult to build a different one..."

"I'm working on it too."

"Did you already forget your transfusion war?"

"Yes, you're right. I'm completely démodé."

I pointed out the coat closet.

"There are some beers and treats if you feel like it."

She opened a can.

"There are new theories coming up: some have started defending the culture of the weak. They defend declarations of vulnerability at the personal and collective level. But, at the same time, they underscore the management of conflict, learning about freedom, the right to dissent..."

"The right to dissent, you said? You sure don't offer it to me."

"Because you practice dissidence in heroic style, with no room for surrender or doubt and always alone, out of pure self-sufficiency. One of the biggest pillars of cultural vulnerability is mistrusting ourselves."

The woman in the next bed woke up.

"Do you happen to have another muffin?"

Irantzu handed her one.

"God bless you, child."

"It's easier for these people," she said. God fills their existential void. We had to manufacture our own little gods. Lacking religion, we've found shelter in ideologies."

I realized the dangerous direction that the conversation was headed in.

"But, shit, what's the alternative: to get comfortable with things the way they are?" Irantzu felt doubtful too. "To go to therapy and live the rest of your life drawing concentric circles while analyzing your traumas? The secret must be in finding balance... You can't deny that building ideologies from one's inabilities is a common practice, at least as broad as going from the analysis of impossibility to a Freudian Reichian Gestaltian homoeopathic doctoral thesis. It's easy to see the indirect plea in anyone who fights passionately for or against a cause. Usually, they ask for your agreement and so are asking for a little bit of love."

"I know the dynamic well."

"I wasn't talking about you. But there is an ideology for each rage. A particular mindset equal to the magnitude of each void. An ideological leader for each orphan. Nevertheless," she lifted her index finger, "are ideologies any less valid because we use them in our favor? Someone must defend them!"

She got quiet and softened her tone.

"The heart of the matter is who defends what: Is it people who defend ideas or do the ideas defend people? You," she took a sip of the beer, "did you fight because you're against medicine or because you needed to fight and decided to go against medicine?"

"A little bit of both, I suppose."

"Those who are talking about the culture of vulnerability are challenging fixed identities and trying to build strategic identities, instead. Identities to put on and take off."

"Then it's really important to choose your underwear carefully."

"No question."

We walked out to the corridor. I proposed going to one of the waiting rooms on the other end of my floor. The second stroll of the day.

"The first time I made it up to here."

I pointed at a door at about ten yards from my room.

"You've advanced a lot."

Once in the waiting room, I pushed the elevator button.

"Where do you want to go?"

"Let's go have coffee."

"Do they allow it?

"Give me your coat."

We entered the elevator. Besides the coat, Irantzu lent me her scarf and I wrapped my head in it, like a turban.

"Elegant."

We burst into laughter. I winked at the server.

"I didn't recognize you!" She leaned on the counter to talk with me. "How is your pneumonia going?"

"Improving."

She served us our order. Irantzu observed us in awe. I told her that I met her the day of the improvisational poetry final.

"She accompanied me to my room."

"Does she know what you have?"

"Pneumonia. You heard her."

"Yes, but…"

"I don't want anyone to know. Maybe because I don't know how to accept my own diminishment."

"The fact that you're confessing your impulse to hide it might be a kind of acceptance."

Holding a cup between my hands, I began observing the people at the tables in the hospital cafeteria.

"People believe that amputees, disabled, crippled, cross-eyed people… are dumber or more evil than others, and that those infected with HIV are good for nothing, human waste. We even think that ourselves, that they got the punishment they deserve, for being drug addicts, for getting involved with people they shouldn't have in ways they shouldn't have, for falling on the wrong side of fate, those poorer, more depraved, more promiscuous than us, for being such night owls."

The server opened the dishwasher; the hot and unpleasant steam interrupted my flow.

"It's ridiculous: I've always fought for the marginalized, but I attack those who push me to the margin."

"The same attitudes that drove you to seize control of your own life now lead you to the loss of control. Holding on to a position for too long makes us weaker. Contradictions are the price we pay for being honest with our own weaknesses."

"Great excuse for hypocrisy."

I pointed at her upper lip; she had beer foam on it.

"The more people are aware of the diagnosis, the more real it becomes. As if others knowing about it is what it makes it real."

"That's right, somehow."

"I don't want them to look at me like *that*. The worst is that I see myself immersed in normalcy, defending the place that I believe belongs to me." I held on to the stool I was sitting on. "I'm trying to be part of the society I criticize, wanting to hang on as long as I can in that indefensible human condition."

"Who doesn't do that? Those on the peripheries want to feel normal in the peripheries too."

I looked at the couple with dreadlocks having tea at the end of the counter and the guy arched his eyebrows.

"Do you think that the stigma is still the same as before?"

"Try it: choose a person in this cafeteria, anyone, and watch."

Irantzu looked around.

"Now think that that person has AIDS, and look at them again. Has anything changed?"

"I see you as I did before."

"No."

"Of course, I do."

"Now you confront me, give me advice; you take care of me."

"What's wrong with that?"

"But you hold yourself above me."

"No way."

"And you like it."

—

When I grew tired of waiting to fall asleep, I spent the night waiting for dawn. The stronger I felt, the more suffocating the hospital became. The corticoids did not let me sleep more than three or four hours; time became long and exasperating. I inhaled the work of Alfonsina Storni. Her admiration for the sea and the insane obsession to seduce death. The unavoidable doomed love common in sensible women.

I watched YouTube videos, one after another all the way to daybreak. Around three in the morning, I came across a video titled *Addiction*. My roommate on her back, asleep. I put on my head phones.

"What causes addiction to heroin? This is a really stupid question, right? It's obvious; we all know it; heroin causes heroin addiction. Here's how it works. If you use heroin for twenty days, by day twenty-one, your body will physically crave the drug ferociously because there are chemical hooks in the drug. That's what addiction means. But there's a catch. Almost everything we think we know about addiction is wrong.

If you, for example, break your hip, you'll be taken to a hospital and you'll be given loads of diamorphine for weeks or even months. Diamorphine is heroin. It's in fact much stronger heroin than any addict can get on the street because it's not contaminated by all the stuff that drug dealers dilute it with. There are people near you being given loads of deluxe heroin in hospitals right now. So at least some of them should become addicts. But this has been closely studied; it doesn't happen. Your grandmother wasn't turned into a junkie by her hip replacement. Why is that?

Our current theory of addiction comes in part from a series of experiments that were carried out earlier in the 20th century. The experiment is simple. You take a rat and put it in a cage with two water bottles; one is just water, the other is water laced with heroin or cocaine. Almost every time you run this experiment, the rat will became obsessed with the drugged water and keep coming for more and more until it kills itself. But in the 1970s, Bruce Alexander, a professor of psychology, noticed something odd about this experiment: the rat is put in the cage all alone, it has nothing to do but take the drugs. What would happen, he wondered, if we tried this differently? So he built *Rat Park* which is basically heaven for rats; it's a lush cage where the rats would have colorful balls, tunnels to scamper down, plenty of friends to play with and they could have loads of sex. Everything a rat about could want. And they would have the drugged water and the normal water bottles. But here's the fascinating thing: in *Rat Park*, rats hardly ever use the drugged water; none of them ever use it compulsively; none of them ever overdose."

I checked the IV drip. Thankfully I did not need to choose. My rat park was not Woodstock nor BBK Live; I could count the friends who came to visit with the fingers on one hand. I had no say about sex, or intravenous drugs, chosen by the doctors.

Father arrived at nine thirty with his crossword puzzle. We finished it in ten minutes. He made me get up for our routine stroll. He smelled like the street.

"Did you drive?"

"Yes."

A one-person metal capsule. The perfect machine to escape in.

"Take me for a ride."

"Are you crazy?"

"Almost. I need to breathe. I lost count of the days I've been here." I grabbed his shirt. "I need to see other things."

We walked by the nurses' station.

"Things? What things? You want me to take you to the Corte Inglés to look at dresses? Or would you prefer I took you to Somera for a drink?" he said sarcastically.

"We wouldn't have to get out of the car: just a ride. Half an hour, that's it."

A man was dragging himself toward us, connected to a serum bag.

"Forget it, Jenisjoplin."

"To the Hanging Bridge."

He stared at me. We used to cross it with Mother when I was a child, by car, at a time when it was not open to pedestrians. It really impressed me, more than when I saw the Eiffel Tower as a teenager.

"Grab your coat. It's cold."

He waited for me in the corridor. We kept our usual pace all the way to the elevator, walking next to each other. I put my coat on inside the elevator. From the twelfth floor down to the sixth, we did not cross paths with anyone. Two nurses came in on the sixth floor. They greeted me. I wasn't sure if they had ever taken care of me. Fortunately, they got off on the fourth floor. A few months earlier, they built a direct entrance to the parking lot and we went straight down to the garage without having to step outside. We quickly found Father's old car. The car stalled on the first try, but it started on the second. We were on the road.

We drove among the buildings. Store clerks had brought their goods outside, to the sidewalks, the butcher shops and fish markets were packed. A man was scolding a child who hadn't looked both ways before crossing the street on his skateboard. Women loaded with grocery bags walked briskly, dark skinned men on a scaffold wearing overalls. The mouth of the metro was vomiting people. A few retirees and a couple of unemployed people in line to buy the last lottery tickets. Two hairdressers taking their coffee-break standing up. We stopped at a traffic light. I rolled down the window and left it open a crack.

"Roll it up."

I obeyed him. I could tell he felt happy by the way he held the steering wheel, laid back, his arm stretched out.

"I could drive through this area blindfolded."

It was the road he took to work. We had never driven it together. We drove through Sestao and came out in Erribera.

Runners and dog walkers up and down the riverbank. On the right side, a scene that belonged to an earlier time. Rusty cranes to unload metal off ships, scrap that never got loaded, small mountains of reddish scrap iron, smoking metal shavings, iron beams and cylinders. On the other side of Ibaizabal, the Areeta houses. He turned left.

"Close your eyes."

He slowed down. The roaring of the motor and the heater. A right turn. He stopped the car.

"Now."

I opened my eyes. I was surprised not to see the river in front of me as I expected. We were at the Maria Diaz de Haro poorly lit housing project, parked next to a line of cars waiting to cross the bridge. The Bizkaia Bridge looked like a monster among the apartment buildings, a giant reddish structure, with its platform hanging from its cables like a pendulum.

"We can't cross it."

He drove the car to the very edge of the bridge. I looked up. The structure built to cross the long beam provoked a sense of vertigo even from below. A four-legged colossal beast, made of equal parts iron and air. We remained silent staring at the giant.

"Some day we will cross it on foot. Now back to the hospital."

—

A year after I finished my degree, in 2005, we started Libre. Karra was the only one who had any previous experience working in radio. For several years he had been a broadcaster who produced an Internationalist show on free radio, writing his own scripts and managing the technical aspect too. We chose him to be the director: he managed the programming and the news show that we coordinated with other stations. Irantzu directed the culture show and the political roundtable, and I began working as an on-the-scene correspondent, reporting from demonstrations, reporting news about strikes and sit-ins. The three of us discussed the radio's ideological orientation in meetings that stretched like chewing gum.

In January of 2006, the Bilbao harbor's longshoremen went on strike. The big shipping companies received new regulations from the European Union allowing them to organize the loading and unloading of their cargo as they saw fit. That meant that the activity at the harbor was at risk and the dock-hands expected to be fired by the hundreds. Of the 5,000 dock-hands working in Spain, 1,700 traveled to Strasburg to protest, Father among them.

We did not act quickly enough to report the news on location. We couldn't seem to be able to keep up with the daily news but, if nothing else, we agreed to do a documentary to shed some light on the plight of the longshoremen, even if it was after the dispute had subsided.

Through Father, I obtained the necessary permits to access the port. His confrontational character must have had something to do with the new regulations being postponed time after time. Finally, they set an appointment to meet with me on a February morning.

I drove my car to the cargo terminal. I showed my identification and accreditation at a window at the entrance. They registered my information and license plate. A few meters ahead, I went through customs. They asked me to move to the side while they searched my car.

The port was bustling with activity. At the entrance, lines of trucks waiting to go through scanners and radioactive material detectors. The ones that got the OK to go ahead drove to the giant dock platform through enormous stacks of containers piled on top of each other. There was also another big line of trucks waiting to exit the port. On the left side, there was a freight-train being loaded. Everything was big, heavy, noisy.

I left the check point behind and parked where they directed me. At another checkpoint, they confirmed my name on a visitor's list and the clerk handed me a helmet and a safety reflective vest. He made a phone call, then opened the automatic gate of the terminal. Father was waiting for me.

It was the first time I saw him dressed in his orange work coveralls. Behind that unfamiliar appearance, co-workers, worries and jobs that I did not recognize, I noticed that he even seemed to walk differently there, more humbly. His bartender confidence, daring, crow-like soul had vanished. His job consisted of controlling traffic and moving machines in the terminal, in three shifts.

He took off his helmet to greet me. The racket was tremendous. They allotted him half an hour to show me the port installations. He drove me through a path between containers. On both sides, colored containers piled on top of each other, forming walls three and four stories high. A moving crane on ground rails transported the heavy Lego-like blocks from one place to another. A forklift took them from the piles and placed them on a truck that took them away one by one. The constant beeping of the machines alerted workers to their presence. We continued on foot. I turned on my recording machine to collect all those sounds around me. Further ahead, at the loading dock, two giant cranes were unloading the *Conmar Gulf* ship, a 121-yard monster. Two minuscule-looking workers walked under a container dangling from 20 yards above ground. Father explained that all cranes were human operated. They worked for eight straight hours from inside a cabin ordering which containers had to be picked up and where they needed to be placed.

"Those of us who work at the port don't know what the containers carry. Our job is to get the cargo organized."

The regular containers weighed between 25 and 28 tons and each ship transported more than a thousand containers. Chemical and metallurgical materials, canned foods, tools, wine, combustibles, building material, paper… There were all types of goods that had to be processed through customs. 800,000 containers were unloaded annually in the Bilbao port.

Father told me about security systems installed at the facilities and the latest work accidents. Two days earlier, a worker had died, smashed by a front-loading machine.

"Vargas, get back to your post."

Father obliged and returned to the place where the supervisor pointed. The foreman escorted me to the exit. He praised the excellence of the terminal and made me guess the size of the biggest freighter ever to dock at the harbor. I saw Father in the distance, among the blocks, signaling the way out for loaded trucks. A blue container flew above him.

I noticed some confusion at Customs. When I stepped in to return my helmet and vest, the administrative assistant informed me that they apprehended 110 pounds of cocaine hidden under a false bottom in a container full of canned tuna fish. He pointed at a pavilion: the national police were sorting the drug bundles.

I had agreed to join Father for lunch at the port cafeteria. They had an hour to eat before returning to their jobs. I waited for him at the bar, having a small beer and jotting down notes in my notepad for my report. The place began filling up around one o'clock. Men in groups of ten, dressed in orange coveralls, bustled in. They hung their helmets and coats on the back of their chairs, sat at the tables, served each other wine from pitchers and lit cigarettes. Father arrived in the second wave.

We shared a table with two other dock-hands. I asked for some carbonated water to mix with the cheap wine. While they mashed the green beans and potatoes on their plates with their forks, they chatted about their work conditions: the personnel losses due to the carelessly scheduled working shifts, the miserable salaries due to subcontracting, the contempt of management toward the workers… The television was turned on too loud; some men stared at the screen, distracted. We were all wrapped in smoke. There were about one hundred people eating lunch, all of them men. The men at my table told me, in a defeated tone, about the petitions they took to Strasburg. I recorded some of what they told me above the background, manly, guttural, murmuring.

When the coffee came, Father stood up.

"Boys, this is my daughter."

Amid the noise, he enveloped my shoulders with his arm and kissed me on the cheek. It provoked an uproar. They lift their glasses and exchanged sad smiles.

"We didn't know you had a daughter," two men who must have been about to retire greeted me.

Everyone stood up when they heard the siren. They drained their coffee and shot glasses in one gulp. They all left in a pack, smelling like cigarettes and dry sweat. The servers in tight skirts began picking up the plates. Men in coveralls headed back to the port. A crew to pile up containers. The freight train started running once again. I lost sight of Father among all the dock-hands.

—

The woman in the next bed died the day before Christmas. The previous day, they sedated her and she spent her last hours in a deep sleep. Two sons stayed with her, caressed her head and held her hand when she drew her last breath.

They moved me to the newly open bed, next to the window. It made me shiver to lie down on the bed where the old woman had just died. I sat on the visitor's chair to read. I added a few drops of the eucalyptus oil that Mother brought me from the perfumery to the scent diffuser. I'm sure that someone must have died in nearly every bed at the hospital: the memory of each body was erased with a fresh set of sheets.

I opened the window. After almost twenty days in that room, I just discovered that it looked out on a humid, interior patio. The window still held metal bars installed during the 80's, to keep junkies from killing themselves. Down on the patio, two young nurses chatted.

They did not bring a new patient to the room that day and Luka spent Christmas Eve on the bed that until then had been mine. We had tuna and egg sandwiches and chocolate cake for dinner. Before we fell asleep, we finished watching the first season of *Utopia*. A brutal sickening bag full of gummies.

The next day, Christmas Day, Dr. Puertas came by the room before lunch time. There was only one week left before the day we agreed to start the anti-retroviral treatment.

"You'll need to choose one of these two drugs."

It was the first time they gave me a choice of drugs. I went straight to read the side effects and listed them in two columns. A: vomit, diarrhea, headache, muscular pain, dizziness, nightmares. B: fatigue, insomnia, depression, suicidal thoughts.

"Think carefully," he advised me.

I did not postpone my decision. I thought it was dangerous to hold the medication responsible for the sadness that could devour me from within. If I blamed my self-neglect during my lowest moments on medication, I would shirk the arduous task of looking for happiness or its more usual substitutes. If I accepted defeat as a side effect, that would be surrender. Besides, I'd had it with insomnia. I favored the side effects that seemed more physical.

And to balance out that "gift," Dr. Puertas promised me that if nothing unexpected happened, he would release me by New Year's Eve.

I called my parents.

Father was at Josune's farm; I caught him outside the house.

"They are eating snails: disgusting."

Josune's whole family was enjoying the annual snail slurping dinner.

"Thank goodness you called me."

He recited the full menu.

"Garlic soup, snails, cabbage, walnut pudding and compote."

He was convinced that the gastronomic line had been purposely drawn to clearly distinguish the Basques from the non-Basques.

It took a lot of effort on our part to convince Mother to take a couple days off and she had gone to a health spa with Patxi. She answered the phone from a lounge chair by the heated pool. She was getting a foot massage. I pictured Mother's skinny legs, disfigured by childhood punishments and so many years of work standing at the bar. It moved me to imagine a pair of strange hands caressing her feet.

I let them know that I was to be released in a few days. From the moment I knew I would be released from the hospital, I had been gathering the courage to ask for what I really wished: I wanted to spend New Year's Eve together. For the first and last time in my life. I accepted my role in the play by taking retroviral medication; now I asked them for one night to set a make-believe scene for me.

My parents, who had been separated since before my illness, had reclaimed a small tenderness toward each other that had resulted from common fears and shared worries, conversations with doctors and moments of tension lived in the hospital hallways.

Luka scolded me.

"By now you should be over the illusion of the united family."

I, adamantly, got what I wanted.

On the morning of December 30, Dr. Puertas released me on probation: he made me promise him that if my temperature went up, even if it seemed insignificant, I would return to the hospital.

I put on the clothes that I wore the day they checked me into the hospital: they looked like they belonged to someone else. I felt like a stranger on the streets. Outside the hospital, people walked quickly, some even ran up the stairs. Cars double parked, buses quickly loaded and unloaded passengers who seemed to be in a rush. Once underground, I calmed down. I felt at ease, thanks to the ceiling of the parking lot above me. I felt protected in that closed, covered space. I sat in the car and lost all my composure when I turned on the radio. At that moment, for the first time in a long while, I was just one of the thousands who were listening to that station, back to normal.

The Christmas lights, all the store windows, the bags full of purchases, the delivery trucks coming and going…, became an unpleasant visual dissonance. I was not in the right mood to land on the runway of the outside world.

Luka drove to Father's house. It was winter and our apartment would be cold, it didn't have an elevator and above all, I did not feel like going back there.

When Father opened the door, I felt an overwhelming wave of happiness within me. Josune would spend New Year's Eve at the farmhouse. We would be alone.

Luka walked me to the sofa and brought me a furry blanket. It smelled like orange flowers. I lay down and took a light nap amid the silence of home and the peaceful atmosphere. There were no slamming doors, no one there but us. I could hear Father's and Luka's voices coming from the kitchen. The rain outside. Someone caressing my hair.

Father lent us his bed and, unlike the hospital, I was able to snuggle up close to Luka.

Father woke us up at nine thirty. He knocked on the door and sharply opened the shutters. He brought us the newspaper. Luka put on a t-shirt and got up. Father sent him grocery shopping for dinner and he sat next to me. We passed it back and forth and completed the crossword.

"Now, get ready."

I had forgotten about Father's obsession: he did not like anyone lazing around the house in their pajamas. He hated slippers and the softness and comfort they represented.

We spent the day watching television. Whenever I felt hungry, I would get up and walk to the refrigerator to eat anything I fancied. Around seven, I took a shower and put on the new dress that I bought online during my stay at the hospital. My barely 110 pounds of flesh were distributed on my 5 feet 9-inch frame.

Mother arrived at eight. She was not comfortable coming to Father and his girlfriend's place. She stopped in the hallway until Father invited her to come into the kitchen. She looked at the photos on the walls from the corner of her eyes. The appetizers were prepared on the kitchen table. Father opened a few beers. We drank them in the living room, mother and I sitting on the sofa and the two men standing.

I knew Mother felt jealous that I decided to seek refuge at Father's after I left the hospital, but the reality was that in the apartment Mother shared with Patxi, there was not a bedroom for me.

We all sat at the table, Luka and I side by side and Father and Mother in front of us. I stood up to get a sweater. Luka quickly noticed that I had a fever. I smiled at him so he would calm down, but the next time I got up to use the bathroom, he followed me. He placed his hand on my forehead.

"You've got a temperature."

When I sat on the toilet, I got goose bumps from the cold porcelain. I was shivering. My temperature was climbing.

"I just took the antibiotic. Let's wait until it starts working."

We returned to the table. Father brought the deviled eggs. He served us wine. I felt happy, over the moon. I felt the urge to tell them that I loved them, and with the push from the corticoid pill I took after the antibiotics, I did. Father grabbed Mother gently, for an instant I thought they were having fun. It brought back memories of Ataka, when they worked side by side wearing torn Hertzaina band t-shirts, while I did my homework on the other side of the bar. Here they were, twenty years later, between their fifties and sixties, at the beginning of their decline, yet full of dignity: Father vain and wild-haired, Mother, serious and beautiful. They still made a good couple.

"Your eyes are all shiny," Father warned me.

I pointed at the nearby full glass of wine. I went to the bathroom again to freshen my face. I checked my temperature. 102.56.

We ate cod in tomato sauce. For dessert, lemon sorbet.

Father and Mother went out to the balcony to smoke a cigarette. Mother was looking at a point in the distance that Father was signaling.

"Do you see them?"

Luka made a gesture of disapproval. I kissed him.

"Your lips are on fire!"

"I feel fine, really."

Father suggested that we eat the year's last twelve grapes on the balcony, following the midnight chimes of the church bells close by. Mother prepared four plates with twelve grapes each. She kept checking the clock on the church.

"Now!"

We heard the first bell. The second. We began swallowing the first grapes. We could hear the ruckus increasing in other flats, the televisions were at full volume. Soon the grapes began piling up in our mouths. We looked at each other and jammed the last grapes in our mouths while bursting into laughter. Father was the first one to swallow them all. He proudly stuck out his tongue.

"Happy New Year!" I said with my mouth full of grapes.

From the building adjacent to ours, neighbors began shooting fireworks; the sparks almost reached us. There was an explosion of fireworks, firecrackers and singing. Someone was even playing a trumpet from a balcony close by. Father opened a bottle of champagne; we were having fun.

—

I felt feverish when I sat at the kitchen table. The apartment was quiet and so were the streets outside. Father and Luka were asleep Mother had left the day before; we called her a taxi around two in the morning. Empty bottles of champagne, wine and beer, containers with nothing to contain were all piled by the sink, like a still life painting of spent happiness. The new 2014 calendar hung on the wall.

I took out three boxes from the opaque pharmacy plastic bag and opened them one-by-one. I tore each information sheet in small pieces and threw them away. I had decided to take the medication as if it were a neutral substance with no hope nor fear of harm at stake. I placed a glass of water on the table and next to it, I arranged them in a row: Truveda blue, Novir white, Precista red. Liberté, égalité, fraternité. I added the corticoid pill and the pneumonia antibiotic to the lineup. I swallowed them all, buttoned my robe and walked out to the balcony.

The cold air did me good. The day was breaking; the garbage trucks were collecting the remains of the collective euphoria from the dumpsters, an old man stealing a few tired steps from the new year helped by his walker. I came inside.

"You've started," Father held the medication boxes in his hands. "Good for you."

He stood in the middle of the kitchen in his jeans with no t-shirt on. He placed yesterday's newspaper on the kitchen table. He scanned it with little interest.

"Go lie down, it might be unpleasant at first."

He followed me to the living room. He put on a Leonard Cohen record and chose the song: Chelsea Hotel.

He handed me a blanket and sat on the chair next to the sofa.

"It was written with Janis Joplin in mind, you know?"

Father was a diehard fan of musicians' gossip, he absorbed the special flavor of their idealized stories of love, sex and death.

"I remember you well in the Chelsea Hotel. You were talking so brave and so sweet. Giving me head on the unmade bed. While the limousines wait in the street."

Father smiled nostalgically.

"They met at three in the morning, inside the Chelsea Hotel elevator. Cohen was staying in room 424; Joplin in 411. Cohen was on his way back from the White Horse Tavern. Apparently, he had gone looking for Dylan Thomas, though he knew he had died. Who knows where Joplin was coming from." Father spoke about them as if they were his close friends.

" 'Are you looking for someone?' Cohen asked her. 'Yes, I'm looking for Kris Kristofferson,' Joplin answered. 'Little lady, you're in luck, I'm Kris Kristofferson.' The young woman though it was a funny reply. They spent the night together."

How nice to listen to Father tell that story while Cohen's voice echoed from the stereo.

"He told the story 20 years later at a concert," he imitated Cohen's voice.

"She wasn't looking for me, she was looking for Kris Kristofferson; I was looking for Brigitte Bardot. But we fell into each other's arms through some process of elimination."

Joplin told him that she loved handsome men, but that she was going to make an exception with him.

"How old were they?"

"Leonard was 33, Janis 25."

I closed my eyes.

"Feel like throwing up?"

"Yes."

"You'll get used to it."

When Luka got up, Father went downstairs to take the garbage out. Luka took my temperature.

"It's not going down, it's strange."

"We need to get to the hospital."

I shook my head.

"Today is a holiday, Puertas won't be there. Let's wait."

I was feverish but felt fine. I was giving my body the necessary rest and felt comfortable and protected in Father's house. Mother called me at midday to ask if I had started taking my retroviral medication.

"Karmen complained about her legs going numb."

"I haven't felt anything yet."

Mother said she would come by later in the day. I scooched to the side so Luka could sit on the sofa. I rested my head on his legs.

"Tell me something."

I told him the story Father told me about Janis Joplin and Leonard Cohen.

"Others like Bukowski, Burroughs, Arthur Miller and Kerouac stayed at the Chelsea Hotel too. That's where he typed *On the Road*.

"I'm not familiar with it."

"Sid Vicious?"

"Yes, I know about him."

"Nancy Spungen died at the Chelsea Hotel, room 100. They founded her half-naked in the bathroom having bled to death and, with Vicious' knife still stuck in her stomach. The worst thing is that people blame poor Nancy for having hooked Sid on heroin and breaking up the Sex Pistols band, more than Sid for having murdered Nancy.

"How old was she?"

"20."

Women who die that young make an impression and stir admiration in me.

"Martyrs of their time."

I began trembling, my forehead became clammy with sweat.

"The antiretroviral medication," I said.

Luka decided to call the hospital. They told him that the trembling and the nausea were normal side effects of the treatment, but the fever must've been related to something else. Apparently, it could be related to the antibiotics I was taking. They advised him to interrupt the pneumonia treatment just in case and to take me directly to the hospital if the fever persisted after twenty-four hours.

We waited for forty-eight hours but the fever did not break; instead, it rose a little. I felt emotionally cheerful and loving, soft.

On January 3rd, Mother came to visit. I heard her talking with Father in the kitchen. The combination of their two voices made a beautiful harmony.

"We're going to take you to the hospital," Mother told me as she approached my bedside.

"OK."

My lack of resistance and gentle mood caught them of guard as I agreed.

The three of them, Father, Mother and Luka assisted me. The nurses were polite. They asked me questions in a soft voice and sent me to get X-rays. The doctor informed us that only one person could accompany me. Mother stood, held my hand and walked in the room.

"You have a new pneumonia. We have to start from scratch, Nagore. We are going to check you in again for at least 21 days."

"OK," I said.

They made me sit in a wheelchair and brought me to the elevator. The same process of a month earlier repeated once again:

the oxygen mask, and antibiotics and corticoids intravenously. When the nurses left, my parents and Luka came into the room. I smiled at them.

"They almost gave me Cohen's Chelsea Hotel room."

I was in room 422.

—

If the first hospitalization felt like an incarceration, the second one felt more like a monastery stay. Once they controlled my pneumonia, the fever went down and the rush I got with the corticoids turned out to be one of the most amazing experiences I had ever had with drugs. I felt an enjoyable inner tranquility, along with a unique calm, emotional openness and clarity. I could organize, effortlessly, all events within an abstract yet simple logic. Everything made sense to me; I felt in unison with the cosmic order, close to all existential secrets. I felt like I could come to understand time and death. Everything that I could not explain was instilled within me. I could spend endless hours in silence, doing nothing, savoring the basic bliss of just being. I had everything within me. I could not think of a more pleasurable exercise than breathing.

Reason, ideologies, discussions, theories, explanations… were, without question, signs of undeveloped minds. Nevertheless, hearing those around me deep into reasoning and discussion did not make my blood boil; on the contrary: I pondered the beauty of human weakness from my bed. Insomnia turned into a gift: during the night, my senses sharpened and, while the world slept, I became one with its pulse. I had no need to speak, the presence of my loved ones embraced me and I did not want to spoil that harmony with words.

"You have to give me some of what they inject you with," Father would tell me.

Wonderful images, moving slowly, came to my mind. It could be a prairie caressed by a breeze. With incredible detail, I could see the swaying of each blade of grass, and perceive how the light hue changed from cold to warm as the sun descended. The images were recurrent, though never exactly the same; the images were alive because they reflected subtle variations or because they made me pay attention to details I had never perceived before. In one of the episodes, I saw myself at a swimming pool. My mind would fill up with light blue water, rays of light filtered in quick flashes, and in the middle of the image, me, swimming. I would hold on to that illusion as if it were a single frame. I registered all my senses: the exact temperature of the water; the arms' angle, rhythm and strength; the gleam of the light; the feeling of penetrating the surface of the water with my fingertips; the warming of my muscles; the weight of the water; the awareness of my body fully enveloped by the water and the feeling of each particular limb of my body; the sound; the cadence of the full scene; the movement of the perfectly coordinated body and displaced liquid; the escape of the oxygen-bubbles… I decided that after being released from the hospital, I would take up swimming.

The connection with Aunt Karmen felt most real during my second stay at the hospital. I recalled forgotten or never-remembered episodes, small, lovely memories, like the exact shape of the wrinkles formed in the corners of her eyes when she smiled or the sound of her laughter. I could hear her clearly. I even perceived her smell, the smell of her skin, and relived how it felt touching her hair.

One night, while awake, yet with my eyes shut, a scene unexpectedly formed in my mind and made me blink my eyes open at once. In the image, Aunt Karmen held me from my arms and whirled me around her. I was flying. It was a clear image, it felt almost real. I heard my own laughter while I flew nonstop around her. Though not visible in the scene, I knew the railroad tracks were behind us, I could smell the rust of the rails. I felt the pressure of my aunt's hands holding on to my small hands, the air on my legs coming from under my flying dress. Suddenly, I would stop turning in circles and Karmen would take me in her arms. At that very moment, I heard my voice clearly: "Mother!" I sat up. I shut my eyes again. Karmen twirled me around her, I wore a dress and she wore a high-waisted pair of jeans. I wore my hair loose and Aunt Karmen's was in a high bun. She took me in her arms. "Mother!"

In that sort of delirium, I let my imagination run: the word in the family was that Mother became pregnant around the time Aunt Karmen was taken to the detox center, and that I was born in March 1982, while she was a patient in the Valencia Cortijo de Santa Elena. My birth and my aunt's detoxing were intertwined in our family's tale, they had even told me that one had led to the other…

Karmen Vargas was pregnant when she was taken to jail. She decided to get clean when she found out she was pregnant, and they took her to "*El Patriarca*." In her letters, she constantly asked about the newborn and explained that the baby gave her the strength to live. In the meantime, Karmen's brother, Rafa Vargas, and his wife took care of the newborn. They barely managed with their cumbersome bar schedule, but it was the least Rafa Vargas could do for his younger sister. As soon as she stopped using heroin and returned home clean, everything would return to normal: the mother would recover her daughter and the daughter, her mother. Karmen returned when the child was two years old. She was eighteen. Karmen held the child in her arms and cried until she no longer had tears left to shed. The young mother was glowing, clean and healthy. She took charge of all the responsibilities related to the care of the child; she fed her, clothed her, took her outside, put her in bed. But everything went wrong when Karmen was diagnosed with AIDS and condemned to an imminent death. Considering everything that was coming their way, they decided not to separate mother and daughter. They kept them together until the very end, but decided never to reveal the truth. From then on, Nagore Vargas would be Rafa Vargas' and Arantzazu Algorta's daughter. With a little luck, the mother would not have passed the HIV virus to the child. In those days, the transmission channels had not yet been studied in depth. The child would grow healthy and protected with the sad yet heroic memory of her diseased aunt.

I fell asleep, and woke up a little later feeling like I was hungover.

That morning, Mother came into the room holding my favorite wheat bread in her hands. I stared at her: we were identical. I had Mother's same long legs and 5 feet and 9 inches of height and almost identical big blue eyes; hers were more beautiful.

During my first hospitalization, poor Mother had been overwhelmed with fear, with no strength to react. After New Year's Eve though, we got closer and she became my main caretaker.

"I'm having hallucinations."

"We must ask them to lower the dosage."

I told her about the dream I had at night under the effect of the corticoid medicine. She listened to me astonished.

"Do I need to show you the C-section scar?"

"Sorry, Mother, I am so high."

"Save a little bit for me, dear."

I felt guilt ridden. Father and I always excluded her from the concentric-conflictive-Oedipal World we both constructed.

"It was the perfect excuse to exonerate me from the burden of being infected."

She caressed my hair. I stared at the woman who always stayed silent but was always within my reach. I stared at her just a few yards away; at her sad, blue eyes. At her unbearable lightness of being. The woman with vague parenting skills, sister, roommate, business partner, travel companion, friend. Mother.

I felt sad on the day I was informed of my discharge. I had grown to feel safe in the hospital. The idea of leaving felt unsettling.

Doctor Puertas came to say goodbye.

"I took a big risk," he reminded me.

He was referring, among other things, to starting the antiretroviral treatment without having first treated my pneumonia.

"Everyone takes risks in their own way."

I spent 26 days in the hospital. Father, Mother and Luka stayed by my side. I had never spent so many days in a row lacking nothing.

—

I opened the balcony doors wide and the sea penetrated all the way inside the house. It extended, foamy and shiny, over the roofs. The Igeldo Castle in the distance; behind, the peak of Jaizkibel. The breeze gently rocked the sheets hanging from the façade balconies of apartment buildings, beach towels likewise placed to dry over the balcony banisters. On the tops of the sandstone church towers, seagulls in the sun.

The house that had belonged to Irantzu's grandmother was almost empty. Irantzu had taken the old furniture away and painted the walls white.

"Whenever you need to be in Formentera, just ask for the keys," she had told me.

The wide bed, now undone, in the room facing the sea, was being freshened with touches of the North Wind. The smell of fish being grilled on the street came all the way up to the room. I eyed Luka coming out of the tunnel, holding the newspaper under his armpit. I whistled at him.

"*Buongiorno mio caro amico*!" I yelled in Italian.

He slowly climbed the stairs; it had not been long ago that he climbed them by twos and threes. Under an archway, he crossed paths with a woman carrying sole to a nearby restaurant. He cheerfully greeted a young girl who carried a fishing pole over her shoulder. He sat down to wait for me at the small square by the church.

"Did you have a good night sleep?"

“Ten straight hours. I can’t remember the last time I slept so much.”

We began walking down the street. Irantzu, through an uncle, had arranged an appointment for us to meet with the manager of a hatchery where he worked. Luka was ecstatic about it; he looked forward more and more to this type of gastronomic plan.

“It kind of frightened me to see that you were gone when I woke up.”

“Where did you think I went?”

The church bells tolled twelve strokes.

“You’ve been reading Gramsci?”

“‘One must think about the pessimism of the intellect and act through the optimism of the will.’”

“That’s what we came for. To put the second part into practice.”

“The sunrise looked amazing: not a single wave on the ocean.”

By then, it had gotten a little rougher, sprinkled with small, whitish waves.

“When everything looks calm, I start getting nervous.”

“Is that why you stepped out onto the balcony?” He held me by my waist. “And me, thinking you were oblivious, looking to the horizon.”

“Yeah, that too.”

We went along the cobblestone street, through another tunnel and found the hatchery on the left. We met Pedro; at that time, there were no clients at the store. We went down to the fish tanks in the freight elevator. All the workers wore knee-high rubber boots, waterproof gloves and aprons that covered their legs all the way to the floor. The floor was soaking wet, slippery, water dripping down the walls. He advised us to put on our sweaters. We could hear the oxygen and cooling system’s motors rumbling.

The crustaceans and mollusks were classified by species in separate tanks: spiny lobster, clawed lobster, shrimp, Norway lobster; spider crab, brown crab, velvet crab; barnacles, clams, oysters, sea snails.

He showed us the snail sifting system.

"We spread them on the floor. We place some vertical panels, close the tank and bring them up and down to the surface three times. We provoke artificial tides and the live snails stick to the panels. We throw away the ones left on the floor."

I walked to the tank with the lobsters.

"We ate one of these in Formentera," I told Luka.

Pedro smiled.

"That one is empty."

He placed his hand in the water and took out an empty lobster shell.

"The female shedding time is about to finish."

He shut off the oxygenation to calm the water.

"You've been fortunate; they usually do it at night. Look there."

He pointed at a medium sized lobster that looked ordinary to us. It was taking tiny steps back and forth. It lay on its side and shook its legs and antennae. It remained like that for a while. Little by little, it revealed an opening on the backside. The creature was pushing against its shell, going through contractions, in a suffocating birthing, working hard to get rid of its old armor. It was anguishing to see it. When it successfully freed its front legs and head from the shell, the animal came out through the opening on the backside of the shell, and remained next to the old skin, exhausted. Pedro caught it with a fish net and placed it in a different tank.

"It's dangerous to leave it with the others: they can attack it."

The others tend to attack the newly-transformed, soft-fleshed lobster.

He showed us the tank for the one-legged lobsters.

"Those are cheaper."

Two workers were picking Norway lobsters with tongs from boxes divided into small compartments. They pulled them from three-square-centimeter cubicles, confirmed that they were alive, and put them back.

We walked into the mollusk unit. He took us to the oyster tank, used a small knife to open two valves and handed them to us to taste.

"No lemon, no black pepper, no nothing. These must be eaten raw."

We brought the soft, delicately folded white-purplish flesh to our mouths. The oyster tank was not the most appropriate place to enjoy oysters: their scarcity was lost in such surroundings.

Pedro considered the visit concluded. We bought a bag of boiled snails and they handed us each a small needle so we could extract the flesh from its shell. We left the hatchery enjoying the snails as we walked away.

We strolled in the shade along the fishermen's market building. An intense smell brought us to a door ajar. On the floor, in 22-pound cans, were anchovies covered in salt. We eyed the back of a small man. On a display shelf, he had a few jars with anchovies.

"These are contraband anchovies," he warned us without turning around. "If you want the kind with labels, you can find them in *delicatessen* stores; there are four or five around here."

We bought two jars from him. He dusted them with a cloth.

We asked him to recommend a place to eat. He squinted his eyes and pointed to the ground floor of an old house by the old port:

"They're trustworthy. I see everything from here."

A group of rowers gathered in a circle was warming up before going out to sea. Young, strong bodies. About a dozen young women lifted the boat to their shoulders and headed toward the small dock. They put it down on the ramp and, after placing their water bottles and towels under the seats, dragged it to the water. We stopped and watched them make their way to the sea.

We walked to the place the small man in the cannery had recommended. It looked like a family-owned, welcoming place. They offered us a table in the shade. The server approached us with the menu in hand.

"You order. I get overwhelmed and always order wrong," I explained.

"It's not that hard."

"Too many choices."

He opened the menu.

"The key is to get the main course right. What type of fish would you like to eat?"

"You already know?"

"I'll order the turbot."

He grabbed the wine list.

"They recommend white wine to accompany fish but I prefer red."

"What an aristocrat."

"I don't like ordering a lot of food."

"Salad?"

The server came. We ordered.

"I almost forgot to tell you: we still have hake cheeks and squid."

I looked at Luka, doubtful.

"A salad and turbot for both, thank you."

They brought us the wine.

"I bet the squid was fresh here."

"Can't have everything at once. Taste the wine."

"Nice."

The server took away the empty salad plate.

"The town looks calm," I commented.

The road to the fishermen's association was closed, and only a few cars drove up and down the port.

"Irantzu told me that this is the last calm weekend before summer."

They brought the turbot on a tray and served us each a piece. Luka filled my glass.

"To hang out with nice people, see beautiful places, eat, live slowly…"

He repositioned himself comfortably on his chair.

"And what about socialism?"

"You don't have to give up pleasure."

He separated the turbot's fleshy cheeks for me.

"Taste it. It's the most tender part."

"So good!"

"What does 'living well' mean to you?"

"Mostly, not feeling guilty about it."

"Try to be more specific."

"To have few clothes and lots of free time."

"I like it."

"We'll need to work too."

"As little as possible."

By the time we got up from the table, it was five in the afternoon.

Young boys with marked ribcages were swimming in the port's murky water. They bumped against each other's still infantile chests and fell backwards with their arms wide open. They fell down into the water in threes and fours, pushing each other in the air, smashing each other in the water. Some pushed each other's heads under the water and pulled down each other pants, a fine line between erotica and war. When they saw us from the water, they asked us to throw them a coin. Luka threw a 20-cent coin as far as he could. They all turned their heads at once and swam together. We saw them dive where the coin sank.

We took the stairs next to the old restaurant following the path to the San Anton summit. On the road, faded blossoms shed from springtime, and in the air, the fragrance of ripening figs. From the seaside, the smell of salt and wet moss on coastal rocks.

"Now is when the days are the longest."

"The boats are off to catch squid."

"In the past, whales swam all the way here."

As we gained altitude, the view of Getaria became breathtaking. The small town settled under a green-vine-covered slope: four streets among the red roofs, and on each side of town the beaches and the sea. The town could not grow any more even if it wanted to. The houses seemed to hang on the edge of the cliff.

Cenere, acero, noccioal, agrifoglio, lauro… Luka kept naming the trees along the way using words that he had not pronounced since he was a child when his mother taught them to him, words that were non-existent in my industrial childhood. We got lost in fragrance-filled paths, sat on benches along the path. We heard the wind rustling against the leaves.

We walked all the way to the lighthouse. On the north-side edge, we extended our bodies from the overlook railing, toward the precipice. Below, seagulls flew close to the wall where the waves crashed. The thrill of finding, below us, what one would expect up above.

We walked to the highest vantage point on the hill. We happened upon an abandoned structure; it could have been the lighthouse's living quarters or a lookout post from the war. The inside was riddled with graffiti: *Sonia and David (07-16-2013)*; *Full amnesty*; *Ane and Martin had sex here.*

We walked outside and lay down on the grass, between the sea and the sky.

"Do you think the locals appreciate this? It would be a tragedy to get used to this beauty."

"It's inevitable: one gets used to everything."

My back itched.

"Scratch me."

I lay face down. He slipped his hand under my t-shirt. He began scratching my waist area.

"A little higher," I guided him, "to the right, a little lower, to the left…Right there."

I sighed.

"I needed you to scratch me exactly there."

We remained staring at the high clouds.

"It would be difficult to have it better than this," I exclaimed.

A southbound plane flew by. I looked at Luka.

"Shush," he said.

We reached town by a trail on other side of the hill. He resumed naming trees: *betulle, ciliegio, pino marittimo…*

The fishing boats were getting ready to leave the port. Net menders working on the ground under the shade of umbrellas; loose scales, pieces of fish and dry algae entangled in the fishing net. A white-haired man was using a fishing line in his hands with his five-year-old-ish granddaughter by his side. The man stood on the edge of the dock, focused, staring at the fishing-line hanging from his index finger. The granddaughter was trying to bait her hook with a piece of ham.

"Got a bite!"

The little girl came close to the edge.

"What is it?"

"A mullet."

Grandpa freed the wriggling fish from the hook and placed it inside a plastic bag. The child put her hand over the fish.

"It stopped."

We saw a group of adolescents playing on the other side of the port: they were getting on a moored fishing boat with no hesitation, without wasting half a second on their jump from the pier to the boat. One of the brutish-looking boys climbed the bow mast agilely and while hanging from the ladder with his bent arm, spit phlegm down on a husky boy standing still on the deck. The fat boy cursed the seagulls flying around.

"Hey, fatso!" The boy mocked him from above.

Beti Piedad (Always merciful), I read the name of the boat.

We looked in another direction, away from the two teenagers: a girl stood on the bow. Her feet and legs tight against each other, her waist lightly pushed back, her eyes looking straight ahead. The others all began to clap. She stretched her arms and lightly lifted her chin. I could swear that she hung still for a second in the air. The perfect swan dive.

We walked down to the dock. The sun was setting. Two chubby guys were flushing water from a small, old row boat. They pulled up the panels under the seats and were scooping out the accumulated water in the keel with plastic *Cola-Cao* containers. They were arguing if it was rain or sea water. The oldest one took a sip from the can.

"Rain."

Luka pointed out the white and blue houses above the port.

"Would you live there?"

"Who wouldn't? I like the attic best. And you?" I asked him.

"The first floor, with the long balcony."

We had a beer before going home. We bought two small bottles and brought them to the west-side vantage point. The sun, big and red, was now approaching the horizon. On the beach, three rows of rocks became exposed due to the low tide and looked like the dark skeleton of a huge whale. The sand wet and soft. Out at sea, a surfer sitting on his board, waiting for waves that didn't come. We eyed a swimmer in the distance, swimming along the shore.

"Should we have dinner on the balcony?"

I fixed gazpacho. The kitchen table did not fit on the balcony so we brought three chairs, one to use as a table. Intense spotlights lit the sandstone wall of the church. Luka brought out the anchovies we had bought earlier in the day.

"We don't have any wine," he explained.

I showed him the bottle of *txakoli*.

"Irantzu left it for us."

We brought the white wine and glasses to the balcony. The outside temperature was nice. Below the house two youngsters, clumsily yet beautifully, touching each other in the dark.

"Tomorrow is Sunday."

I looked in the distance. A few blinking street lights reflected on the water. A bird paused on a terrace. Luka asked:

"What will we do from now on?"

"I'd like to have the skill of crows to know the future."

I observed the section that the roofs cut out of the sky.

"I can hardly see any stars," I pointed out.

"I know the constellations on your skin by heart."

The warm breeze enveloped us. We could hear, somewhere out there, people singing and the cling-clanging of the boats coming from the port. The fishing boats were out at sea. Dark water. The beach looked calm and lonely. The boats that had gone to catch squid were returning to port, distant lights resembling stars. Soon they would all be home.

www.ingramcontent.com/pod-product-compliance
Lightning Source LLC
LaVergne TN
LVHW010055110826
845155LV00028B/345